D0055641

Miss Meteor

TEHLOR KAY MEJIA and
ANNA-MARIE McLEMORE

An Imprint of HarperCollinsPublishers

HarperTeen is an imprint of HarperCollins Publishers.

Miss Meteor
Copyright © 2020 by Tehlor Kay Mejia and Anna-Marie McLemore
All rights reserved. Printed in the United States of America.
No part of this book may be used or reproduced in any manner whatsoever without
written permission except in the case of brief quotations embodied in critical articles
and reviews. For information address HarperCollins Children's Books, a division of
HarperCollins Publishers, 195 Broadway, New York, NY 10007.
www.epicreads.com

ISBN 978-0-06-286991-3

Typography by Corina Lupp
20 21 22 23 24   PC/LSCH   10 9 8 7 6 5 4 3 2 1
❖
First Edition

To friends lost, then found again

LITA

THIS IS THE first thing anyone will tell you about Meteor, New Mexico: it was named for a piece of iron and nickel that fell from the sky and cratered into the earth a few miles outside town.

This is the last thing I'll ever tell you about me: I came here with it.

I don't remember the moment I turned from star-stuff thrown off a meteor into a girl. But I guess that part's not so strange. No one really remembers being born.

Some days, Bruja Lupe will almost—almost—admit that we came from the same star-sprinkled patch of sky. That we came here with that small but very overheated rock that fell through the atmosphere more than fifty years ago.

To everyone around Meteor, Bruja Lupe and I are mother and daughter.

And I am enough of a daughter to her to know that, at this moment, she is seething.

Our last appointment of the day is twenty-three minutes late.

A gringa, no doubt. The gringos are always the latest, assuming we have all day to wait.

People can make any jokes they want about Mexicans being late, but anyone like us knows better than to show up late to see a curandera.

When the knock at the door does come, it comes forty-five minutes late.

Bruja Lupe will show the woman no mercy.

She huffs over the tablecloth and candles while I answer the front door.

The woman looks me up and down. She is so thin, her nails so neatly manicured, that I can't help wondering if she's looking at my soft arms and bitten-down cuticles.

"Are you the witch?" she asks.

I shake my head and lead her inside, where a glaring Bruja Lupe gestures for the woman to lie down on our repurposed dining room table.

"Yeah, I don't have a lot of time," the woman says, dropping her purse on the table, wrinkling the cloth I pressed this morning.

I try not to gasp. She's using the table where Bruja Lupe does our remedios like a hat rack.

Bruja Lupe gives a placid smile.

No, no mercy at all.

"I just need to know what color to dye my hair for my reunion," the woman says. "My ex is gonna be there, and I need him to suffer."

Bruja Lupe looks at me, and I try not to sigh.

What a waste. Doesn't this woman have a better question to spend her money on?

"Look into my daughter's eyes." Bruja Lupe pushes me forward. "And we will find the answers, for this child holds the heavens within her."

Leave it to Bruja Lupe to use poetry to tell our secrets without telling our secrets.

By now, I've seen enough movies to understand I'm not what anyone would expect of a girl who shares blood with the stars. They'd expect thin, fragile, with hair of pale gold or silver and eyes as light as the Out of This World Motel pool. Not a rounded-out girl with skin the color of desert rock, my hair so brown that indoors it looks black, my eyes as dark as our deep-stained dresser.

I count this as a singular lack of imagination on the part of all those movies. Girls like me don't all look the same, any more than stars do.

The woman gives a solemn nod.

She slouches to gaze into my eyes, as though they might swirl like pinwheels, or like I might shake my head like a Magic 8 Ball, a different answer showing up in each iris.

3

Bruja Lupe begins to hum.

And then screech, like she's possessed by a spirit.

She grabs her prop scarves, the ones she never uses except for clients who have thoroughly pissed her off, and throws them in every direction.

The woman's eyes widen at the flying cloth, while Bruja Lupe lets her own roll back into her head.

Then, finally, she wails, "Platinum blond!"

It's an unfeeling choice. This woman's eyes and skin are so pale that with such light hair she'll have little color at all. When the woman pays and tips us, leaving with a teary "Thank you," I almost consider following her into the parking lot and saying so.

But I let the woman leave.

We have to pay rent somehow.

Only, soon, Bruja Lupe's going to have to do it without me.

The front door clicks shut.

"Was that really necessary?" I ask.

"Who's the mother here?" Bruja Lupe asks, pulling the cloth off the table, blowing out each of the candles she lit for absolutely no reason. "You or me?"

Why Bruja Lupe got to be the older one, and thus in charge, I'll never know. One theory is that I'm just slower at everything, including making a girl out of myself. Another is that the stuff I am made of spooled off a young star, while the star-stuff that became Bruja Lupe is steady as an iron core, molten and metal.

Whatever the reason, it's always struck me as highly unfair that she got to skip being my age entirely, and I have to spend four years at Meteor Central High.

To everyone here in Meteor, I am fifteen years old. And that's just as well, because I may know I am made of star-stuff, but I don't remember the way it feels to be anything but the girl I am.

Bruja Lupe glances my direction. "I only cheat those who ask for the wrong things. Lo sabes."

It's true. For those who want to know if they'll become rich, she pretends to see the future between the coffee maker and the microwave. Last month, she gave a useless tincture to a woman who wanted her sister written out of their parents' will. For the man who wanted a spell to keep his wife from noticing he was cheating, she kept screaming without warning and throwing hierbas in the man's face.

Bruja Lupe puts some of the money in her purse, some in a drawer, and hands some to me.

Any further complaint disappears off my tongue.

I'll add the little bit of money to the other little bits of money I keep under my bed. Bruja Lupe probably thinks I use it on soda or lipstick, but I've saved it all for her, a small offering left behind for when I'm gone.

After the woman drives away, I lie on my bed, clutching my stomach, trying to hold myself together. I don't lift my shirt because I don't want to see it, the strip of my stomach that looks like a little Milky Way, the first part of me that is turning back into stardust.

"Oh, Estrellita." Bruja Lupe sighs from the door.

Her pity is never a good sign. Bruja Lupe doesn't offer pity for fevers, stomach flu, or sprained ankles. The fact that she offers it now means I can't ignore this.

I am turning back into the stardust I once was.

She knows it. And her knowing it means I have to know it.

I could feel sorry for myself. I could stay curled up on my bed and lament the ways in which the sky is taking me back, the ways in which I am losing myself. But the truth is, I started losing myself a while ago.

It happened around the same time my best friend stopped being my best friend.

Sometimes I wonder if Chicky and I stopped being friends because she saw it, the stardust under my skin. Maybe she realized that the name everyone calls me—Lita—is short for Estrellita. Little star. Maybe she began to think of me like a mermaid or a unicorn or something else she had to decide didn't exist.

I doubt it though. I may be made out of the same dust and glow as the lights in the sky, but if you read any of the astronomy books in the library—you'll realize, isn't everyone?

CHICKY

WHEN YOU LIVE in a three-bedroom house with five other people, you learn quickly how to minimize your time in the bathroom.

Heels click impatiently outside, manicured nails rapping. There's always a ride coming, or a party starting, or a shift to get to. There's always an emergency, and it's never mine. Tonight, the voices increase, decibel by decibel. I don't answer, because I don't have to. What can they do? It's the only door in the house that locks from the inside.

In front of me, in a bathroom shared between four sisters, stands an arsenal of beauty supplies. Liners, shadows, powders, masks. Polishes and mascaras and highlighters. In front of me, my face's own reflection stands staunchly naked, brown and a little freckled. A protest flag.

My name is Chicky Quintanilla, it says. *And I won't be painted like a doll.*

The mantra is almost enough to get me out the door unscathed.

"It's about time!"

"Are you serious?! What were you even doing in there? You look the same!"

"Berto's gonna be here any second! Move!"

"Girls, let's keep it to a dull roar, please. Your mother's balancing the books."

The hallway creaks under the boots my mom raised her eyebrows at in the department store, and I like the sound. It means I'm causing a small reaction, even in the din. It says I was here, even if it doesn't say it loudly. I'm never saying anything loudly. Not here, not anywhere.

"Chicky?" my mom calls from her office—a renovated closet once full of board games with missing pieces. She sits in there like a queen on a throne with the accounting books she barely keeps out of the red, so proud of the space she's earned by keeping our family's diner running for a decade. Dad fixed up the closet/office for her on her thirty-fifth birthday. He's not great with practical stuff like bills, but he cares, you know?

"Hey," I say, shaking my hair out of my eyes, exposing them for once.

Brown today, green tomorrow, my dad always says. But that sunflower in the middle always stays the same.

"Sit with me while I balance?"

There's loud music to listen to, and magazine pictures to

cut out and stick to the walls, and sure, homework to do, if I get that desperate. But I make myself at home on the rag rug in the corner anyway, not caring about the tiny cat hairs that immediately adhere to my diner uniform.

I wish I could say I stay because I love my mom. I mean, I really do, but tonight it's about something more. My eyes are scanning everything—the chair with the stuffing poking through, the three-light-bulb lamp with two burned out, the worn spot on her shoe that's about to become a full-on hole.

To everyone in Meteor, New Mexico, the Quintanillas are a family of self-starters, immigrant parents who came across the border "the right way" (as if there's a right way to run from danger) and built a business that's become a town institution.

Never mind that half the customers have tabs in the triple digits that they never intend to pay. Never mind the worry lines beside my mom's eyes, and the sleepless pacing of my dad's sneakers down the hallways during tax season.

Four beautiful girls, the neighbors say. Though the youngest is a little odd with her flannel shirts and her boy's haircut.

We get good grades, we help out at the diner, and we stay out of trouble for the most part. Between that and the neon Open sign that clicks on every day at seven a.m., we must have it all, right? Not like those other immigrants. The "lowlifes and criminals" the news is always screaming about.

As if financial security is any measure of a person's character. Or their humanity.

9

Personally, I consider those stereotypes a singular and offensive lack of imagination on the part of the news. But I probably shouldn't be surprised by that.

"What's on your mind, Banana?" my mom asks, and I grimace.

"Mom, please," I say for at least the billionth time.

She laughs, and the sound is so bright and rare, like a butterfly in a rainstorm that lands right on your finger and just makes you marvel at the fact that life can exist. I vow at that moment to never give her grief about my name again. She deserves better.

"Should I say Chiquita instead?" she asks, her smile young, her pen forgotten atop the painstaking columns of numbers that never seem to add up to a new dryer, or a radiator for the car. "Your grandmother was awfully fond of it." She looks up at the picture above her makeshift desk, and her smile changes temperatures, cools into something nostalgic like the autumn wind that only blows one week out of the year in the New Mexico desert.

The photo should be in the Smithsonian, and that's not an exaggeration. Not because it's particularly good artistically, but because it documents an actual, modern-day miracle. My sisters and I, existing in the same two feet of space, without anyone being maimed or ridiculed.

In the picture, we almost look happy.

The Quintanilla girls are all named by an archaic tradition that has persisted through you don't want to know how many generations. Exactly twenty-six days before a Quintanilla baby's birth, her bisabuela will have a dream that decides her name. She hands it down like the verdict of a grand jury, and no one dares question it. Even if the name is something really stupid, like say, Chiquita.

From oldest to youngest my sisters smile from the frame, and as my mother gazes at it I swear I will try to love them, if only for this moment, and if only for her sake.

Cereza, the eldest, tart and sweet like the fruit our father's grandmother dreamed of picking in a summer rainstorm. No one argues with Cereza, not even Papa. With her dyed red hair curling to her waist and every diner customer wrapped around her nude manicure, she's juggling nursing college, too. She's the queen of the family, the daughter we should all aspire to be. Sometimes we all secretly hate her for it.

Next to her is Uva, named for bisabuela's dream about stomping grapes between her bare brown toes. Round and smiling, full of the giddy headiness of young wine (bisabuela's words, not mine, Uva's the peacekeeper. The common thread. The comic relief. She's the kindest and the best of us.

Beside her is Fresa, la princesa, the apple of Papa's eye and the cruelest and most beautiful of us all. I've thought on more than one occasion that my parents should have stopped there, with this sweet and wicked sister, the balancing fire, the face and figure that made her the second runner-up in the Miss Meteor pageant last year. She tells anyone who'll listen that if there wasn't a rule against entering twice, she'd have the crown this year.

Her boyfriend, Berto, who drives a vintage Camaro, claims she tastes like the strawberries she was named for when bisabuela dreamed of flowering vines crawling across the desert, digging in deep and cracking open the ground before their fruit swelled bloodred.

I know it's just her lip gloss. Two ninety-nine at Meteor Mart. She buys them five at a time.

Mama clucks her tongue, drawing me out of the photo, as if her disapproval can change the earning and spending totals her neat hand follows down each column.

There's only one sister left to examine, and of course, it's me.

Twenty-six days before my birth, my bisabuela dreamed of the dancing girl with the fruit-filled hat from the banana commercials, smiling and spinning circles beneath a thousand twinkling lights. No one dared name me banana, of course, but bisabuela didn't hesitate. She'd always liked that girl, with her bold dress and her wide smile, and so she handed down my name. Decided my future.

Chiquita, she said. And that was that.

I decided the rest for myself, by becoming as unlike a girl

named Chiquita as I could. With my awkward, gangly limbs and my perpetual slouch, straight black hair that flops heavily into my eyes with or without my permission, I'm more likely to scowl than smile, more likely to stay up worrying than to drunkenly giggle at a boy around a desert fire in an oil can.

I like dark jeans, and sweatshirts with thumbholes in the sleeves, and when I'm older, I'm going to convince Mom to let me get a nose ring.

But until then I'm just Chicky, a tomboy at best, the least popular girl in Meteor Central High's sophomore class. The girl who should have been as pretty as her sisters, but just isn't. The girl who doesn't have a single friend.

I had a friend once, who was bright where I was dull, who smiled where I scowled. I caught her like a falling star one night just after kindergarten let out for the summer, and I never dreamed I'd let her go.

My mom asked me once, what happened to Estrellita, the girl who saw worlds, and I mumbled something about growing up and growing apart.

It wasn't the truth.

The truth is this: Bisabuela wasn't wrong when she dreamed of the dancing girl on the surface, toes barely touching the earth. But she should have named me for the earth below her feet. The depths she never plunged. Because when people start to dig in, I run. There's too much darkness down there.

Lita found that out the hard way, and we never quite recovered.

In a town this small, for girls like us, survival is based mostly on how well you can camouflage, not on dredging up the bloodred and sunshine yellow of your secrets and splattering them across your chest.

But if you read about warfare in any of the history books in the library you'll ask yourself: Isn't it that way for everyone?

LITA

MY FAVORITE PART of the morning used to be when I got on my bike and my fingers brushed the streamers. The slight movement of the tinsel strips and the desert sun, already bright early in the morning, would cast pink bands of light over the ground as I got the wheels started. It always felt like our nearest star's way of winking at me.

Now the little flickers of light make me sick to my stomach. It reminds me how my body is dissolving, how I'm turning back to what I once was but can't remember being.

I pack up my backpack.

"Still you go to school?" Bruja Lupe asks. "I'll write you a note."

I'll write you a note. Like I have a cold.

Bruja Lupe's thinks I should be out getting fresh air, talking to my cactuses, breathing in the world.

But I'm taking as much of Meteor into me as I can before I dissolve all the way.

Even Meteor Central High.

Math class is there. So are Cole Kendall and Junior Cortes.

"Buenos días, Señorita Opuntia." I greet the cactuses as I fly by on my bike. "Bon matin, Monsieur Cereus. Good morning, Mr. Hedgehog Cactus."

I stop my bike in front of the school.

"Looks like My Little Pony decided to show up." I hear them whisper—the kind of whisper I'm meant to hear.

If the tinsel flashing in the sun used to be the best of my morning, this was my worst. These are the same girls who make fun of how I wear the powder-blue tights Bruja Lupe bought me, or how my lunch always comes in old plastic Tupperware instead of between slices of white bread.

I don't look at them.

I never look at them. Because I already know how they look at me and my bike, which is clearly designed for someone half my age. But really, I'd like to see these girls try handling their beach cruisers with legs as short as mine.

"What is she even riding?" one of them asks.

Cole Kendall steps off the curb, and his shadow cools the back of my neck.

"My old bike," he says.

That shuts them up.

How comfortable Cole is with himself often makes other people uncomfortable. I've heard him joke about borrowing his brother's old clothes, which were usually several sizes too big. About how his habit of collecting earthworms as pets horrified his mother and sister. About how he doesn't have the luxury of hating sparkles, because in a family that's won three Miss Meteor pageant titles, he had to become immune to them sticking to his backpack and socks.

And now he makes a crack about this bike. A little girl's bike, all shimmery pink varnish and those glittering streamers. I was there the day his grandmother, not yet understanding just how much of a boy Cole was, bought it for him for his seventh birthday, and Cole walked it around the neighborhood with a look of both pain and obligation.

I was six, and even though I barely knew him, I shouted across the street, "That's the best bike in the world!"

Because it really was, and I thought he should know.

"You want it?" he asked, looking so much like a light had come on inside him that I couldn't even open my mouth to ask if he was sure.

The one thing Cole never jokes about is the name he was given when he was born. Why would he? There's nothing funny about being called something that's wrong.

He's Cole. He's always been Cole, even before he told everyone. Not that it took him long. He was five.

"Personally," Cole says now, "I think we should give that bike a round of applause for still running after a decade. Don't you?"

Even with his back to me, I hear the undertone, his warning of "lay off her." I'm one of many people Cole breaks out this tone for. Daniel Lamas, who sometimes dresses up as Amelia Earhart or Frida Kahlo for Halloween. Beth Cox, who got made fun of every day for having scoliosis until Cole and his older brother made clear that anyone who did would answer to them. Oliver Hedlesky, who probably never would have tried out for the soccer team if Cole's presence didn't make Royce a little less, well, Royce.

And when Cole Kendall uses his "lay off" voice, they do. Because Cole is not just one of the boys who anchors the soccer team (striker) and the baseball team (shortstop or second base, depending on the lineup). He is one of the boys carrying the weight of the cornhole team.

Yes, cornhole.

In seventh grade, they made us memorize a William Carlos Williams poem about how much depends on some chickens and some rain and a red wheelbarrow. And I didn't understand it until I realized that the poem could have been about Meteor, because around here a lot depends on boys throwing beanbags into wooden boards with holes in them (boards that Junior Cortes almost undoubtedly painted).

This whole region has a circuit of teams who play each

other. Cornhole officials debate the merits of nylon versus polyester. Boys shave their arms because they want their throws to
be as aerodynamic as possible. Wooden boards and the holes set
therein are inspected months in advance (I don't know what
you can do to sabotage a cornhole board, but around here, it's
treated with the gravity of state secrets).

Along with the pageant, the cornhole championship
jams Meteor full of tourists, and we need every one of them.
Our motels and restaurants and souvenir shops depend on it.
Thanks in large part to Cole's older brother, Meteor Central
High School won last year. This year, Meteor wants a win even
worse—not just to hold on to the title, but because this year
even more tourists will be watching, ones with money in their
wallets. This year is the fiftieth-annual Miss Meteor pageant,
and they're already expecting the biggest crowds this town has
ever seen. Cole has been practicing his signature shot ("the air-
mail," the one his brother taught him).

Those girls shuffle off.

I kiss Cole on the cheek to tell him thank you.

He used to pull away when I did this, pulling his palm
across his cheek and saying something about girl-germs.

He doesn't do that as much anymore.

I don't think about how, once I turn back into stardust, I'll
never see Cole Kendall again. I make it a point not to. Because
when I do, it gives me a hollow feeling, like the whole inside of
me has already crumbled into dust.

Maybe it's good that I already lost Chicky. We already got it over with. She's not someone I'll have to figure out how to say goodbye to.

I hand Cole the bag of galletas dulces I brought him, because I won't be at lunch today.

I always bring him sugar cookies on the last days of school. Before winter break. Before summer. Before the break in the school calendar for the annual festival. It's my continued thank you for this bike that keeps bringing me to and from Meteor Central High, and everywhere else in town.

"Thanks," he says. "I'll consider this fortification."

"For what?" I ask.

He nods toward a banner getting hoisted up across the street.

We stand next to each other, reading the calligraphy-like blue script:

The Fiftieth-Annual Meteor Regional Pageant and Talent Competition Showcase

"It's a beauty pageant," Cole says. "Can we all just call it a beauty pageant?"

I glance at him.

"Sorry," he says. "When I was born my mother expected me to take the title one day. I have strong feelings." He opens the bag. "Especially this time of year."

This time of year.

It's not so much a break as the school's way of acknowledging how many of our families need our help once the tourists flood in. Chicky Quintanilla, my once-friend, and her sisters will be trading off at the diner, and I will pretend my heart doesn't pinch every time I pass Selena's and see Chicky in the window. Evie Lewis will make sure her aunt's souvenir shop never closes, so there's no hour that tourists can't buy Meteor town postcards or nebula scarves or tiny replicas of the space rock. Junior Cortes will have his hands full both with his hours at the museum and with painting. Thanks to his skill at turning famous works into cornhole boards, our practice field always looks like a gallery. Where else but Meteor can you find a board identical to Frida Kahlo's *Self-Portrait with Thorn Necklace and Hummingbird*, or one a perfect match to Edvard Munch's *The Scream*? (The hole is the round O of the subject's mouth.)

Junior is bound for some art school that's so sophisticated I (and half of Meteor) have probably never heard of it.

"Kendra's gearing up," Cole says.

"What?" I ask. "Already?" Cole's sister is in my grade. Almost no sophomores ever try for the crown. Since you can only enter Miss Meteor once, you only get one shot. You can take it whenever you want, but almost everyone who enters waits until they're seventeen, the last time they're eligible. "She's not waiting until next year?"

"Yeah, apparently not," Cole says. "It's a whole thing."

21

Of course Kendra's not waiting. Why would she? While we're all still waiting to grow into ourselves, she's already the pale kind of beautiful I used to see on almost every page of Fresa Quintanilla's magazines.

And this year's the fiftieth. Why wouldn't she go after the crown?

"I'm already bracing for the bathroom to be covered in eyeshadow and duct tape," Cole says.

My head snaps toward him. "Duct tape?"

"Trust me," he says. "You don't wanna know."

But I do.

I want to know everything about the pageant, even though it stings just to look at the banner. I even want to know whatever horrifying magic Kendra works with duct tape.

Right now, the thing I want most in the world is to stop turning back into stardust.

But once, the thing that I wanted, more than anything else, was to be Miss Meteor.

CHICKY

PEOPLE SOMETIMES MAKE fun of me for eating lunch at home, but none of them live with the best cook in Meteor.

I'm already exhausted from half a day of school by the time I dump my shoulder bag on the floor inside the door, but the smell of bean tlacoyos revives me slightly, and I stagger into the kitchen with my mouth watering.

"Just in time, Banana." Dad puts two of them on a plate and slides it down the weathered, farm-style kitchen table that used to belong to Bisabuela Gloriana.

"Thank you." I grab one and take a huge bite despite the still sizzling oil on the outside.

Dad's tlacoyos are so much more than stuffed tortillas. The gently spiced masa, the black beans he cooks for two days before mashing them in garlic oil. The slight crunch of the cilantro and onion he adds just before he fries it all together into a little pocket of heaven.

23

"Chicky!" Uva exclaims from the front door. "Stop leaving your bag on the floor! You know what Abuela says."

"Abuela says a lot of weird stuff," I mumble, my mouth still full.

"Don't underestimate her," Uva says, her green-gray eyes far too intense for the matter at hand. "Remember that time there was no purse hook at the restaurant we went to in Santa Fe?"

I stare at her blankly, finally swallowing. "No?"

"Chicky! I put my bag on the floor! And the very next day I got seventeen dollars stolen on the Rail Runner."

When I don't answer, she rolls her eyes, hanging my bag carefully on the back of my chair. "I'm just saying."

"Give it a rest, Uva," says Fresa, who's slouched over a bowl at the end of the table. "Just because you're prematurely ninety years old doesn't mean the rest of us should have to suffer." I'm about to agree, but she turns on me next. "Although, putting shit on the floor is gross, Flaca."

Only Fresa can somehow disagree with two people who disagree with each other.

"Anyway," I say, when Dad turns to the fridge to grab a pitcher of horchata. "It's not like I have any money to lose." Uva shushes me, but it's true. I used to get twenty dollars a month allowance, but sometime last spring it just stopped showing up in the painted bowl on the hall table.

Cereza told us all not to complain, that Mom and Dad were

24

doing their best, but I didn't want to complain anyway. I was just worried.

"Nobody has any money in this junk heap," Fresa mutters now, rocking the crooked-legged chair at the table loudly for emphasis. Uva tries to shush her, too, but this time she's not quick enough. Dad hears her.

"I've been meaning to fix that chair," he says. His voice is too bright, the tops of his ears turning purplish as he pours us each a glass, cinnamon flecks spinning around the ice cubes.

I can smell the orange blossom water he calls his "secret ingredient," and I feel terrible for bringing up money. I should have known Fresa couldn't keep her mouth shut.

"And . . ." He digs into his wallet and pulls out three crumpled five-dollar bills. "I forgot to put allowance in the bowl this week."

"Dad, it's fine," I say, just as Uva says, "I'm too old for allowance, Papa." Fresa, of course, pockets hers without looking up. Uva kicks her under the table.

"Girls, your sister is right," he says. "You've all been working hard. Have a little fun."

I don't bother telling him you can't do anything fun with five dollars anymore. Not even in Meteor. Not even if I had anyone to do fun things with instead of just sisters who look at me like I'm a bug and classmates who have pretty much stopped looking at me at all.

"Thanks, Dad," I mutter, shoving more food in my mouth

so I won't have to come up with anything else to say. Fresa is still staring moodily into her bowl. She doesn't say thank you. She doesn't even acknowledge him.

An awkward silence falls, and suddenly I wish Cereza was here, instead of working the lunch shift at the diner with Mom. She would know exactly what to say to get us all laughing again.

"Hey, Fresa," I say, taking the number one play out of Cereza's well-worn oldest-daughter handbook: Make fun of Fresa. "Is that another grapefruit? No wonder your face looks all pinched up like that all the time."

Uva looks at me gratefully, then back at Fresa. "Her face *is* kind of pinched up," she says, picking up a fresh tlacoyo from the plate. "Here, Fres, have some caaaarbs." She says it in a spooky Halloween voice, and I snort into my horchata.

"Girls, be nice," Dad says, but there's a glimmer of mischief in his eye. Sometimes Dad is a bigger kid than any of us. "I hear grapefruit is good for skin rashes. Maybe your sister has a rash."

This time, I almost choke. Fresa's skin care regimen is more detailed than some astronaut training programs. The word "rash" is the stuff of her nightmares, and it shows in her eyes, which have narrowed to angry slits.

"Oh, maybe you're right, Dad," Uva says. "Fresa, if you have a rash, it's nothing to be ashamed of. I hope the grapefruit helps."

"I do not have a rash!" she shouts.

I would almost feel bad, except Fresa gives five times as good as she gets, so anytime you can best her, it's a victory.

"It's called. A cleanse." She stands up, stomping to the sink and dumping the bowl too loudly.

"Oh yeah," I say. "There's a little redness there, on the back of her neck. Maybe that's where it starts."

"I hate all of you!" she shrieks, taking the stairs two at a time, but I hear the bathroom door slam, and I would bet this five dollars in my pocket she's checking the back of her neck.

Dad is laughing as he sets my school bag on my shoulder, but as he returns to the kitchen he bumps into Fresa's abandoned chair, which wobbles with a loud, wooden thunk that echoes down the hall.

LITA

TODAY IS SEÑORA Strawberry's birthday.

Like always, I bring aguas frescas to pour over the cactuses, and streamers in the same pastels as their spines, and party horns.

I would never tell the other cactuses—I give birthday parties to all of them who've told me their names—but she's one of my favorites. She cheered up her neighbor, Herr Rainbow Hedgehog, enough to bring him back to life. Herr Rainbow was drooping like an overwatered daisy until Señora Strawberry burst into magenta bloom right next to him. Then his base filled out green, and he grew a fine coating of pink and yellow spines.

Now I think they're a little bit in love. I swear his spines blush a deeper pink as I sing "Happy Birthday" to Señora Strawberry.

"Señora Strawberry," I say, holding her birthday candle in

front of her. "I wouldn't ask you this unless I absolutely had to. But I need you to make a birthday wish for me."

I've asked other cactuses to wish that I wouldn't turn back to stardust. They have, every time. Monsieur Cereus even wished it so hard I felt it in the air.

A dust-covered pink wrapper blows across the ground. It's about to blow right through Señora Strawberry's birthday party. I stomp over to it. If I catch the tourists littering as much as they did last year, they are going to see me throw a fit bigger than they thought possible from a girl this short.

I pluck it from the dirt.

It's not a wrapper.

It's a flyer.

I unfold it and find the same words from the banner. *The Fiftieth-Annual Meteor Regional Pageant and Talent Competition Showcase.*

Something about those letters traces down my spine.

Señora Strawberry's birthday candle still flickers in my hand.

Once, being Miss Meteor was my dream, as big as the whole desert sky. I wanted to earn that crown for Bruja Lupe and me and the stardust under our skin. I wanted to wear the name of this town I love and the rock they named it after.

But then Royce Bradley and his friends taught me, in ways that feel as hot on my skin now as my tears felt on my cheeks then, that girls like me are never Miss Meteor.

The Miss Meteor judges pick the same girl every year, like

29

blond and blue-eyed and size-nothing is the best thing in the whole universe.

I am nothing like those girls, like Kendra Kendall. And I'm two years younger than almost every other girl who enters.

But the sky is going to take me back anyway. So what if I went for what I wanted all those years ago?

I hold the candle to Señora Strawberry, and I swear I can feel her waiting for the wind to blow it out for her. Then I leave the cactuses to their celebration. Because before lunch period is over, I have another stop.

I take the second bag of galletas dulces I brought with me today, and I go visit the rock.

Well, it's not the whole rock. Most of the rock turned to dust and fire as it streaked through the atmosphere all those years ago.

But a piece did survive, so big that there's not enough of me to give it a full hug. A few men and one woman (the history books usually forget her) claimed the meteorite as property of the town they just then decided to establish.

"About time," Buzz says when he lets me into the Meteor Meteorite Museum. "It's been waiting."

I haven't figured out if the museum is called this because Meteor is the town name and the museum houses the meteorite, or because no one can agree on whether this town is actually called Meteor or Meteorite.

Except for the poor clerks in the town hall, this is less of a

30

problem than you'd expect. Until festival season, when it's time to make banners. A tourist has an equal chance of seeing either name proclaimed in a window or draped above the main street. *Celebrating Meteor* flutters alongside *Meteorite: The Pride of New Mexico.*

I hand Buzz the other bag of galletas dulces, my thank-you for letting me in when the Meteor Meteorite Museum isn't technically open.

From the outside, the museum looks like a weather-beaten house with a lit sign above it. But here, under Buzz's care, is my favorite rock in the whole world, with a bulb-lighted billboard and even a velvet rope that keeps tourists from trying to chip off pieces of it.

This is probably the quietest moment I will get with the rock until the end of next week, when the tourists leave.

"Buzz?" I ask.

Buzz uncoils the twist-tie from the galleta bag. "Hmm?"

"Could we have a minute?"

He combs down a few stray pieces of his white hair, nods, and leaves me to it.

I ease into setting both hands on the rock; lightly, so I don't startle it.

"So, what do you think?" I ask.

The rock hums under my hands.

"Should I do it?" I ask. "Before I . . ." I can't say it, even to this rock, especially to this rock. I can't say that I will turn to stardust, and there will be nothing left of the girl I am now. "Before I go?"

You can enter Miss Meteor up until you turn eighteen, and most girls wait until their last possible year.

Almost no one enters as a sophomore.

But this is probably the last chance I'll get.

A vein of silver flashes through the rock. It could be some trick of the light, but I know better. The rock is telling me what I already know.

I have nothing to lose. And if the sky's going to take me back, I'm going out as a girl who goes after what she wants.

CHICKY

AT SCHOOL, I'M even more invisible than usual. You'd think it would be hard to go unnoticed when you're about four inches taller than every other girl in your class, stomp around in combat boots, and perpetually smell a little like diner grease, but the kids in my class are very talented at erasing me.

Plus, it's Friday, the last day before the entire town takes two weeks off for the annual suck-up-to-tourists-fest known as the Meteor Regional Pageant and Talent Competition Showcase.

Some schools get homecoming, we get this. And as usual, I seem to be the only one in town who sees what a joke it is.

To some of the people at this school, it's about town unity, or a break from school, or a ridiculous dress and world peace. To some of them, it's about the glittering hope that for one night, they'll transcend their small-town mediocrity and brush up against greatness.

33

You can already see it in the halls. Long, fake nails painted sparkly blue and orange (Meteor Central High colors), fake eyelashes fluttering. The only salon in town is booked weeks in advance, so the girls without an in have to be careful with their manicures.

Mine, of course, are bitten ragged and unpainted as usual.

No one notices.

In the air, there's the futile hope that Kendra Kendall and Royce Bradley won't fulfill their genetic destiny to be Miss Meteor and Cornhole MVP respectively, golden and chosen, lip-locking over the spiked punch bowl before one of them inevitably pukes electric red on the other's super-shiny shoes.

And before Kendra Kendall, who already lives in one of the nicest houses in town, walks away with a check for ten thousand dollars.

What I wouldn't give.

"Listen up, I know you all have pageant week on the brain, but there are still ten more minutes of school, and we're gonna make them count, okay! Look alive!" Mr. Hamilton hasn't had his spirit crushed by the profound disinterest of Meteor Central High's sophomore class yet. He's the kind of teacher who cares so much, he can make you not care just to compensate.

Also, he makes history puns about his own name, which is just humiliating.

"With all this extra time over the break, I want you guys to do a little . . ." He actually gives himself a drumroll on the edge of Amelia Perkins's desk. "Partner project!"

An audible groan goes up from the crowd, but I don't bother joining in. It's survival time. My eyes dart around the room until I find the familiar dark, glossy curtain of hair atop Junior Cortes's head. Junior's different than the rest of the people here, in that he's not altogether horrible. At least, as other people go.

Case-in-point: He's already looking at me when I find him, eyebrows raised in silent solidarity. He doesn't have to do this anymore. Hide. He could be sitting with them back there if he wanted to, but instead he sticks with me. We were both awkward in middle school, so it made sense to band together, but while my body doubled down on it, growing taller and more gangly by the second, his sprouted a jawline and muscles in all the right places to give him "potential."

On me, five-nine looks like a circus sideshow, but on him, even another two inches looks effortless. It's deeply unfair.

In a town the weather-beaten color of the desert, a sandy brown like mine blends right in. But Junior's is darker, like the stones of the seventeenth-century Spanish ruins we visited on a field trip when we were twelve. His skin is warm, even under these torturous fluorescent lights.

People notice him these days. I notice them noticing. But if Junior knows it, he hasn't changed to fit the mold. That's what makes him the one I look to when I'm forced to leave my invisible bubble.

Unfortunately, it's not up to us today.

"I can already see you all partnering up with your eyes out there," says Mr. Hamilton, "but we're gonna do things a little differently this time . . ."

It's all I can do not to slam my head against my graffitied desk. Like he's the first teacher in history to ever assign partners. Like it's so different and quirky and cool. Like if he picks just right, he'll be responsible for the total upending of a decades-old, rigid high school hierarchy.

I should already see where he's going with this, but somehow, I'm still surprised when he calls my name.

"Chicky Quintanilla?" He goes overboard on the accent, why does that embarrass me? "Why don't you try . . . Kendra Kendall?"

My mute horror must show on my face, because Junior shoots me a pitying look. He might be the closest thing to a friend I have in this town, but he's definitely not the only one who knows Kendra and I have been mortal enemies since fourth grade. The whole class snickers, looking between Kendra and me like the air might catch fire.

To his credit, Junior doesn't look away until Mr. Hamilton pairs him with Kendra's brother, Cole Kendall, who's just leaning back in his chair with that half smile he always wears, like he knows something we don't.

Meteor's so small we've had blended classes since second grade, so even though Cole is a grade ahead of us he's still subject to Mr. Hamilton's bad fourth period puns.

My secret is this: As much as I loathe his sister, I've always secretly envied Cole. We've never spoken a word to each other, but it's clear just from proximity that he knows who he wants to be, and he's brave enough to be it out loud.

Case-in-point: He was the only one who ever tried to stop his friends from going after me in middle school, when the lunch room was my daily torture. The only one who nodded or said "hey" in the hallways when everyone else was pretending I didn't exist.

I wasn't the only one he stuck up for, either. Royce calls him the patron saint of losers because he's always talking them down from their latest bullying escapade, but he just takes it in stride.

Well, unless they started teasing him. Then he clams up just as fast as I do.

I always wished I could return the favor, but I've never had the guts to even talk to him, not really. I mean, besides the occasional mumbled "thanks" when he distracts Royce with something and lets me escape to the bathroom to eat in peace.

But sometimes I wonder if we could have been friends. You know, in another life.

In this one, I'm too busy trying to sink into the floor as Mr. Hamilton moves on to pair up some other unfortunate social misfits with their cool-kid counterparts, I pray that I'll disappear as Kendra rolls her eyes at the girls around her. She doesn't even bother to glare at me.

The rest of the period passes in a fog of wishful thinking. That this is all a bad dream. That the bell ringing will project us all into an alternate reality where the Kendall family never moved to Meteor, or I skipped fourth grade like my teacher said I could, or even that my parents really did stop having kids after Fresa and I don't even exist.

Unfortunately, when the bell does ring, all it does is cause a stampede. School is out. Pageant week has finally arrived.

Junior hangs back, and I fall in step with him as we walk out the door in comfortable silence.

"Hey, Ring Pop!" comes Kendra's voice from behind us.

Every one of my muscles clenches at the nickname. I quickly scan the hallway to see who heard her and how much damage has been done. It's the first time she's addressed me directly since we started high school.

And I guess Kendra is ready to remind me of that. Maybe I've gotten too comfortable in my anonymity, but this throwback to the most humiliating moment of my school career is like being thrown into the deep end.

Fourth grade. A field trip where I was lucky enough to be seated next to Allison Davis on the bus after admiring her shiny, golden hair since the beginning of the year.

And look, I was nine, I wasn't sure what my feelings meant

yet. If I wanted to be best friends with Allison, or if I wanted to be her, or if I wanted something else altogether. Something I didn't even know the shape of yet. All I knew was that my mom had given me two Ring Pops in my lunch and told me to share one with a friend, and the saints had sat me next to Allison.

I didn't get up the nerve to offer her one until the bus ride back, after she leaned close to show me a rock that looked like a horse head, and I got goose bumps because her hair smelled like flowers.

Later, I'd kick myself for not just handing her the candy like a normal person, but I was carried away on the wings of what I didn't yet know was my first crush, so I took Allison's hand and went to slide the plastic ring onto her finger. My heart was beating so hard I was sure she could hear it, and she smiled.

But that was before Royce Bradley, seated behind us with Cole, leaned over the seat. "Ew, what are you guys, lesbos?" he asked, loud enough for the whole bus to hear, elbowing Cole, whose eyes widened for just a fraction of a second with something I knew even then was fear. Cole had never been under fire from Royce, but he had to have known he was protected by very thin social armor.

Kendra was behind them of course, she and Royce already an item at nine and ten. While Royce was usually the instigator, Kendra was cruel, and I saw it in her eyes. She'd remember this moment long after Royce lost interest.

She'd make me pay for my mistake.

I froze. *Lesbo.* I'd never heard the word, but I knew what it must mean. My summer-brown skin hid my blush, but Allison's was spreading like strawberry jam, and she yanked the ring off her finger and threw it at me.

"I'm not gay," she sneered. Kendra laughed loudly, and I knew I should have said I wasn't either—because I wasn't, right?—but I knew if I spoke I would cry, so I just sat there as Allison turned a stony shoulder toward me and spent the rest of the trip looking out the window.

She moved again, at the end of the year, and Cole punched Royce on the arm and asked him a question about some sports thing, and eventually they moved on to ridicule someone else. But Kendra called me "Ring Pop" until well into middle school, and absolutely everyone knew why.

Forget asking questions, or exploring, or coming out. From the moment Jeff Hanson peed his pants at the blackboard at the end of seventh grade and my daily harassment ended, I knew I was lucky to be left alone. Even if being left alone was some-times lonely.

Even if the weight of the secret cost me my best friend.

"Kendra," I mumble when she reaches me, trying and fail-ing to present a smaller target by collapsing my shoulders. I know I'm ruining months of what Cereza calls *posture training* (which is just her jabbing me in the spine whenever she catches me slouching, anyway).

Kendra glides up to me with her usual precise steps, her

long legs golden beneath a sunflower sundress. "I thought we should talk about the project before you take off to serve . . . whatever it is your family serves out of that tin can." Her entourage of long-legged, perfectly made-up lackies laugh, like the bleating of sheep.

My face heats up, but I don't answer, just shrink even further into myself.

She rolls her eyes. "Well, even you must know the Miss Meteor pageant is next week." She gestures to the banner just being strung up in the school's main hallway, as if the event needs to be announced. "I'm gonna be doing my duty to the town by being the fourth woman in my family to be crowned . . ."

The girls around her whoop, twirling, showing off their tiny dresses and blindingly white braces-corrected smiles.

"So, I'm just saying, if my duty is to attract tourists to save this town and all the sad little businesses in it—like, what's that little lunch shack called? Se-Loser's?" Another chorus of bleating fills the hallway. "I'm gonna need you to do your duty, too, do we understand each other?"

"It's called Selena's," I say, because my parents deserve it, but honestly, I'm not even sure she hears me, and I don't try again. If I upset her too much, she'll forget whoever is in her crosshairs this week and I'll be right back where I started.

"Hey, Kendra," says Cole from the group behind her, and my stomach flip flops. His voice is usually mild, laid back, but there's something tense in it as he takes the target from me again.

41

He must be afraid of them, I think. Afraid of what they'll do if he steps *too* far out of line. But he doesn't let it stop him. Even though he doesn't know me. Even though this isn't his fight.

"Cole," Kendra says, in a way that grants permission and relaxes the crowd. Her gaze is imperious, unearned, and directed at Cole. It makes me feel something closer to anger than fear. Just for a second.

"It's weird," Cole says. "But I'm actually on the cornhole team—which some say is an even bigger draw than the pageant—and I don't have a problem finishing my homework."

"Yeah, Kendall?" Royce Bradley says, approaching in a crowd of letterman jackets with little beanbags sewn onto the chests. "Well some of us are busy getting laid."

Cole's jaw tightens. Just a little. Not enough for anyone to see. Anyone but me, anyway. Because I think Cole Kendall has just helped me transcend my fear, if only for a second. At this moment, I don't feel totally alone, and that feeling lights a tiny, reckless flame in me. Like a single match.

Something small, but with the potential to be utterly destructive.

"Is that any way to talk about a man's sister?" Cole asks, but there's more effort behind that casual tone now, and my tiny flame finds more fuel. What right do Kendra and Royce have? Why doesn't anyone ever stop them?

"The project," Kendra says to me, glowing even brighter with her upperclassman boyfriend draped around her, already turning to go. "It's all yours. Don't expect any cozy late-night study sessions or anything . . ."

My face burns, my hair in my eyes again, my only armor against this place.

"Yeah, don't get any ideas about my girl, Ring Pop."

Not everyone laughs, but enough people do, and the flame of my anger withers and dies as the panic sets in. *Please no*, I think. *Not here, not today.*

The shape of the word has occurred to me, peeking up and out no matter how invisible I stay.

Pansexual. I didn't know the word when I needed it, but I know it now. It's a word that means it's okay if I don't notice "boy" or "girl" or any other gender first. It's a word that means it's okay the way I notice the spark of a person, and that what's on the outside doesn't change the way I'm drawn to it like a moth.

And it's a beautiful word. I loved it the moment I overheard one of Cereza's friends say it through the thin wall separating our bedrooms. But as beautiful as it is, it doesn't belong in this hallway. It belongs in a someday future maybe, far from here when I don't have to hide. Today, being pansexual, being anything outside the norm, is a liability. A disaster waiting to happen.

See, Meteor prides itself on being a place where you "look out for your fellow man" (I actually think I lifted that straight from the town brochure). But it's also the kind of place where

43

you're expected to fit in, to earn that down-home courtesy. To be one of the smiling faces on the brochure. To let the town pretend it's tolerant by not making them reach too far to prove it.

For instance, probably a third of our town's five-thousand residents are Latinx—but Meteor "doesn't care if we're purple," so long as we're not too loud about it.

Ms. Jacobs and Ms. McNeil have been "roommates" for twenty years in a one-bedroom house on Spruce Street, and no one bats an eye because they don't make a spectacle of themselves in public.

And then there's Cole Kendall, who's treated like one of the golden boys as long as he's calling little old ladies ma'am, keeping his hair neat, and scoring half the soccer team's goals all season.

But here, in the hallway, with Royce sneering at me, it's all too obvious that this town has already given me my maximum allowance for weird. I'm already the black sheep Quintanilla sister with the bad haircut and the weird clothes. I'm already a different color than the families with money and clout.

My answer is all over Royce's face right now, and he's right. Meteor isn't going to let me be any more different. Not unless I give something up first.

Junior steps forward, toward Royce, but I shake my head. Fighting back here, on their turf, will only make things worse. Even he should know that by now.

Royce waits, his chest puffed out, his arms at his sides. Cole won't meet my eyes this time, and I can tell whatever moment we almost had is over. Kendra has reminded us all of her power, her boyfriend like some mythical amplifying staff on her arm, the Miss Meteor crown in her hot-pink-taloned grasp. The darkness of all my secrets is folding in on itself again, willing to do whatever it takes to stay hidden.

The show over, the members of the crowd seem to remember they don't have to be here anymore and scatter.

"Tell me what's going on in there," Junior asks when we're the only ones left in the hallway. For a moment I wonder: Should I tell him? Make myself a little less invisible just for a minute? Paint a Chicky-sized outline in this hallway even though it will fade away?

I know he wouldn't judge me, but can I really do it? Say: What's going on, Junior, is that I'm different and I'm afraid?

But that's when I see Lita, peeking around a doorway down the hallway, her eyes round and shiny as quarters in the road. I don't let myself smile when I see what she's wearing, but it's hard not to. It's one of her cactus birthday party outfits. A yellow sweater covered in little, fuzzy pom-poms, and a shiny skirt over hot-pink tights. There's even a tiny, matching mylar balloon stuck behind her ear like a pencil.

Feliz cumpleaños, Señora Strawberry, I think sadly, but then it hits me, and the sight of Lita is all it takes to force me back into sixth-grade Chicky's shell. I remember what it felt like, to be on the verge of telling, to not be able to. How much it hurt. How it made me pull back into a cocoon of my own making and push everyone around me away to keep the secret safe.

Since then, I've kept everyone at arm's distance. Even when Lita looked hurt and confused in the hallways and eventually started sitting somewhere else at lunch. Even when Junior tries to get closer.

I can't risk it. Telling Junior. Because I couldn't even tell my best friend. The girl closer to me than a sister. The truth was too big to confront, sharing it too big a risk to take.

The truth that I might not be like everyone else.

That I might be worthy of the nasty names that flew around behind me at school.

I couldn't tell her. And it destroyed us. But telling her would have destroyed me.

In the hallway now, Junior looks at me quizzically, waiting for an answer I still can't give, because some stupid flouncing princess and her rock-headed prince made it their mission to make me feel unworthy. Small. Cornered and alone.

They're still just as smug, as self-important and drunk on their own power as they were then, and in my building anger I realize:

Maybe I couldn't tell Lita then. Maybe I can't tell Junior now. But there's one thing I can do. Something I should have done a long time ago.

I can take something from that girl, who took so much

46

from me with just a sneer and a nickname, and the thing she cares about most is all around us.

Miss Meteor. Kendra expects to win. Everyone expects her to win. But you can only enter Miss Meteor once. If I can find a way to stop her, she'll never get another chance.

Her family legacy broken, humiliated in front of the school and the town and the tourists? It would be a start.

Leaving Junior shaking his head in the hallway, I walk as fast as my baby-horse legs can carry me to the bike rack outside school. Because there's only one place to go when you need a secret, insidious plan, and that's straight to my older sisters.

LITA

ALL THROUGH AFTERNOON classes I think about it. It distracts me when we talk about phytoplankton in biology. It makes my mind wander away from a lecture on the ancient Romans. It even draws my attention away from the flowery graphs we make of polar equations in Mrs. LaRoux's class.

But my thoughts keep circling around Miss Meteor.

Am I really thinking of doing this? Am I really considering making what might be my last big act on Planet Earth this, something that might end in my complete humiliation?

And if I am, how am I even gonna do it?

I want to tell Bruja Lupe.

Except I can't tell Bruja Lupe anything until I have the plan of all plans. Because I know exactly how she's going to react to "I know you're losing me, how about in the little time we have together, I parade around a stage for everyone in town to laugh at?"

"Lita," Mrs. LaRoux says as I leave class. "Are you feeling all right?"

Mrs. LaRoux knows math is my favorite subject. I listen to my math teachers with the attention Bruja Lupe gives old Grace Kelly movies. Last time I seemed distracted, it was an hour before I got sent home with walking pneumonia. Nothing takes me out of math class.

Except this.

"Yeah," I say. "All vital signs normal."

That makes her relax enough to let me out into the hall.

Through one of the school windows, I can see that banner.

The Fiftieth-Annual Meteor Regional Pageant and Talent Competition Showcase

Bruja Lupe knows that, a long time ago, I wanted to be Miss Meteor. I wanted to embody all the cosmic magic of this town, the same way the space rock does. I used to trip around in old Goodwill ballgowns with Chicky pretending to be my manager (back then, bids for Miss Meteor seemed like such a big deal to us that we thought they were like political campaigns).

But ever since what happened with Royce and his friends, I stopped talking about it, to anyone, including Bruja Lupe.

Now I stand in the hall, my brain toggling back and forth between wondering if Bruja Lupe might lend me her lipsticks and trying to come up with any talent I could do on a pageant stage.

Whenever I catch Cole at the edge of my vision, like I do right now, the things I notice are the things that have been the same since we were small. The cornhusk blond of his hair. His khakis that are cut like jeans. Collared shirts or plain T-shirts, never polos. He breaks from the uniform the rest of the corn-hole team wears.

"Bye, Lita," Cole says.

I register him there, but I'm thinking too hard to answer.

"Little out in space today?" Cole asks.

The words catch me, like my toe snagging on the edge of the carpet that's peeling away in Bruja Lupe's living room.

My attention snaps back. "What?"

"Are you okay?" Cole asks.

"Yeah," I say. "Are you?"

I say it out of instinct, like when someone asks "How are you?" and you say "Fine, and you?" without thinking. But there's something sad flickering in his eyes.

"Cole," I say. "What's wrong?"

"Nothing," he says. "Just thinking about practice. Coach has me working on this wrist-flick thing."

I know what it is probably, even without knowing what it is. It's all the little slights he lives with.

It's how sometimes people are so busy congratulating themselves on being accepting that there's no room in them for anything else. Including being accepting. Meteor(ite), New Mexico, may have a dozen gringos each Halloween dress up in flying-saucer-sized sombreros and fake mustaches, but point out the flaws in their costumes or opinions, and they'll respond like you've told Martha Stewart her angel food cake is dry. It's just not something they consider possible, that they are anything less than small-town neighborly. They act as though they've always embraced Cole Kendall as the guy he is. They don't want to remember the ridiculous meetings debating whether he should be allowed in the boys' locker room, or where to put him for sex ed. (That was how they phrased it too. *Where do we put him?*)

"Is your dad gonna make it home this week?" I ask.

Cole shakes his head. "Can't."

He holds his jaw tight, keeping his face from falling. Every time I ask Cole about his father, Mr. Kendall seems to be in a different city, giving a presentation or smoothing over a project in a different regional office. All of which seems to be more important than making it home for Cole's games.

Even this week's cornhole championship.

"He's gonna have to stay in Buffalo." Cole shrugs like it's nothing. "Some kind of deal going through. It's fine though. When I'm throwing, it's not like I notice who's there. Hubert Humphrey himself could stop by and I'd miss it." He tries to laugh.

Hubert Humphrey. Everyone around here knows he was vice president when Meteor was founded. Everyone knows there's a statue of him in the park. But Cole Kendall is probably the only one who remembers what number vice president he was. I definitely don't know. Just like I don't know why Cole still talks to me.

Probably because I am little (Bruja Lupe's word) in a way that makes him look out for me, cute (Mrs. Quintanilla's word) in a way that's easy to feel sorry for, and made fun of enough that his conscience won't let him forget me entirely.

You can't really know what makes people keep caring or stop caring. I learned that from Chicky.

Right now, I catch a last glimpse of Chicky, watching Junior's back as he goes.

And an idea hums through the desert, landing on me like a blown-loose party streamer. It's bright as yellow-and-pink crepe paper, waving and fluttering to get my attention.

Fresa Quintanilla was second runner-up in last year's Miss Meteor pageant. Before her, Uva and Cereza placed high, the crown almost in reach. And they did it while older versions of Kendra Kendall hid their talent ribbons and mascara wands.

Scheming is in the Quintanilla blood. I know that from Chicky. It was Chicky who figured out that putting out the right wind chime late at night would, to Bruja Lupe's dreaming brain, sound like our laugh behind my bedroom door. It let us sneak out while Bruja Lupe stayed asleep.

When we wanted to make nopales, it was Chicky who

managed to borrow Fresa's tweezers for the spines and get them back before she noticed.

If anyone knows how to hatch a plan, it's Chicky.

Chicky, my old campaign manager.

Maybe Chicky isn't my friend anymore. But maybe it doesn't matter. Maybe there's something I could offer her. The prize money? Me live-serenading her and Junior on their first (long overdue) official date? Whatever it is, she can have it.

"Earth to Estrellita Perez?" Cole says, a laugh in his voice.

"Huh?" I startle back to him. "What?"

"Okay, I'm starting to worry," he says. "You're way far out there. Even for you. Are you okay?"

I watch Chicky fleeing down the hall. I can't ask her here. First, I have shorter legs than she does, I'll never catch up.

Second, I still remember the last time I talked about being Miss Meteor at school, and I'm never making that mistake again.

"Yeah," I tell Cole. "I just had an idea."

CHICKY

SELENA'S DINER IS one of those all-chrome anachronisms you see in fifties horror movies. You know, with a giant praying mantis standing over them, holding a screaming blond lady in a red evening gown?

On my way there, I take the only hill in town as fast as I can on my bike. The burning in my muscles won't slow me down, because I am a girl on a mission. I fly past the low, drab buildings and the scrubby trees and the cactuses that grow like weeds.

I fly past out-of-date storefronts with bulbs burned out of their signs, benches that desperately need to be repainted, and so much cheesy space-inspired stuff it kind of makes me sick to my stomach.

Would it kill them to clean the place up a little? I wonder. Repaint some stuff? Make it look like something besides the dusty, nowhere town where every campy sci-fi movie starts?

The people in those movies never end up staying in the town once the threat has been neutralized.

I can take some comfort from that, at least.

When I stop, finally, I lean my bike up against the stack of pallets in the back, catching my reflection in the dingy, scratched surface of the diner. I don't look any different than normal. There are the too-long legs that I call "stick brown" and my mom calls "sepia." The black cutoffs I've been wearing since seventh grade. The striped T-shirt I wear when Fresa hides all my black tank tops and tells me to stop being so weird.

As if I can help it.

I might look the same on the outside, but on the inside I've been totally rearranged. Today, *I'm* the meteor, hurtling forward on a collision course. Only this time it's not a ramshackle town in danger, it's a long-legged blonde with her nose in the air.

Because at the end of next week, Kendra Kendall will be watching someone else don the Miss Meteor crown with a frozen smile on her face. For me. For Cole. For the absence of Lita. For everyone who has ever felt like a demoted dwarf planet in the presence of her sun.

And I'm gonna be the one to make it happen.

So far, I've thought of itching powder in her strapless bra, blue Kool-Aid in her shampoo, foot cream in her expensive moisturizer, but I know that's kid stuff compared to what I need.

Luckily, my sister Fresa is working today, and no one can scheme for nefarious purposes quite like she can.

Trust me, I learned that the hard way when she caught me borrowing her purple high tops in sixth grade without asking. Revenge came low and slow, and my left eyebrow never grew back the same.

I walk into Selena's filled with righteous fire, but when I push through the back doors, my heart sinks down to join my stomach. I can tell from the kitchen window there are no customers here. Not even old Buzz, who sometimes drinks coffee at the counter all day long when the museum is closed. It's too late in the day to hope for an after-school rush, so we just have to cross our fingers for dinner. Again.

"Chicky! Good thing you're here. We need all the help we can get!"

My dad approaches from the empty grill, and the sinking feeling just gets worse. Dad's doing the same thing he did at home during lunch, pretending everything is all fine and well. I wish that, for once, my parents would just be honest with me.

Selena's is a family business, which means my parents run it most of the time, and the four of us help out after school and on weekends. Five women, and yet my dad is the one prancing around the kitchen, singing "Como La Flor" into a spatula.

"Pero, aaaaaaayyyy, como me duele . . . ," he serenades me. "Aaaaaay, como me duele! Come on, sing with me!"

But the sinking feeling is too heavy, I can't even smile. How can he be dancing around back here like nothing's wrong when even the lights being on in this room is like throwing money into the gutter?

"Sorry, Dad," I mutter. "Just looking for Fresa."

He stops singing, turning the music down. "You okay, Mija?" he asks, concern putting a crease in his unibrow. My dad is so handsome, he could have been in movies, but instead he's stuck back here, in an empty kitchen, singing a dead girl's songs to no one.

"Just thought there'd be more people here," I mumble, before I can help myself.

My dad's too-bright smile falters. "You know pageant week's coming up," he says. "We'll get plenty of business. We're okay, Mijita."

But the question lingers between us: Will pageant week be enough to make up for a year's worth of empty lunch tables?

"Yeah, okay," I say, not meeting his eyes. "Um, Fresa?"

"Uh-oh, what'd she do now?" he asks, obviously trying to cover up the worry thick in the fryer-smelling air between us, but I can't even answer around the lump in my throat.

"In the alley breaking down cardboard," he says when I don't reply.

"Fat chance," I say, cracking half a smile. An offering.

Dad rolls his eyes affectionately, taking it. "Okay, okay. More like convincing the dishwashers from next door to break down cardboard for her," he amends.

I try to widen my smile, but on my way through the diner there are tears pricking the backs of my eyes. "What are you looking at?" I ask Selena's life-size cutout by the counter. She doesn't answer; she just keeps smiling.

There's a flickering neon moon on the sign outside, a thinly veiled attempt to fit in with the space craze this town is famous for, but the Tejana queen reigns supreme inside. Signed photos, cutouts, and album covers are all over the walls.

In other parts of the country, nostalgic places like this one pay homage to Elvis, but we don't kneel for kings in here. Only for La Reina. "Don't you know?" my dad asks tourists with Meteor T-shirts from Buzz's gift shop. "Selena is a moon-goddess's name, and all the Quintanillas are blessed by proxy."

No one has the heart to tell him we're not those Quintanillas, and we pretend we don't see him combing genealogy free trials at night when everyone else is asleep.

Through the side door, Fresa examines a nail haughtily while sure enough, two dishwasher boys from the Milky Way Ice Cream Parlor across the street break down a stack of Selena's cardboard boxes and toss them in the shared dumpster.

"Fres," I say, and she looks up. "I need your help."

She sizes me up for a second, taking in my cooling cheeks and my eyes that must still be reflecting all my destructive urges.

"Fine, I was getting bored anyway." She turns imperiously to the boys sweating over her afternoon task. "Shoo," she says, waving a hand, and they do it. Just like that. Scamper back off to their soft serve like she has the authority to physically move them through space. Like she's not just an almost-nineteen-year-old girl who spends an absurd amount of time on her hair.

This, more than anything so far, convinces me I've come to the right place.

"Okay," she says when they're gone. "Let's talk while you help me clear tables."

"I need to make Kendra Kendall lose Miss Meteor," I blurt out before she can go inside. The effort of not saying it since the hallway is finally too much. "With, like, as much suffering as I can inflict along the way."

Fresa raises one perfectly shaped eyebrow. "I'm not even gonna ask why," she says, and I know she means it. She doesn't care. I probably had her at "suffering."

She considers me again, something else gleaming in her eye this time. It says maybe I'm not just the useless weirdo that sleeps across the hall, after all. That maybe I do share an iota of her DNA after she's spent years trying to prove I was adopted.

She's still thinking when the bell rings, and I hate myself for the hope that jumps into my throat. Maybe it's a group of old ladies after book club, or a bus trip to Santa Fe that stopped off to see the rock . . .

I run to the counter even though I'm not technically working today, ready to put on my best "you want to eat here" smile, but it's only Lita, her wide eyes taking the place in like she's never seen it before. Like she didn't practically grow up across from Bruja Lupe in the third booth on the left—the one you can see the moon sign from. Back when she was working her way through the menu from top to bottom, looking for something that felt like home.

The distance between us tugs at my chest, just like always, the piles of words left unsaid not enough to fill the hole our friendship left when it faded like a comet's tail in the sky.

"Hey," I say, like I'd say it to anyone.

"Hey," she says back, imitating my casual nod.

Don't be awkward, I tell myself, right before I say: "So, the weather, it's . . . uh . . . tater tot nachos. The special is tater tot nachos."

Even Lita Perez, the strangest girl in Meteor by a landslide, looks at me like she's worried maybe I have a concussion.

I sigh. "Sorry, can I get you something?"

She pretends to look over the menu, even though we both know she doesn't need to, and I try to remember the last time we actually spoke. We see each other constantly, it's the curse of the small town. But I avoid Bruja Lupe's neighborhood, even though it means riding my bike the long way to school, and Lita avoids the diner.

At least, she used to.

"I'll take a cupcake with . . ."

"Jalapeños?" I can't help finishing for her.

"Jalapeños," she confirms, and we both smile.

"Chicky," Lita says as I pull a red velvet cupcake from the

glass pastry display (she was never picky about the flavor) and a jar of pickled jalapeños from below the counter. I arrange five of the green discs on top of the frosting and push it across the counter on a plate.

"Lita?"

"Do you remember when we used to play Miss Meteor?"

It's the absolute last question I expected her to ask, and my first reaction is to curl up like a porcupine against the memories. All the togetherness that I distanced myself from because I couldn't tell her the truth.

But before I can, her words start to stir something in me. Something as old as paper dolls and cactus-flower crowns. Something that makes itching powder seem like child's play.

"I do," I say cautiously, because with Lita you never know what's coming next.

"Remember how you used to be my manager?" Her voice is high and breathless, her eyes sparkling.

I can't help it, I sparkle back. "I do."

"We always won," she says. "Every pageant."

"The other contestants were Señora Strawberry and three of Cereza's old dolls," I reply, trying not to smile too much. It's just going to hurt when I have to put it away again later.

"Señora Strawberry was always our stiffest competition," she reminisces, smiling, but then she pauses, a long thing with plenty of space for imagining inside it.

"What if it wasn't pretend?" she says when the silence has run its course. "No cactuses, no bent-spoon tiaras. The real deal."

"You're not thinking of entering . . . ," I say, because I can't picture it, even though I remember the way she daydreamed about it back then. But then, just as suddenly, I *can* picture it. Kendra Kendall, losing Miss Meteor. But not just losing. Losing to Lita Perez . . .

"Not without your help," she says in a wheedling tone. "I mean, you know I never could have beat Señora Strawberry if you hadn't coached me through the Q&A."

She's steeled herself, I can see it on her face. Despite her jokes, this is what she walked through those doors to ask me.

It breaks my heart and makes me hopeful all at once, that even after years of distance and avoiding and the terrible sadness of growing apart, we're still scheming in tandem.

Lita's still watching me, her brave face faltering a little as I think it over.

It's a crazy idea. Worse than crazy. Lita and I barely know each other anymore, and honestly the itching powder probably has a higher probability of success than the two weirdest girls in Meteor staging the biggest pageant upset in the event's fifty-year history.

And so I'm about to say no. Ask Bruja Lupe for something itchy from her hierba drawer when Lita's out and go the easy route. But then I remember the end of our pretend pageants, where we'd crack open the shoebox full of chocolate coins and split our winnings.

Ten thousand dollars. Even a portion of it would keep the lights on a little while longer around here. Maybe fix some cracking paint or replace the chairs with the wobbly legs.

"Never mind," Lita says, her voice small. "I shouldn't have—"

"I'll do it," I say, my voice clear and decisive even though alarm bells are ringing louder than the ancient fire bell in the town square and every cell in my body is demanding an explanation. "I'll help you become Miss Meteor."

Lita's jaw drops. "You . . . I . . . What?"

"I'll help you. But we're not competing against dolls and cactuses anymore. You're gonna need more help."

Luckily, I know exactly who to ask.

LITA

I WOULD HAVE been less surprised to see Hubert Humphrey, vice president of the United States when Meteor was incorporated, waltz into Selena's than I am at this moment.

Because Chicky saying yes—so quickly and so surely—is as odd as having a politician who died in 1978 sit down and order onion rings.

"Really?" I ask. I was ready to offer her the prize money I may or may not win. I was ready to learn to play mariachi for the Chicky-Junior first date. I was ready to scrub plates the next time the dishwasher in the diner kitchen breaks down.

"To be clear," Chicky says. "I'm not entering with you. It'd be you up there in sequins and fake eyelashes, not me."

I can't help laughing. Not because Chicky couldn't rock an evening gown (probably with combat boots), but because she would be stomping across the stage and rolling her eyes through the entire promenade.

"I know," I say.

A memory hangs between us, of when we used to play dress up, pretending to be actors in Bruja Lupe's favorite movies that no one our age had ever heard of but us. I'd borrow one of Bruja Lupe's dresses and pretend I was Rita Hayworth, and she'd borrow one of her dad's old suits and strut around with the style of Marlene Dietrich and the suaveness of Humphrey Bogart.

It brings the familiar ache of something that faded and just got lost.

Friendships don't always end with a big fight, a sudden silence. Sometimes it's a sad, slow drifting apart. Sometimes it's one of you getting the flu so bad you're out of school for two weeks, and then when you come back you just don't sit together at lunch anymore. Sometimes it's realizing there's something big you're not saying and something big she's not saying, and that you're both not telling each other the big things anymore.

This is how you stop being friends, a little at a time.

"Can I ask you something?" I say.

She nods.

"What made you say yes?" I ask.

I'm ready for her to say, "Do you want my help or not?" Or something about a gifted horse—a phrase people on this planet seem to really like when it comes to questioning favors, but that I've never gotten up the nerve to ask the meaning of.

But Chicky shakes her head at the glitter-flecked Formica

65

tabletop. "You ever just wake up one day and realize you've taken something for years and you can't do it for another day? Like, literally can't do it anymore?"

Mr. Hamilton might pick on her use of the word "literally," but from the look in her eyes, I get the feeling she means it.

I think of the skin on my stomach turning to stardust, my desperate wish to hold on to my body and my life on Earth.

I think of how I can't leave this town, this planet, without trying for the dream I had all those years ago. Because then I would have stayed small and afraid forever, right up until the sky takes me back.

"Yeah," I say. "I know that feeling."

"Now can I ask you something?" Chicky says.

I nod.

"Why now?" she asks. "You have two years. No one in our grade enters. You know that."

"Except Kendra."

"Right. Exactly."

If she says I'm too brown/too chubby/too wobbly on high heels to win a pageant, I'm leaving. I know all that, and I don't need to hear it from her.

When she doesn't, I answer her question.

"You know how you literally can't do it anymore?" I ask.

She nods.

"I literally can't wait two years," I say.

I wince, waiting for her to ask why, knowing I won't tell her.

I only told Bruja Lupe—weeks ago, when the first ribbon of stardust appeared—because I thought she'd know how to make it stop. The air in our house has felt a little sadder ever since the night she told me she couldn't, didn't know how. Ever since every remedio didn't turn it back.

But Chicky doesn't ask why.

Instead, the sunflowers in the centers of her eyes brighten, as sudden as clouds clearing. "And you're sure you have this in you? Prancing around in sparkles?"

"If I had the stomach to help you steal Fresa's tweezers, I have the stomach for anything."

"Oh my God!" Fresa comes thundering toward the booth. "That was you two! I knew it!"

"Run," Chicky says under her breath.

I slide out of the booth.

Chicky lopes after me.

Our only salvation is that I'm pretty sure Fresa's nails are wet—I can tell by how they're shining—so she won't grab the door and come after us.

But we're still running and laughing, and we could almost be out with the cactuses again, years ago, when we were friends and Miss Meteor was something we acted out in old evening gowns under the desert sky.

CHICKY

I'M SITTING AT the kitchen table, stress-eating pickles and wondering what I've gotten myself into, when the fight breaks out.

"Give me back my leggings!"

"You guys, can't we handle this without screaming?"

"I'm gonna KILL you!"

I roll my eyes, putting the pickle jar back before taking the stairs two at a time. I've been avoiding this moment. Asking Fresa for help with the pageant makes it more than just nostalgia. More than remembering Lita and I in the cactus field, her in too-big high heels, me with a clipboard shouting out instructions.

If I get Fresa involved, that means we're doing this. For real. In front of God and Kendra Kendall and Junior and Mr. Hamilton and everyone.

Everyone . . .

In the hallway outside our bedrooms, Uva is still standing between Cereza and Fresa, but I can tell her courage won't last much longer.

"You know those are my leggings," Cereza says, in a voice that will probably convince patients to agree to risky medical treatments someday, but it does nothing for Fresa, whose pupils are dilated in a way I have associated with danger since I was six years old.

"They're my leggings," she says. "I bought them because Berto said my ass looks good in them. Like I would forget that."

"Oh yes, because the objectifying comments of a guy who drinks tall cans of Modelo out of paper bags in the gas station parking lot hold any sway in this argument whatsoever."

"Hey, Fresa," I say, knowing I'd be better off waiting for the next ice age than the end of one of their legendary arguments. She doesn't even turn.

"Maybe you wouldn't be so mad if anyone ever told you your ass looks good in something," Fresa retorts. "In fact, you know what, Rez, you can have them. My gift to you. Maybe you'll get laid and stop being such a b—"

"Oh, like I even want your ho charity!" Cereza screeches.

"So you admit they're mine!"

"OH MY G—"

"HEY, FRESA!" I yell, and for once, they all go silent. Three pairs of surprised eyes turn my way. "Can I talk to you for a minute?"

"Uh, sure, Flaca," she says, turning back to Cereza. "You're lucky I'm such a good sister, bitch. Wear those leggings tonight, and your hoops. Thank me later." She turns and beckons me into her room before Cereza's face can go from red to purple.

"So, what's up?" She pulls a pillow onto her lap. I haven't been in this room for months. There are cutout photos of greased abs on every flat surface. It's nauseating.

"It's . . . about Miss Meteor," I begin, and she perks up instantly. "I'm not entering," I clarify quickly. "But . . . Lita wants to."

I wait for her to laugh.

"You mean in the cactus field like you guys used to when you were little, right?" she asks, her eyes narrowing. "Great, I'm glad you found a hobby, hermanita. Because you can't possibly be talking about Lita Perez and the *actual* Miss Meteor pageant."

I exhale loudly. "Except that I am."

"Take it from me," Fresa says, with an expertly arched eyebrow. "Try underwater welding or something. It'll be safer."

"I'm . . . pretty determined."

Fresa blows her bangs up, then fixes me with a penetrating stare.

"Why on earth would you do something that stupid? Is this about your weird obsession with Kendra Kendall again?"

"No," I say, instantly defensive. "Okay, yes."

"I thought you wanted to humiliate her, not yourself."

"Think about it, though," I say, some of the delusional

70

magic that made me say yes to Lita's diner pitch infecting me again. "Losing to Lita? It would be total social devastation."

Fresa would never admit it, but her eyes start to sparkle, just a little. It's dangerous, like the glint of a streetlight on the barrel of a gun.

"To not just lose, but to lose to people like us?"

Fresa twirls a strand of perfectly blown out hair around her French-manicured index finger. "Okay, I mean, in theory I kind of love it. But Lita, really? I mean . . . she has even less of a chance at winning than you do, and that's . . . really saying something."

"Why do you think we need you?"

Fresa's eyes unfocus, like she's gone somewhere deeper in search of an answer. It's a few minutes before she comes back.

"Fuck it, I'm in," she says.

"Just like that?" I ask, halfway through coming up with another prong of attack. I'm instantly suspicious. "What's in it for you?"

"Duh, justice," she says. "I mean, everyone knows I was robbed last year. And the only thing this world loves more than a dynasty blond girl is a good Cinderella story, right? So, we make Lita fucking Perez a real contender for the tiara. We upset the balance. We piss off the Kendalls and all their weird groupies."

I can tell she's serious, because she hasn't said "bitch" in, like, five minutes.

"Worst-case scenario, she doesn't win, but everyone's

71

talking about this for years to come. Kendra's spotlight gets stolen. Best-case scenario, she actually wins, Kendra is ruined, and there's finally a brown girl wearing that sash."

In Fresa's no-nonsense tone, it almost sounds like it makes sense.

"But if you think I'm getting Lita onto that stage by myself you're—and I never say this—overestimating me."

"What do you mean?"

"I mean you have three sisters. Go get the rest of them on board. We're going to need them."

LITA

"YOU WANT TO what?" Bruja Lupe asks.

I can almost feel the sky vibrating above us, even through the popcorn ceiling.

I weight my feet into the worn-down carpet. "I'm going to enter Miss Meteor."

"Do you have a fever?" Bruja Lupe reaches for my forehead.

"No," I answer slowly, because this sounds like a trick question.

"So this is a decision you made in your right mind?" she asks. "This is what you want? Spending your precious hours fluttering your eyelashes?"

"It's my choice what I do with . . . ," I can't say it.

The time I still have.

Bruja Lupe sighs. "And the choice you want to make is to invite the whole town to make fun of you?"

Now I don't have to try to plant my weight. I feel like I'm going to sink into the carpet.

"That's what you think?" I ask. "That I'll just fail completely?"

"Towns like this don't want girls like us to succeed. You know that."

My brain slips down a familiar path. I want to pull it back, but it keeps going. It slides into an old memory that still stings no matter how many times it's played in my head. How I was stupid enough to come to school in a rhinestone tiara and polyester sash on Halloween, playing at being the beauty queen I thought I could one day become. How ridiculous Royce and his friends thought I was.

Worse than ridiculous.

Something they had to crush.

They weren't happy until they'd scared me down onto the locker room floor, gotten me small and crying and hating that I ever thought I could be anything but what they decided. They weren't happy until they ripped the tiara off my head, its plastic teeth taking pieces of my hair, and put something else, something they considered more appropriate, in its place.

Maybe I'm not much bigger now than I was back then. But I have something I didn't have then, the recklessness of having so little left to lose.

"Chicky's going to help me," I say.

"Chicky Quintanilla?" A laugh rattles through Bruja Lupe's

74

throat. "You chose the one Quintanilla girl who's never been on that stage?"

I almost say how she used to be my coach in our fake Miss Meteor pageants, but now all that feels so small and babyish.

A knock comes at the door. The back one, the one we go through, not the one Bruja Lupe lets tourists in through.

Bruja Lupe gives the biggest sigh of this whole conversation. "What now?"

"I'll get it," I say before she can stomp toward the door.

I open the door, and a whirl of styled hair and fruit-bright color rushes at me. Six eyelinered eyes all fall on me. Six manicured hands grab me and pull me into the center of the three oldest Quintanilla girls.

"Thank goodness we got here in time!" Fresa rushes toward me and takes my face in her hands. "Well, she's pretty, or at least she will be when we're done with her." She says it less like she's paying me a compliment and more like she's identifying a type of duck. She looks at her sister Cereza. "Some highlighter would make her drop-dead perfect, no?"

"You don't heat-style, do you?" Cereza asks. "Don't worry, we'll teach you."

Fresa taps my upper lip and glances at Uva Quintanilla. "Depilatory or cream bleach?"

"Fresa!" Cereza shouts.

"What?" Uva says.

Cereza steps back to consider me. "If we start now, we

might just be able to find her perfect lip color in time," she says. "Do you see yourself as more of as a red girl, a plum girl, a coral girl?"

I look down at my arms. "I see myself as the color I am?"

"Stand up straight, lovely"—Uva pokes me between the shoulder blades—"you need every inch you've got."

Cereza taps my ankle. "If we find her a pair of heels that match her skintone, her legs'll look longer than you think."

"Love these big eyes," Fresa says. "She looks like a cartoon cow."

"Fresa!" Uva says.

"I meant in a cute way." Fresa rolls her eyes at Uva and then brushes her fingers along my temples. "But we have to do something about those brows. Have you ever tweezed?"

Uva steps back, considering. "I wanna see her dressed in blue."

"Blue?" Cereza asks. "A girl with coloring like this and you're gonna count out red and purple?"

"Just trust me on this one," Uva says. "We'll try a few different shades. We don't like it, we go with red."

"Conditioner." Fresa takes a lock of my hair between her fingers. "Say it with me. Lots of conditioner. Sleep with it in every night. I always did it the week before a dance. You'll thank me later."

Fresa moves just enough to let me see into the kitchen.

Bruja Lupe rushes around the stove. She's probably making

tlayudas, her standard people-coming-over-unannounced dinner (her secret ingredient: ground jalapeño. They're good not
just in whole pepper form, and not just on top of cupcakes).

I can tell from the size of the pan that she's cooking for all
five of us.

Six of us.

Chicky leans against the counter and crosses her arms.
She gives me a smile that's half weary, half smirking, a look of
"careful what you wish for."

"Thank you," I mouth.

Miss Meteor, here we come.

CHICKY

YOU HAVEN'T DIED of boredom until you've watched three former beauty queens teach their new protégé how to smile.

Yeah, I thought it was a natural reflex too. Apparently, there's a lot more Vaseline involved than I ever knew.

"Did you put it on?"

"Pendeja, I'm holding the damn tub in my hand, aren't I? My finger all smeared with the stuff? What do you think I'm doing?"

"Well it's not enough! I can't see her canines!"

"It's because she keeps licking it off!"

"Lita bonita, it's supposed to stay on, okay? Just try to forget it's there."

They're gathered around her like vultures on a carcass. My sisters couldn't be more different from each other, but with a common goal they become a three-headed beast, dangerous to all who cross its path.

"Chicky! How do I look?" Lita calls, as Uva balances a book on her head to "promote good posture." It falls to the ground, pages splayed, when she does a ridiculous twirl to face me, her teeth bared in what I can only describe as a rabid Barbie smile.

"Sorry, is there a scaring-neighborhood-children event I'm not aware of?" I ask before I can think twice. Honestly, I haven't flexed my friend muscles in a while, especially not with Lita, and when her face falls I know I messed up.

"No! Lita! Don't close your mouth!"

"The Vaseline!"

But it's too late. They all groan before whirling on me.

"I'm sorry," I say, meaning it. With maneuvering skills I've had a lifetime to practice, I dodge their swatting hands and offer Lita an apologetic shrug. "You know I don't get this beauty pageant crap," I say, tugging at my own DIY haircut. "And I didn't think your regular smile needed improvement."

She rewards me for this with exactly the smile I mean, like a beam of light through a dark sky.

"Your posture, Lita!" Uva groans, shoving me aside just as Cereza swoops in with another glop of Vaseline on the tip of her finger.

"Reza, get a Q-tip or something!" shrieks Fresa as she sticks the offending finger right in Lita's mouth, spreading the fourth coat of slime across her teeth.

"Ha! You think this is gross," Cereza says, "you should spend a day in the Meteor Clinic."

"Hard pass," Fresa says with a withering glare.

They've just got her Barbie smiling again when a voice from behind me freezes me in my tracks.

"So, is now a bad time, or . . . ?"

Junior Cortes is standing at the end of the driveway, his face halfway between alarm and amusement.

"What are you doing here?" I ask, a little more harshly than I should. It's just that I can't stop seeing this through his eyes. How ridiculous we must all look.

His eyes say he's a little hurt, even though he's trying not to show it.

"It's . . . Wednesday." He shrugs. "But I can come back another time."

"Don't be silly," Uva says in that high voice she always uses around company. "Chicky, visit with your friend, we can take care of Lita for a little while."

Lubricated teeth shining in the afternoon sun, Lita gives me the double thumbs-up.

"Come on," I mumble, leading the way into the kitchen, still too embarrassed to meet his eyes.

On Tuesdays Selena does mac and cheese, with the nacho cheese and the little green chilies in it. My dad keeps making it even though Junior is the only one who likes it—and he works at the museum on Tuesdays.

The compromise they worked out is this: Junior comes over every Wednesday, and my dad makes sure there's a plate of leftovers waiting for him. Usually we do homework while he eats it, but today, with Lita, with the pageant, I forgot all about it.

"I'm thinking of getting my schedule switched just so I can eat it fresh," he says, obviously trying to get me out of my head. "Your dad never lets me pay for the leftovers, and plus there's a certain Meteor landmark I'm dying to visit . . ." He raises an eyebrow, and I sigh because I know he doesn't mean the life-size statue of Vice President Hubert Humphrey on the downtown plaza.

Although if I were picking landmarks, Hubert would be way above the one Junior means on the list.

See, there's a gross, sagging, dingy, grease-stained wall in the usually empty second dining room of Selena's, and Junior's been offering to paint something on it since eighth grade. It's one of our longest ongoing disagreements, and with Junior and I that's really saying something.

"Still no," I say, trying to hide how sad it makes me. His art is amazing. It deserves a bigger stage than Selena's failing diner. Bigger than the cornhole boards, even. Bigger than anything this sorry place has to offer.

He shrugs as I uncover the plate of mac and cheese and put it in the microwave, like he was expecting it.

"You know," he says, "centuries from now, they're gonna find a fossilized can of Ortega chilies beside a bag of elbow noodles and this will be venerated as a sacred ancient dish."

"I keep telling my dad this stuff is an abomination, but he doesn't care." Despite my grumbling, when the microwave beeps I get two forks.

"What's not to love?" he asks with his mouth full. Even though it's ridiculous, I think he means it.

I can't help it. I smile back. He pokes me in the cheek, where I have a dimple that makes me look about five years younger than I am.

"So, are we gonna talk about what's going on out there?" he asks, careful to look at the plate and not my face, which I appreciate. It's easier to talk when both people are looking straight ahead. It was Mrs. Cortes who told me that, which is probably why Junior knows. She's the only shrink in town.

"Lita's entering Miss Meteor," I say quickly, like ripping off a Band-Aid.

"I see that," he says, taking another bite. "But . . . why is she doing it here? You guys cool again?" He asks this like it's no big deal. Like it wouldn't be the second-biggest cosmic event in Meteor for Lita and I to make up.

"It's not about that," I say, deflecting because I don't know. "It's about . . . you're gonna think it's stupid."

"Chicky, when have I ever thought anything you said was stupid?" His amber-brown eyes are too big when he asks, and he's turned them on me, like he's asking something without really asking.

This makes me nervous enough that everything just spills

out, with what Mr. Hamilton would call "a disappointing lack of punctuation."

"It's because I want Kendra Kendall to lose Miss Meteor so she knows what it's like to feel humiliated and Lita's wanted to enter the pageant since we were kids so for a second it seemed like it made sense but now it seems crazy and they're putting Vaseline on her teeth and I—"

"Whoa, whoa, whoa, slow down," Junior says.

I do him one better. I stop completely.

"What?" I ask when he doesn't respond right away, and it sounds snappier than I meant it to but I don't apologize.

"Nothing," he says, shaking his head. "Forget it. It sounds like you've got it all figured out." The mac and cheese is only half gone, but he stands up anyway, and suddenly I'm panicky.

"I have nothing figured out!" I say, feeling bad for the snapping, and for my less-than-warm welcome. "I'm floundering in my own life! And I can tell by that thing you do with your forehead that you have an opinion about it, so let's just have it already."

Junior smiles grudgingly, sitting back down. "Look, I just think if you want to hang out with Lita you could probably just ask. You don't have to go all elaborate destructive plan about it. I never really got what happened with you guys anyway."

"That's not what this is," I say, sticking my fork in the congealing cheese and leaving it standing there. You know, in case I have to flee. "I can't explain what happened. And this

Kendra thing isn't a ruse, it's for real. She and Royce are the worst, and I want them to pay for it, and I didn't have any better ideas and—"

"Okay, okay!" Junior holds up his hands, but he's laughing. "Look, they're flawed, no question. I just think if you happen to get your friend back in the process, it's not the end of the world, right?"

For a minute, I picture it. Lita and I. Friends again. It's something I haven't let myself wonder about—not further than reminiscing about our outside-town pretend pageants anyway.

I can only get so far in my imagining, though, even now, because I can't picture telling her. I'm still not ready. And if I can't tell her, I already know how this ends.

"It's not gonna be a thing," I say, looking him in the eye this time so he knows I mean it. "We're just working together. We have a mutual goal. And I should probably be getting back to it."

"World domination to follow," Junior says, but he looks kind of bummed.

And I'm kind of bummed, too, so I just bump his shoulder with mine and say, "I know being my only friend is a big burden to carry, but you're not getting rid of me that easily, Cortes."

He looks at me with those big question eyes again, the sadness all but gone.

"I'm not going anywhere," he says, and hands me my fork. "Maybe you better fuel up, just in case things get ugly out there."

I strain my ear toward the open kitchen window.

"No screaming, maybe I can steal another minute?"

He smiles.

When the plate is empty, I realize maybe I was too hard on the mac and cheese. It really isn't bad.

LITA

"EVERY TIME I think we've found the basement, they start digging," Bruja Lupe whispers to me.

She's referring to her latest customer, a man asking if we can make him a potion that will render him irresistible to women.

"If you have any essence of musk-ox," he says.

Bruja Lupe has promised to stop trying to talk me out of Miss Meteor if I let this man stare into my eyes.

"Gaze into them as you might gaze into the firmament," she urges, her voice dreamy and light as she flicks her wrist, "and therein you shall discover all the secrets of love held in the universe."

At first, he seems ill at ease. But then his look shifts, as all their looks do.

"Do you understand?" Bruja Lupe breathes.

"Yes," the man answers in a hypnotized voice. "I understand it all."

Because would a man like this ever really admit otherwise? She sells him a few overpriced sachets.

"Steep in hot water and drink a half hour before going out," she tells him. "It will give you the confidence of a hundred kings and the charm of a hundred gentlemen."

The mesh bags are probably full of lemon balm. The only thing it will give him is a desire to take a nap. But he nods with the solemn look that tells us he intends to follow her directions precisely.

After he leaves, I hand Bruja Lupe the parent permission form for the pageant, and she pretends to have to look around for a pen. "You sure this is what you want?"

"I have to do this," I say.

"Okay." She scrawls off her signature. "Just don't expect me to put in hair pins or fix your lipstick."

"Don't worry." I beam at her. "I have four whole coaches."

I will not let this be sadder than it has to be, the sky taking me back. Instead, I will show Bruja Lupe that I am not just turning to stardust.

I am leaving a streak of light across this town.

I grab a sweater off the wooden hooks near the front door. Bruja Lupe never lets me go out without one, afraid I'll catch cold even when it's ninety degrees. That's another way I know she's made of the same star-stuff as me. Something in her remembers the blaze of burning through the atmosphere with the meteor that brought us here. In comparison, New Mexico heat is like the ice tail off a comet.

"Wanna come with me?" I ask.

"What, you want a fifth opinion about lipstick?" She ropes her hair into a bun. Her hair goes halfway down her back, but it never takes her more than three pins. Threads of gray glint among the coiled black.

"Don't even pretend you don't want to see Cereza and Fresa claw each other's eyes out over types of hairspray."

"I do, realmente." Bruja Lupe grins. "But I'm meeting the girls."

"The girls" usually means the Meteorite Birding Club. Leanne Cortes has gotten Bruja Lupe to care deeply about the number of cactus wrens and Costa's hummingbirds in the desert around town. She's had that effect on enough Meteor residents to double the membership.

"Lita?" Bruja Lupe says.

I stop just before the door. "I'm glad you and Chicky are partners-in-crime again."

If she'd said friends, I would have felt the wavering guilt of having to lie to her. But she said it right. Partners-in-crime. We are doing this one thing together.

On my way out, I stand on tiptoes enough to kiss Bruja

Lupe on her hair. She rolls her eyes, and I know she'll get me back, leaving a plum-red lipstick print on my cheek when I'm not expecting it. But it's worth it.

The neatest handwriting of my life on Earth goes on this registration form for Miss Meteor. Or—it occurs to me that I better learn the whole name—the Fiftieth-Annual Meteor Regional Pageant and Talent Competition Showcase.

Because I won't just be competing against the prettiest and most talented girls in Meteor. I'll be competing against girls from every town around that's too small to have a pageant of its own.

Buzz's wife, Edna, sits at the registration table, the street and sidewalk around her humming with all the festival preparation. I present the form like Elizabeth Taylor showing off her latest engagement ring, and I give Edna the smile the Quintanilla sisters have spent hours teaching me.

Edna looks frightened more than delighted.

Maybe the smile reads better from the stage?

Edna stamps the form and hands me back a registration number. "And that's for you, sweetheart. Best of luck to you. And don't forget, show up early to the question and answer so we can check you in."

The fluttery feeling in my stomach settles partway between excitement and nausea from all the Vaseline I've swallowed. I'll be up against the Kendra Kendalls of the whole region, girls whose families are legends in the Miss Meteor pageant.

But I can do this. The Quintanilla sisters will make sure I can do this.

And I've already done the first part. I have an official contestant number and a place in the Fiftieth-Annual Meteor Regional . . . I mess it up in my head the first time I try to say it back to myself.

I turn around to step out of line, reading the top of my contestant badge over again.

The Fiftieth-Annual Meteor Regional Pageant and Talent Competition Showcase.

I read it again and again, trying to stick it in my brain.

Meteor Regional Pageant and Talent Competition Showcase.

Meteor Regional Pageant and Talent Competition Showcase.

When I look up, there's Kendra Kendall, looking more polished and with better posture than I'll probably look on my best day of the pageant. She wears a sundress that seems both like she bought it new from a store yesterday and like it came from some boutique half a century ago, the first dress store that ever existed in Meteor.

"You've got to be kidding me," she says with more disdain, more pity, than anger, like the way Bruja Lupe sounds when she gets yet another request for her to fortune-tell winning lottery ticket numbers.

Cole stands behind her, drinking from a green water bottle that he will carry with him from now until the championship later in the week. Every cornhole player has their rituals. Some eat bowls of spaghetti the size of their heads. Cole drinks the most disgusting flavor of Powerade there is (the green kind).

"Did you really just enter?" Kendra asks.

"Kendra," Cole says. "We do not have time for pageant stuff right now."

Kendra looks back at him. "This"—her eyes flash back at me, and I realize I'm the *this*—"is not pageant stuff." She glances at Cole once more. Then her eyes cling to me. "You are not pageant stuff."

"What's the matter, Kendra, can't take a little competition?" Cole asks.

"Yeah, real competition." She looks at my chest, but not in an admiring way. I know what admiring looks like between girls from seeing the way Chicky sometimes notices other girls, that kind of light, glancing consideration.

This is not that.

This is evaluating, like the school nurse checking our spines for scoliosis.

"She doesn't even have boobs," Kendra says.

That makes something in me flare. Maybe I was flat all the way up until the fall of freshman year. Maybe even now I don't have much compared to Kendra or Fresa. Maybe my boobs took their sweet time coming in, but they did get here.

And the fact that Kendra doesn't know it means she probably hasn't taken a good look at me since I came to her house for Cole's birthday party in eighth grade.

I am nothing to her but the chubby girl her brother talks to because no one else does.

"Yes, I do." I draw down the V-neck of my shirt, just enough to show her the cleavage Fresa insists we're going to show off during the swimsuit competition. I don't just have boobs, I have a bra that fits them right, something Bruja Lupe is as proud of as she is of teaching me to make chiles rellenos. Your body is worth something that makes you feel good, she always tells me. Never forget it.

This is even one of my new bras, patterned with pink and yellow flower shapes. I'm almost glad to get to show it off. Maybe it'll show Kendra I can be a little like her, wearing pretty clothes that fit me.

Cole, drinking from the water bottle the same moment I tug my shirt down, does a spit-take worthy of the best old comedies Bruja Lupe has ever shown me. He practically mists the back of his sister's hair.

He puts a hand to his mouth, either to cover it or wipe it. Kendra glares back at him. "Ew."

"What, you think I meant to do that?"

"You're a guy and so inherently gross, so yes, I do."

"I'm gross? You're dating Royce Bradley."

"He's your teammate."

The second of them bickering gives me enough time to realize everyone is staring.

Everyone is staring at the bra I only meant to show Kendra Kendall.

Edna comes up behind me. "Let's save those for the swimsuit competition, shall we, dear?" She urges my hands away from my neckline.

Kendra snaps her head back toward me. "Thank you for that demonstration, because you've just proved my point. Every girl from Meteor who enters is representing the whole town of Meteor."

"Meteorite!" someone calls out from half a block away.

"Shut up, Alex!" Kendra calls back. She looks at me again. "You know you can't win, so you just want to embarrass us all, right? Make fun of this whole thing? You're just like your friend."

I perk up. "I have a friend?"

"Your little lesbian friend. She's always acting like she's better than all this."

Chicky.

I almost correct Kendra and tell her that Chicky isn't a lesbian, that I've seen her crushes on girls and her crush on Junior, the boy who makes her laugh in the halls at school. But it wouldn't matter. I'm not telling Kendra anything she hasn't noticed herself. Besides, anyone who says lesbian like it's a bad thing doesn't care about getting words right.

93

It makes me wonder how she fits in her head the truth that Cole is a guy, and her sureness that anyone else's truth isn't worth considering.

"So think about what you're doing." Kendra pivots, shifting her weight. "Because you're just gonna make our whole town look bad."

She takes her first step away.

"You're right," I say.

She stops and looks back.

"Maybe I don't have boobs compared to someone like you," I say.

Kendra looks less satisfied than pitying, like she's softening. "We don't all store our fat the way we wish we did."

"Can we leave already?" Cole says. "I'm not covering for you this time when Mom asks why we're late."

She ignores him. This time she looks at my stomach, at the softness Uva told me never to be ashamed of, and my hips, wide enough to match Fresa's even though I'm shorter.

And I don't know what I'm doing next, but it's like Cereza and Uva and Fresa all have their hands at my back, urging me on as though teaching me good posture or the beauty queen stride

The sky is going to take me back anyway.

Why do I have to let Kendra and Royce and everyone like them make me small anymore?

What do I have to lose?

"But at least I have an ass," I say.

A satisfied *ohhhh* rises up from the crowd, like they're watching a fight and I just got in a good shot. It comes with the stifled, sudden laugh of half a dozen people, and the unstifled, shocked smile on Cole Kendall's face.

I stride away, feeling everyone's eyes on my back, and for once, it makes me stand up straighter.

It also leaves a deeper, weirder fluttery feeling on my skin, like the time I got heat exhaustion.

As soon as I'm out of sight of the crowd, I duck behind the Space Bar and lift up my shirt.

The second I see my stomach, I am breathless, air shuddering in my throat.

The patch of stardust is smaller.

More of my skin is skin instead of glimmering light.

Maybe Miss Meteor isn't just something I have to do before I turn back to stardust.

Maybe it's something that can save me from turning back.

CHICKY

I BARELY SLEEP at all, but I still manage to stay in bed too late.

"No, no, no, no!" comes Cereza's voice through my open window, followed by a scream (Lita) and a metallic crash (Uva's unicycle?). But I don't actually throw off the blankets until the neighbors' car alarm starts going off.

I can't believe they started without me.

The scene in the yard is worse than I imagined it. I squint into the too-bright morning, my plaid boy's pajama pants and black T-shirt the exact wrong uniform for the relentless desert heat.

Lita is disengaging herself from an upended, yes, unicycle, which has somehow made its way beneath Mr. Miller's minivan. Uva hovers worriedly, although whether she's more concerned for Lita or the precious one-wheeled death trap that won her crowd favorite four years ago is not immediately clear.

"Sorry, Mr. Miller!" Cereza calls, flashing the same grin she uses at the diner when Fresa burns someone's grilled cheese con nopal.

"You girls practicing for the pageant?" he asks, his scowl gone in the face of Reza's perfect-Mexican-daughter radiance. With the press of a button, the incessant honking of the alarm mercifully ceases.

"More like practicing for having wrinkles before I'm twenty," Fresa mutters, stalking over to untangle a glittery purple ribbon from the van's rearview mirror. Even angry, she wields it like the girl that, in an American flag swimsuit and white leather cowboy boots with fringe, won second runner-up in the Forty-Ninth-Annual Meteor Regional Pageant and Talent Competition Showcase.

"What are you doing?" I ask, trying to keep my voice even. "I have a list of possible talents upstairs and literally none of these things are on it."

When we were younger, the talent portion of our pretend pageants usually involved both of us singing karaoke into cactus flowers until we collapsed into giggles on the ground.

Let's just say it was a good thing none of our audience members were human. Or in possession of working eardrums.

"Like I told Lita," says Cereza, the same intense gleam in her eye that she gets when she's talking about scalpels and contagious skin rashes. "I know other talents might seem showier, but I think you'll agree that Shakespeare"—she thumps the heavily dog-eared volume for emphasis—"never goes out of style."

Fresa tosses her hair, narrowly missing Uva's face. "Spoken like someone who didn't even make the top five . . . how long ago was it, Reza, ten years?"

Uva backs away slowly. It's the best idea she's had all week.

"Excuse me," Cereza says, Lita forgotten as she rounds on Fresa. "I graduated six years ago, and you know that."

Fresa shrugs in that infuriating way of hers, like nothing you say can possibly get under her skin. "If that's your story."

"Oh, you did not!" Cereza, nursing student, five-time *Meteor Monthly* best service industry professional, lunges at her little sister like they're roosters in a ring, going for the only thing Fresa Quintanilla truly cares about.

Her hair.

"Okay, seriously? ENOUGH!" I yell, stomping across the heat-withered grass in my bare feet.

They don't even hear me. Fresa is quitting, and Cereza is firing her somehow, and even Uva is yelling. I know they'll get over it eventually, they always do, but that's not what I'm worried about right now.

Lita is still standing against Mr. Miller's van, twisting the end of her braid and biting her lip like she's physically forcing herself not to apologize. And suddenly I remember, one night during our last pretend pageant together, when I found twelve-year-old Lita crying at the base of Herr Rainbow, clutching a copy of the newspaper, which was running a retrospective on all the past Miss Meteors.

All the tall, leggy, blond, past Miss Meteors.

She'd been sure she could never fit in, the pretend pageant clashing with the real one in her mind, her dreams seeming out of reach.

Lita looks just like that now, and I find my friend-muscles aren't so out of shape after all. I sidestep the sister cyclone and grab her arm.

Junior's words from yesterday are in my ear, painting the picture of Lita and me as friends again like he painted a perfect Frida on last year's championship cornhole board. But this isn't that, I tell myself. This isn't friendship. This is just protecting the asset.

"Do you want to get out of here?" I ask her, trying not to add to the overload.

She turns to me with wide, grateful eyes that look almost on the edge of tearful, and nods. It's enough for me.

I go inside and shove my feet into the first shoes I lay eyes on. The pajama pants and oversized T-shirt that I'm wearing will have to do. Lita's already standing by the door when I get back to the porch.

"Wait," she says when I take the stairs two at a time. "I need to get my bike. What if someone steals it?"

I don't have the heart to tell her that scuffed, scratched, fifty-times-repaired bike with ten-year-old streamers isn't the least bit valuable to anyone but her.

We walk without a destination in mind, just a little space from my sisters while I think of a pep talk worthy of a real pageant contestant, but I shouldn't be surprised when we end up outside the Meteor/Meteorite museum.

I sigh, leaning on the wall outside the rock room, trying not to notice the peeling paint, the billboard with the missing letters, the velvet rope that was probably really plush, like, thirty years ago.

"Are you okay?" I ask.

Her smile is sad, but it's a smile. "Your sisters are all just so . . . determined. They're proud of their talents. But I'm not sure any of them are really *me*. And I want to be me in this pageant. I . . . have to be. One last time."

I know she's talking about the one-time entry rule, but there's something strange about her voice. I'm about to ask when she turns to me, eyes blazing like twin stars. "I want to make your sisters proud after all they've done for me. I want the town to see not only the Kendra Kendalls of the world deserve this. I want to get that money for your parents. And I want Meteor to . . ."

She trails off here, looking away, like she's not saying something so big it's actually stuck in her throat. But I barely notice, because my face is heating up.

"Wait, what do my parents have to do with this?"

Her eyes are as round as an owl's, brown and kind of fathomless, as she looks at me. "They need the money." She says this like it's obvious, and it is, but I didn't know it was obvious to everyone.

"We're fine," I mutter, scuffing my shoes. "I mean, I figured we'd split the prize, but for like, normal stuff, you know? College or whatever."

It's a feeble argument, and Lita's eyes say she knows it. "Sure," she says. "I didn't mean to say . . ."

I'm dreading what she'll say next, the pity already seeping in around her eyes. But her expression is replaced by wild delight before I can find a way to escape.

"What?" I ask, hoping for nothing more than a radical subject change.

"I think I just had an amazing idea! Get excited!"

She's got color in her cheeks again, life back in her eyes. I always thought I was imagining it, the way she got shinier the closer we came to the rock, but right now she's almost . . . glowing . . .

"I can't tell you what it is right now," she's saying, grabbing the sparkly pink bike and throwing her leg over it. "There's something I have to do, but I'll tell you everything this afternoon! On the practice field! At three o'clock sharp! And bring your sisters!"

I know better than to try to stop her now. She pushes into

101

wobbly motion on the bike, and I'm sure she's going to fall, but at the last second, she rights herself and makes it across the parking lot unscathed.

"This terrifies me!" I call after her.

"It's gonna be great," she calls back. "Three o'clock! Trust me!"

I want to, but it doesn't help that a neighborhood cat runs screeching out of her irregular path the moment the words have left her lips.

LITA

THE QUINTANILLA SISTERS all mostly want me to do the same things. Smile. Smile bigger. Stand up straighter. Let them pull at my hair and poke at my face until they turn me into a pretty enough version of myself that they'll let me onstage.

Then they tried to agree on a talent for me.

Cereza says if I perform Juliet's death monologue right, I'll have all the judges and half the audience reaching for their tissue packs. Uva insists that if I can manage a unicycle, I'll charm them all into adoring me. And Fresa is sure that her shimmery white ribbon wand will not only look perfect against the brown of my skin but will mesmerize the audience like they're all fish watching a shiny object.

If I pick any one of their talents, I hurt two of their feelings. And I can't do it, not to these women who are fixing my hair and my beauty pageant stance and staying up nights debating what color evening gown we should try to find at the Goodwill for the final stage walk.

The answer was obvious. Or it should have been. I just didn't see it until Chicky gave me the idea.

Chicky's sisters are helping me, so shouldn't I pay tribute to all of them?

I show up to the park with Vaseline freshly applied to my teeth. My cheeks hurt from smiling so hard, but I will give them a pageant smile even if I have to ice my face afterward.

Hubert Humphrey Memorial Park is the biggest green space in Meteor, and considering the water restrictions in our county, we're lucky to have it. In a feat of civic engineering that's truly shocking from a town that can't even decide its name, the planners doubled what would have been its size by setting nine cement paths in the grass. They're all rings, like the orbits of a planet. A playground is at its center, with sand-filled arms like the rays of the sun.

The downside: Once Pluto was declared not a planet, even our park became out of date. I would feel sorry for Pluto if the classifications the men on Earth make mattered beyond the atmosphere of this planet.

To make it seem like we have even more grass, they set the park next to Meteor Central High's track and field. The scrub sod they laid down might look cheap to everyone else, but right now, I'm ready to put on a show so great, it'll look like the rolling hillsides from the finale of *Hello, Dolly!*

The Quintanilla sisters all show up at the school track like I ask, and I'm ready. I don't even care that the field on the slope next to it is all cornhole players and wooden practice boards and flying beanbags. I don't care that they're watching while I unfurl Fresa's ribbon wand (I folded it the precise way she asked) or while I kickstand the decades-old bike I borrowed from Buzz (I'll never manage the unicycle in time, and I'm pretty sure if Uva really thinks about it, she'll realize that).

I don't even care that Royce and half the guys who shoved me into the locker room are here, because this time, I'm going to win.

"Just wait there!" I call across the track. I want them to keep their distance, so they can see exactly what this will look like onstage. If it looks awful, they'll tell me, just like they told me never to wear a lemon-yellow shirt or magenta lipstick again.

I throw a leg over the bike, run through Juliet's lines in my head, and poise the ribbon wand.

All these talents will squish together into the best talent the Meteor Regional Pageant and Talent Competition Showcase has ever seen.

I push off and start pedaling, steering the bike with one hand and twirling the ribbon wand behind me with the other, and proclaiming lines about love and poison in the clear, loud voice Cereza coached me into.

"Arm higher!" Fresa calls. "Imagine they're taking your picture!"

If she's correcting me, she likes what she sees. Criticism, I've learned, is the way Fresa Quintanilla shows she cares.

One sister on board, two to go.

"Posture!" Uva calls. "Don't slump."

Then I know Uva doesn't hold it against me that I decided against the unicycle.

But nothing from Cereza.

She stands across the track, arms unfolding, eyes wide.

"Please stop," she calls.

Maybe I'm not doing the voice right. I try to open up my lungs like she talks about, and project across the track. *"I do remember well where I should be!"*

Chicky stands a step behind them, watching with horror I can't quite place. Is she afraid I'm going to run myself off the track? (I might the first couple times. That's why I picked somewhere with grass.) Does she think this is the worst talent idea ever dreamed up in this town? (She won't once Fresa and Uva polish up my form.)

Or does she regret agreeing to help me in the first place?

"This is a bad idea," Cereza shouts. "Please. You're gonna hurt yourself."

"And there I am," I call. *"Where is my Romeo?"*

On the word "Romeo," a beanbag grazes my arm, and a shock of laughter comes from the cornhole practice.

106

The bike wobbles, but I right it.

"Okay, not cool," I hear Cole say.

Another one strikes my ribbon wand, ruining the perfect spiral. But I snap it into a zigzag. Fresa has to be proud of that. It's her first rule of ribboning. If the shape you're in isn't working, twirl the ribbon into another one.

Cole objects again, and this time a couple other boys echo him with, "Yeah, come on."

I guess I'm too pathetic to throw at.

I think of the guys in the locker room backing away when I curled up on the floor, crying into my knees, and the bike's handlebars wobble.

Another beanbag flies my way.

I pretend I am Cereza and Uva and Fresa all at once. I am not the little girl Royce Bradley got to sob on the floor of the locker room because he wanted me to know how much I didn't belong.

I am three Quintanilla beauty queens put together.

"Go, get thee hence"—I lift my chin at the cornhole practice—*"for I will not away!"*

The next beanbag misses me by a bicycle's length. It lands on the track in front of me and bursts, spilling its dried beans everywhere.

I give a smug smile to the cornhole players.

Until I feel my front bike wheel bump on a cluster of beans.

"What the hell, Bradley?" I hear Cole call. "That's not funny."

There's a reason I usually ride a little girl's bike even though I'm not a little girl anymore. God and all his stars in the sky did not bless me with long legs.

So when the old bike Buzz let me borrow from the Meteor Meteorite Museum decides it wants to go its own way, I don't have the muscle memory to argue.

The ribbon falls, catching and tangling in the spokes, and now I'm skidding more than rolling.

"There rust, and let me diiiiiiieeeeee!"

The last line of Juliet's death monologue turns into a shriek as I careen off the track.

I debate whether abandoning the ribbon wand will make things worse (will the wand break in the gears?), or if I should just jump off the bike and into the grass.

Until I see Cole in my path, braced to try to catch me.

I try to stop the bike, but the ribbon balls up in the brakes.

In the second of us both going down, I realize six things at once:

1) I am headed straight for the boy who gave me my first bike nine years ago.

2) Nine years later this is the way I'm managing to thank him.

3) Chicky's sisters are not three braided-together voices;

they are each their own woman, and their ideas do not always go together, especially when their ideas involve ribbons and wheel spokes.

4) My perfect talent idea for Miss Meteor is turning into a perfect disaster the cornhole players are first laughing and then gasping at.

5) I hate this whole stupid little planet. I hate it, and if it wasn't for everything I'd miss I'd say turn me back into stardust right now. I would welcome the second great meteor of this town's history landing on me right now.

6) Especially if it could show up before I run this old bike, which I cannot seem to stop, into Cole.

It doesn't.

I end up on top of Cole, with the bike on top of me. When I shove it off of us, I realize Cole's arm took the force of the back gears and wheel.

His left arm.

The one he throws with.

And it's worse than that. Cole's eyes are shut, and I wonder what part of the bike cracked him in the head when we fell.

I put my hands on the sides of his face and say his name, over and over, my words wobbling and panicked but still loud in my leftover Cereza-Shakespeare-recitation voice.

"Cole," I call his name again.

He opens his eyes, which look clouded over, the pupils wide even with the sun behind me.

"Cole." Now the word sounds strangled. Nothing like how Cereza is teaching me to talk. "Say something."

He gives me a weak smile. "You're so sparkly." His voice is dry and soft, like he's been asleep all day.

My throat tightens. "What?"

His eyes clear a little. "You're all stardust."

I look around to see if anyone heard that, those few words that could make everyone look at me twice. Not like I'm a beauty queen.

Like I'm something to be explained.

"This man is severely concussed," I project, exactly like Cereza taught me, like there's a whole audience who needs to hear. "He's making no sense at all. He needs immediate medical attention."

I look across the field to the cornhole team, waiting for them to do something, to show up and be at Cereza's command so she won't be the only one trying to help Cole.

And some of them are running across the field or running for help.

But Royce just stands where he is, grinning at me, like this is how he always saw it going the whole time, all the way back to elementary school.

CHICKY

HERE LIES CHICKY *Quintanilla. Worst pageant campaign manager in history.*

I can almost see the tombstone between where I'm still frozen and where everyone has rushed to help Lita and Cole. I don't actually move until I see Royce and Kendra approaching, and then it's pure rage at the controls.

I'm storming across the field before I can think better of it, nothing in my head but incoherent rage-sounds that will hopefully form themselves into words by the time I reach him.

Except they don't.

Kendra is already at work by the time I reach them, unloading on Lita as she stares tremulously at Cole. "What is wrong with you?" Kendra asks in a deadly voice. "Being an utter failure wasn't enough? You have to drag everyone else down with you? Look at my brother! How is he supposed to play cornhole? How—"

"Lay off!" I shout, storming up to them without a single thought for self-preservation. "It's his fault this happened, not Lita's!"

Royce steps between Kendra and I, six feet, four inches of pissed-off jock.

"What did you say, dyke?"

Really? I imagine saying, my voice calm and level and devastating. *Your teammate is down because of your stupidity, and your first order of business is to get a homophobic insult in. What team spirit, Bradley. What fucking solidarity.*

The words are there, but my mouth won't move, because his word, his one little word, is big enough to swallow them all.

Dyke.

"I asked you a question, you little psycho. What did you say?"

All I can say is "Nothing" in a pathetic voice that doesn't even sound like mine.

"That's what I thought," he says, and he looks so tall, so impossibly square-jawed, and his teeth are white and straight, and even his little, mean, beady eyes are terrifying somehow, and I feel like a slug at his feet because he has all the power.

And then Kendra steps up beside him, furious and shining like a golden statue, beautiful and terrible and cruel, and I wonder how I ever thought I could destroy them. How could I even make a dent? Even before this horrible disaster it was a stupid, childish plan.

"Chicky!" Fresa is coming toward me, eyes narrowed at

my tormenters as Cereza kneels beside Cole, and I can tell she wants to tell Royce and Kendra off, protect me like the pathetic little sister I am, but if she gets too close she might find out what they have on me. Ring Pop and Allison and everything that came after, and I just can't.

Not in front of Fresa.

Not now.

"Forget it," I say, walking past her, deactivating her seek-and-destroy eyes. "It's nothing."

"Chicky, I need some help over here," Reza is saying from behind me. But look at me. I'm nothing. How can I help anyone?

I glance once more at Lita, who looks shaken but not hurt. Cole is beneath her, clutching his arm while she shouts his name again and again.

"Chicky! Now!" But she's all focused fire and I'm water vapor, scattering into the air. I can't do it. I can't face them. Not like this.

"I'm sorry," I whisper to my sister, but maybe it's really to Lita, for being too much of a coward to help her. Or to stay and be her friend.

I'm backing away before Cereza realizes what I'm doing. "Don't," she says. "They need you." But she's wrong. No one needs me.

"I'm sorry," I say again, a little louder, and then I walk away. Not just to the sidelines to wait, or to be there for Lita.

113

Not just to the park where we used to trace planetary orbits, or where Lita made us light a candle for poor Pluto in its time of need.

I keep walking until walking is running. Until the sounds of the crowd and Cole's moans of pain and Lita's panicked shouting have faded, and it's just me and the beating sun in the streets.

I'm already almost back downtown when it hits me:

Lita Perez, the Cinderella story of the Fiftieth Miss Meteor Pageant has just done the unthinkable. The unforgiveable. She injured the throwing arm of the cornhole team's second-best player less than a week before the match of the half-century.

Even if we give up, it won't be enough for the town we needed to love us.

Forget loving us, I think. They're going to hate us.

Forget hating us. They're going to destroy us.

LITA

IN A VOICE that sounds half-asleep, Cole insists he's fine, he's absolutely fine, that it's nothing some ice and Advil won't fix.

Cereza wants to take him to the hospital. But I can think of a hundred reasons we're not doing that unless Cole says we can.

We compromise. Cereza puts Cole's arm in a makeshift sling with the wand's stick and the cloth from the ribbon, and we take him to Bruja Lupe. Not through the front door with the dimmer lighting and the globes of polished gemstone, but the back way, into our apartment.

Cole looks both in pain and nervous all the way there. Bruja Lupe can feel it on him. She puts her hand under his chin and makes him look at her.

"No te preocupes," she says. "I'm not gonna give you the tourist treatment. You're one of our own, and we take care of our own."

His expression clears, just for that second, and I think maybe he understands.

"It's not a break," Bruja Lupe says once she gets to checking him. "At least I don't think so. What do you think?" she asks Cereza.

"That's what I thought. But it's a sprain. He's still out until it heals." Now Cereza talks to Cole. "No cornhole practice, young man, entiendes?"

He's still a little foggy, but he understands enough to deflate at the news.

I want to sink into the textured carpet our landlord keeps promising to replace.

Cereza and Bruja Lupe set his arm, and I talk to him to distract him, so it'll hurt less.

"You can sprain my arm back if you want," I say.

"Lita," Cole says, like me suggesting this is the worst thing I've done all day, not the thing that got us here.

"Fine, then Kendra can if she wants."

"Don't offer. She might take you up on it."

"It'd be fair. I broke you."

"You didn't break me." He grinds his teeth as Cereza and Bruja Lupe finish, so the words come out flat and coarse. They tighten the sling into place, and he swears under his breath. "I'm gonna break Royce, though."

We put ice on where they think he hit his head, me holding it in place and him staying so still I wonder how often he's had

116

to take the chill of cold packs against his skin after practice. Drops fall onto the back of his neck and snake into his collarbone. He doesn't flinch.

I set the pads of my fingers against the fallen drops, soaking them up with my fingerprints.

He looks between my hand and my face. "You're never gonna answer my question, are you?"

I pat my forefinger against another drop. Underneath I can feel how warm his skin is. "What question?"

"Okay." His smile is pained but patient. "You can play it that way if you want."

The way he looks at me, it's like he can see the star-stuff in me.

It's a fizzy feeling I would've loved before I started turning back into stardust.

I only have a second to think about it before I hear Cereza and Bruja Lupe in the kitchen.

They're shaking out doses of painkillers. Prepping the hierbas that will bring the swelling down and let Cole sleep tonight and the next few nights. And in that moment, it's a kind of beautiful that makes me glad the world will have Cereza Quintanilla as a nurse as soon as she graduates, a woman who believes in both penicillin and cures for susto.

Cole's first dose works a little too well. He falls asleep on our so-ugly-it's-perfect plaid sofa. *Midnight* is on TV. It's another one of Bruja Lupe's favorites. Sometimes she puts a movie like this on in the background when she's giving a real cura, like the sound might distract from pain or worry. And they're always on when she needs them. She gets old episodes of *The Twilight Zone* on channels I can never quite find.

I sit at the other end of the sofa, leaving space between Cole and me in case I might find another way to accidentally break him.

Cole Kendall, the one guy on the cornhole team who bothers trying to stand up for those of us Royce Bradley sees as nothing but living, breathing targets, and I broke him.

I can feel a new shimmer of stardust inside me. Whatever patch of my skin I reclaimed after I told off Kendra, it'll be stardust again by morning. I know it. Stardust is already creeping over my hips and stomach, and considering today, where will it show up next? My ankle? My forehead? Somewhere I can't hide without a floppy hat or a turtleneck or my hair in my face? Do they even make turtleneck evening gowns?

Cereza perches on the arm of the sofa.

"I ruined everything," I say.

"Oh, honey, it's not like that."

Honey. Cereza says it the same way her mother does.

"Yeah, it is like that," I say. "What happened to Cole. Giving Royce a chance to go at Chicky like that."

Cereza's face hardens. "You did not give Royce a chance, he took it himself. Do you understand?"

I slump back into the sofa.

"Don't give up so easily." Cereza crosses one leg over the other.

The Quintanilla sisters are so beautiful, all four of them. If Fresa, beautiful, fearless Fresa, got as far as second runner-up, why did I think I had any chance at winning this? Why did I think I could do any better than embarrassing myself and Bruja Lupe and the Quintanillas?

"Didn't my sister ever tell you about her first ribbon practices?" Cereza asks.

I shake my head.

Cereza laughs slightly, and I can tell she's keeping herself quiet so she won't wake Cole.

I almost tell her that thanks to Bruja Lupe's hierbas, nothing short of that meteor I wished for is gonna wake Cole Kendall, at least not for the next couple hours.

"Fresa accidentally lassoed my mother's favorite glass bowl." Cereza giggles. This most serious and poised Quintanilla sister giggles. "She smashed it to pieces. My mother didn't talk to her for a week."

I try not to laugh, but I do. "Really?"

"Really." She watches the screen. "I'll kill you if you ever tell her this, but sometimes I'm sure she would've won if she were white."

Cereza's words seep into me. I'm not just a girl made of star-stuff. I'm a brown-skinned girl in a town that's chosen fifty years of blond, milk-faced beauty queens.

I'm quiet long enough that Cereza flashes me a look.

"I mean it," she says. "You breathe a word to her, I'll deny this whole conversation."

"No," I say. "It's not that."

"Then why do you look even more worried than you did a minute ago?"

Because I dragged so many people into what was just a stupid dream I had to try for.

Because, for a minute, it seemed like that stupid dream might save me.

Because whatever patch of my skin I got back, I can already feel stardust closing over it.

"Because if girls like us can't even win when they're as good as Fresa," I say, "I have no chance."

"Don't throw in your contestant number yet." Cereza settles back into watching the movie. "You shouldn't give up, because we're not giving up on you."

CHICKY

THE STREETS OF Meteor look different when you're a coward and a traitor.

I walk them anyway, the pavement unfriendly beneath my sneakers. I can't go home. I can't go to the diner. I can't go to Lita's—not that I ever could. I can't go anywhere I'll have to look into the eyes of someone who knows me.

Not after shrinking down into nothing in front of Royce and Kendra again.

As I walk aimlessly, the tin siding of mobile homes catching the afternoon sun, I can practically hear the gossip spreading from the telltale heart of town—the cornhole practice field. They'll talk about how Loca Lita Perez took out Cole Kendall doing something totally batty and weird.

They'll say what a shame it is, that the Meteor cornhole winning streak is over after just one year thanks to Lita and those Quintanilla girls.

They'll talk about *boys being boys* whenever anyone mentions Royce's wayward beanbag, just like they do every time. The blatant bullying. The complete refusal to acknowledge the humanity of anyone not like him. The joy he seems to get from making people feel small and weak and bad.

There are never consequences for him, so why would he stop? It occurs to me as I mourn the dying possibility of taking him down for good that Royce wouldn't be so scary if everyone in this town wasn't so predisposed to congratulate him.

As if being white and rich and a boy makes up for being a monster.

I'm almost to the highway, the houses giving way to empty desert, before I turn my sneakers back toward town. Honestly, I don't even know where they're taking me until I see the Meteor Meteorite Museum looming in the distance, and by then I'm already resigned to it.

No matter how much I hate this place, I always seem to be drawn back to it—and to the people who love it.

Junior is out back as usual, deeply concentrated on painting the final cornhole boards for the match next week. He's already done *Starry Night*, the famous Warhol soup can, and the cover of Nirvana's *Nevermind* flawlessly. Like the artists themselves were painting through him.

It's a little mesmerizing, I'll admit it. Even if he won't.

Tonight he's priming, which I know he loves. Turning a splintery, unusable surface into something ready to shine.

For the second time in a week, I feel guilty for not giving him the diner wall.

"Hey," he says, without looking up.

"Hey."

It's something I've always liked about Junior, the fact that he doesn't feel the need to fill every silence with chatter. After a lifetime as a Quintanilla, you really start to value silence.

Well, if you can still imagine what it must be like.

When the last brush strokes have been applied and the board is a uniform, gleaming white, Junior meets my eyes for the first time.

"So, funny story . . . ," I begin, trying to be casual even as my traitorous voice catches in my throat.

"I, uh . . . ," he begins, rubbing the back of his neck. "I heard."

"Already?" I ask, getting to my feet and pacing, like it'll dull the next blow.

Junior stands, too, but he shifts on his feet. "You know how it is, Chicky. It's a small town. People talk."

"Who told you?" I ask. "What did they say?"

He looks right at me, while I try to look anywhere else. "Do you really want me to tell you?"

I deflate at his words. He's right. Who cares who it was or what they said? It's not like it wasn't always gonna be all over town before the start of the evening news. Hell, with what passes for content in Meteor, it probably is the evening news.

I can hear the intro now: "Local Pageant Underdog Maims Town's Favorite Athlete in Freak Shakespeare/Ribbon/Antique Cycle Accident—TONIGHT on *Meteor News!*"

"Stop catastrophizing," Junior says, reading my thoughts as usual.

Stupid psychologist mom.

"I'm not," I say, even though I totally am.

He tosses his paint roller in the water bucket, pacing around the lot for at least a minute before turning to face me. His eyes are uncharacteristically intense, and he holds my gaze until my blood starts to buzz and I have to glance away.

"You should go get a soda from inside," he says, tossing me his key. "It's on the house."

I should stay. Ask him what's going on. Offer to help. But honestly, I'm a little afraid of him right now. I came here for chill, for unconditional, but it looks like neither of those things are on the menu tonight.

Inside the museum, the lights are dim, barely showcasing the treasures of Meteor's past. Here's the newspaper article—Vice President Hubert Humphrey with his arm around a much younger Buzz, the crater on the edge of town blotting out the background, looking totally otherworldly.

In the photo, there are two guys with hard hats from some obscure government agency, flashlights pointing into the darkest parts of the crater. Nineteen sixty-six was probably the last time anyone went down there. The story went that after one of the investigators disappeared, they roped it off with caution tape and forbade entrance until more tests could be done.

But no one ever came back. At the south end of the crater there are still two stakes in the ground, a last piece of sun-bleached warning tape stretched between like a museum exhibit itself. A couple seniors when we were in eighth grade took pictures of it for the school newspaper, and the administration refused to print them on the grounds of disrupting an ongoing government investigation.

"Ongoing," I always thought, was an interesting way to put it.

The museum's soda machine has a special trick to it that only staff members—plus Lita and I, of course—are allowed to know. I punch in B65E4 and the lights flash festively, allowing me to press A6 twice for two ice-cold, old-fashioned Coca-Colas in glass bottles.

Buzz imports them from Mexico. He says they make them with real sugar there, but I don't know enough Spanish to read the ingredients, so I have to take his word for it.

Normally I'd go straight back out to Junior and we'd drink them perched on the low wall enclosing the parking lot, talking about everything and nothing, but tonight isn't normal, and I make an uncharacteristic detour.

The room that houses the space rock is like a tiny amphitheater with no seats. The patchy velvet rope, the red curtains that haven't been closed in so long they have permanent dust streaks, and then the rock itself, which at first glance just looks like any other giant, slightly metallic rock.

Not that I'd ever admit this, but it's kind of more than that. There's this luster to it, like nothing you've ever seen before unless you've watched Lita's eyes while she dances in a thunderstorm. And maybe, beneath that, a melody. Something beautiful but just a little lonely.

It's always been the sound, or the idea of it, anyway, that draws me in.

I open my Coke and slide under the rope, turning my back to the Biggest Roadside Attraction Between Las Vegas and Santa Fe and letting it pull me back against it, like it's inviting me to take a load off for once. I feel that weird song in my bones and close my eyes against the emotion it calls up, like I'll never quite know where I fit, but maybe that's okay.

Like Royce Bradley and all his Meteor-sanctioned destruction are a million light-years away.

After a few minutes of that, I'm ready to go back.

In the shadowy alcove of the museum's back door, I pause for a second, thinking about that fiery look in Junior's eyes before he tossed me the keys. But then I see what's happening outside.

Into the finished Nirvana board, Junior Cortes is tossing cornhole bags. I wait for the thwacking sound as they hit the board beside the hole, or the skittering of gravel as they miss the mark completely, but I don't hear a thing save the *swish, swish,*

swish of beanbags passing through a perfectly sized hole.

After the fourth, I step out from the shadows, wheels turning in my head.

After the tenth, I'm actually smiling.

Junior nearly jumps out of his skin when I approach. "What the hell, Chicky!"

"What the hell, Chicky?" I ask, incredulous, still smiling. "What the hell, Junior! You're amazing with those stupid things!"

"So?" he asks, clearly embarrassed, which means he hasn't yet seen the path forward that I've seen.

"Oh, don't be embarrassed," I say, waving a hand, the Cokes forgotten on the counter inside. "Sure, it's a sad hobby and everyone who does it is soulless, but man is this gonna come in handy for me right now."

In my mind's eye, it's all coming together perfectly. Junior can take Cole's place. The town won't hate us for ruining its chances at the cornhole championship. We're saved.

"I'm not doing it," Junior says, before I've even explained what I want him to do.

I shake my head like a wet dog, just to rid myself of the sound of him saying no. "Wait, what?"

"I said I'm not doing it."

His eyebrows are drawn together, that normal, easy confidence in his face vanishing. He looks pissed, like I've let him down somehow by even thinking of it.

"But, Junior," I say, pushing through it because he so clearly doesn't understand. "This . . . You . . . could fix it. Everything we ruined today. You could save Lita's chances. You could help me."

He stops, looking right at me, that molten metal back in his eyes.

It makes me want to run and not look back.

"Chicky, I can't do it. I can't play cornhole with those jerks. Not after the way they've treated . . . everyone." But his eyes say he's talking about me. About Ring Pop.

"But you always fix everything." I think back to a lifetime of him saving me from group projects, inviting me over to his quiet house when my sisters are too much, going the long way around Lita's house with me even though I didn't ask him to.

"Yeah," he says, "I always do." He takes a step toward me, the angles of his face their own work of art beneath the orange parking lot light. They're softer now, and that line between his eyebrows has smoothed out. "But why do you think I always do?"

Something is swelling between us. Something like the gas and space dust and ethereal whatever that combines to make its own, unique star. And I'm terrified of it.

"Junior . . ." He waits, but I have nothing else to say. He's closer than ever, but the distance feels like light-years. "Don't."

"What if I want to?" He takes one more step, the one that makes the heat coming off him my responsibility. And there it

128

is, the feeling I've always felt. That I just don't fit.

"What if I don't?" I whisper.

"Chicky," he says, and the way he says my name is like connecting the dots in one of those kids' coloring books. "What if you do?"

There's a small flutter between my fourth and fifth ribs on the left side, but it stops when he reaches out and touches my face. I can't help it, I step back.

"Please," I say, my voice cracking. "I just . . . I need you to . . ."

But he's already turning away. "No," he says. "You don't need me. You've made that totally clear."

Here lies Chicky, I think for the second time tonight as Junior lingers, not looking but not leaving. Waiting for me to prove him wrong. *She was a horrible friend.*

And then I run.

Again.

LITA

WHEN COLE KENDALL walks into his own family's kitchen the next day, I'm not sure who jumps higher. Him when he sees me checking the temperature on the oven. Or me when I realize he has no idea I was coming over. I thought for sure his sister would warn him.

"What are you doing in my house?" He's yelling it, but not in an angry way. He's coming down from the shock.

I probably should have announced myself when I crawled in the open window. His hair is after-shower wet, and I feel like I've just walked into his bedroom.

"Look, Lita." Cole readjusts his posture, like he's still getting used to the sling. "I'm good with you coming over anytime. But you do not wanna run into Kendra right now. And I do not wanna see what'll happen to you if you do. Also I'm hoping you don't show up randomly in other people's kitchens, but we're gonna leave that conversation for another time."

"I called Kendra. She said it was okay."

"She what?" Cole asks.

"She said, 'Yeah, sure, why don't you just move in while you're at it?'"

"Do we need to have a discussion about sarcasm?"

"I know what sarcasm is. But she shouldn't have said it if she didn't mean it. People shouldn't say things they don't mean."

I reach for the cellophane-and-brown-paper-wrapped bouquet on the counter. The early-morning light softens the edges of the flowers. I hold them out to him, a fluffy mix of delphinium and larkspur, the only really blue flowers Kari keeps stocked at Cosmos, Meteor's one and only flower shop. "Is blue still your favorite color?"

"You brought me flowers?"

"That's what you do when you want someone to get better, right?" I ask.

Behind the amused look, I catch something else, like this means something to him.

"Give me two minutes," he says. "I can't talk to you looking like I just got out of bed."

The kitchen table is covered in library books he's probably gotten out for the social studies project he and Junior Cortes are partnered on. "You look like you've been up for a while."

"Still." He pulls down the same kind of glass jar Bruja Lupe saves from spaghetti sauce. "This is probably really rude, but I'm down a wing, so I'm gonna ask you to do this part."

He is a boy, so he doesn't think of the fact that I need scissors. Most boys just stuff flowers into vases without cutting them.

"You're lucky Kendra's not home," he says.

"Not lucky. Just listening. She's not quiet about her voice lessons."

"Ah, yes. The rousing rendition of the musical classic I've had to hear her practice for the last three months."

"Should I ask?"

"You're the competition." His voice is more teasing than suspicious. "I'm not sure I should tell you."

Then he's out of the kitchen and down the hall toward his room.

"In case you missed it," I call after him. "I have no talent. I don't think I'm the competition anymore."

When I hear his door close, I open the junk drawer where I remember the Kendalls keeping their scissors and spare nails and tape measures.

But it's not scissors inside.

There's a layer of paper. As soon as I see the envelopes with the words PAST DUE highlighted in red, I close the drawer. These are not for me to see.

But I've already seen enough. It casts the whole house in a different hue, like a camera filter.

How the weathering on the shutters might not be because

Mrs. Kendall wants them that way, it might be because she can't get them repainted.

How a cracked window that looks out over the backyard hasn't been fixed, or the lower door gasket of the refrigerator, masking tape sealing the accordion of plastic.

These are small things. Mrs. Kendall still keeps a neat house, with recently washed flowered curtains and pictures in tidy frames on every dusted surface.

They are things I would not have noticed if the red letters had not made me look again.

These are things that, to Bruja Lupe and me, just mean our landlord hasn't returned our phone calls. But to families who own their houses, it means they can't afford to fix a place that is theirs.

I don't look for scissors after that. I put the flowers in the glass jar without cutting the stems, adding a penny to the water like Kari told me to.

Cole comes back with his hair combed, and I can't tell if he changed his shirt or if it's the one he was wearing before. The blue almost matches the lightest shade of the larkspur flowers.

He's still buttoning the last buttons with one hand when he says, "Sorry about how hot it is in here. And loud."

I hadn't caught it before. But he means all the fans blowing, one or two set up in every room. All the windows open, even this early in the day. Another thing I would not have noticed because Bruja Lupe and I do the same thing all the time. Families who can afford it just leave their air-conditioning running.

"We don't really turn on the AC unless it's over a hundred," Cole says, and I hear the nervousness, the self-consciousness under the words. "Saves energy. Good for the environment."

I never thought that Kendra Kendall might be showing me the sharp edges of her French-manicured nails for any reason but that she wanted a crown and a title.

"I'm really sorry, Cole," I say, and I don't know if I'm talking just about plowing into him with a piece of museum memorabilia or the fact that his family has a drawer full of red-lettered bills.

His glance at his arm is involuntary. "You have to know that wasn't your fault."

"It was at least a lot my fault," I say.

"It was a little your fault. Let's save the 'lot' for where it's deserved."

"Ribbon. Bike wheel. I should know better."

"Yeah, well, Bradley should know better too."

Sports at Meteor Central High were the one thing Cole always had, and I took that from him.

"You're out for the season," I say.

"Just the cornhole championship," he answers, like it's nothing. "The doctor my mom made me see agrees with Cereza and Lupe. He says I'll be good for soccer in the winter and I can work up to the baseball stuff for the spring. He just doesn't want me throwing right now."

It's just then that I put something together.

Sports aren't just something Cole loves.

They're his future.

He's talked about college, close enough that he could drive back to Meteor on weekends if he wanted to, far enough that no one would expect him to if he didn't. I know he both loves this town, and needs breathing room from it. And how good he is on the field is how he's gonna make that happen.

It was how his older brother got to UNM. The same older brother that, according to rumor, set down the rules of how his teammates were gonna treat the first transgender guy to join their team. "So you guys are gonna look out for my little brother or I'm gonna kick all your asses, sound good?"

I finish with the flowers in time for the oven to beep.

"I hope you're hungry," I say.

Cole laughs. "Always."

"Good." I borrow Mrs. Kendall's oven mitts to pull the casserole dish out. Bruja Lupe helped me put the enchiladas together before her Barbara Stanwyck movie marathon with Liz Peterford. "Because I brought you something else."

But now Cole sighs. "Please don't serve it for me, my mother keeps trying to do that. I do have full use of my other arm."

"I won't." I set the casserole dish down and stick a serving spoon in it. "You're gonna do it yourself."

Now he looks wary. "Is this some kind of exam?"

"Not an exam. Practice." I pull down plates. "Green enchiladas stain less than anything else Bruja Lupe and I make. This is good experience learning to eat with your other arm. Before you have to do spaghetti or something."

He shakes his head, like he's humoring me. But he does it. He pushes the books aside, and we sit at the kitchen table together, Cole as patient learning to eat with his nondominant hand as he is waiting for the right moment on the soccer field.

I say a prayer of thanks that the enchiladas turned out, that I learned how to make something more than the same sugar cookies.

Cole spears his fork into one. "It's 'Somewhere Over the Rainbow.'"

"What?" I ask.

"Kendra's song. It's 'Somewhere Over the Rainbow.'"

I look down at my plate so he won't see me cringing. Even I know how many past Miss Meteor contestants have tried that one.

"Oh wait, I'm not done." Cole sets down his fork and holds up a hand to stop me reaching for words. "Modified to 'Somewhere Over the Space Rock.'"

Now I set down my fork. "Oh no."

"Oh yes. I wish I didn't, but I now know the words by heart. And no, I'm not gonna sing it." He picks the fork back up and stabs the tines into another piece of enchilada. "Not even for you."

"Is she gonna wear the Dorothy Gale dress?"

"In Meteor Central High colors."

"Leave this town while you still can, Cole," I deadpan.

"Oh, I plan on it," he says. "But I'm probably not gonna go that far, you know that."

"And why is that, exactly?" I ask. Probably a hundred colleges—some of them far from Meteor—would want him for their baseball team. Maybe soccer even more. There's not a striker in the district who hasn't wished they had Cole Kendall's mix of patience and speed.

"Because I love this place," he says, in a way that almost makes me believe his relationship with this town isn't as complicated as it is. But only almost. "And I want to be able to get back here when I want to. I just don't want to live here. I want to live somewhere I don't have to follow everyone else's rules to get to be who I am. I wish that place was here, but it's just not, at least not right now." Cole shakes his head, smiling. "Believe it or not though, I am gonna miss some things about this place."

"So am I," I say, and I feel like my heart's crumbling to stardust.

"Oh yeah?" he asks. "You're out of here, too, when you get the chance?"

"Yeah."

"Where are you going?"

I'm trying to figure out how to give an answer that's not *far away, like, galactically far away,* when the sound of keys being set down makes me stand up.

I brace for the sight of Kendra's curling-iron curls.

Worse.

Mrs. Kendall's high heels click into the kitchen. They match her shell tank that looks like it came from a sweater set. She dresses like this even on her days off. I wonder if it rubbed off on her son. Cole always looks a little nicer than he has to.

I realize, just now, that it's the richest guys in town who always show up in wrinkled shorts and flip-flops in brands none of us know because nowhere in Meteor sells them.

Before my brain has a chance to give Meteor men's fashion any further consideration, it lands on something else.

Cole's father's trips to Chicago, and Duluth, and Omaha.

Is he never here for Cole's games not because he's busy with deals and presentations, but because he's looking for work?

Mrs. Kendall sets her eyes on us. "What is going on here?"

Cole stands up. "Mom."

"Haven't you done enough?" she asks me.

"Mom, please."

But I don't want Cole to have to defend me to his mother. I broke her son. I'd hate me too. So I don't even take the time to walk to the front door.

"Lita," Cole says.

But I'm already climbing out one of those wide-open windows.

Before I can scramble out of Mrs. Kendall's hydrangea bushes, I hear more than I want to.

"That's the girl who almost cost you your future, and you let her into this house?" Mrs. Kendall asks.

"She didn't cost me anything," Cole says. "I'm back in soccer in the winter and baseball in the spring. For all I know, this'll be good for me. I actually get some time off before soccer season. Maybe I actually get time for the fifteen things that hurt every day to heal a little instead of just icing them down and going back to practice."

I crouch down in the hydrangeas, more to make myself small than to hide.

"You can't lose focus now," Mrs. Kendall says.

"My focus should be cornhole?" Cole asks. "There's no college in the world that's gonna give me a scholarship for it. I don't even like it. I just do it because everyone wants me to."

"You can't get distracted."

"Do I look distracted? I'm doing homework. How many of the guys in my class do you think are gonna touch any of this before next Sunday night?"

"That's its own distraction."

"School?" Cole laughs. "Really?"

I shut my eyes.

Sports isn't just Cole's future.

It's a weight on him.

Whatever nerves I feel about Miss Meteor is nothing next to the pressure that's on him. Because nobody expects me to win. Everyone expects him to.

"Don't worry," Cole says. "I get it, Mom. We all get it."

Whatever jokes we make about my grasp on sarcasm, I catch it. I hear it hardening his voice. "I'm too much of a dumb jock to get a scholarship with my grades or my test scores, so I better make sure I stay at the top of the team lineup. Message received."

CHICKY

IT'S A MARK of how bad I feel that no one speaks to me
the next morning. No well-meaning lecture from my mom, no
goofy jokes from my dad, not even a catty remark from Fresa.
It's like they know I can't feel any better or worse than I already
do, so they don't even try.

When the sun is high in the sky and everyone's at the diner,
I finally make my way out of my room and downstairs. My dad
has left out carnitas and pinto beans de la olla and rice from last
night's dinner—he knows I like to fry an egg on top of my leftovers for breakfast—and it all smells amazing as usual, but I'm
not even tempted. I don't deserve the joy of food.

I don't deserve anything good.

Not after I set Lita on a path to destruction, abandoned her
and Cole on the field, and utterly failed to stand up to Royce
Bradley. Not after I walked away from another best friend who
just wanted to know me.

Even if he was kind of pushy.

Even if he made it pretty clear he wants to do more than just be my friend.

I groan as I shove my feet into my shoes, hating myself for obsessing about it when there are so many worse things to obsess about. More immediate things. More disastrous, catastrophic things.

No more Junior drama, I tell myself, stern and uncompromising. Not today.

But even my strictest ban isn't enough. As I wander aimlessly through the residential streets of Meteor—avoiding the museum, and the diner, and Lita's house, and even the Kendalls' block—he's all I can think about. Him and our friendship, which until last night was the least complicated thing in my life.

Would it be so bad? I wonder, as I walk past the bench where we mock people, just out of view of the diner windows. Would it be so bad to hold his hand? Kiss him? Laugh at the dumb jokes that usually make me roll my eyes? When I picture it, the early afternoon sun beating accusingly down, it's not bad at all.

But it's not good either.

Not the kind of good that makes your stomach swoop and your palms sweat.

Not the kind of good that leads to more than kissing . . .

Turning west, I skulk past Hubert Humphrey Memorial Park, remembering the long summer after seventh grade—my first summer without Lita—and the way Junior and I would eat paletas in the grass and talk around all the things that made me sad.

He never pushed me. Never pressured me. He's always just been home base. A place I felt safe. And that's something, maybe even something big.

But now he's pushing, and it's making me realize I don't *know* him. Not in the deep, enduring way that my mom knows my dad, not even in the destructive but intense way my sister knows Berto. I don't know what fuels him or what makes him tick or who he'd be if he could be anyone.

Not even close.

And how are you supposed to decide if you want more, when you don't even know what you have? I replay this question over and over, walking the orbit of Pluto until long after I should have been chased indoors by the heat.

No answer comes.

After I start recycling reasons to berate myself, I realize people are looking at me. And not just in the way they usually do.

First, two girls from school giggle behind their hands as they pass me on their way to the track. This in and of itself wouldn't be particularly alarming—especially after what happened on the field. But as I scowl at their backs, a few words of their conversation drift back to me on the scrap of a breeze:

"I heard they attacked him, like, screaming and stuff."

"Oh, I totally believe it. They are such freaks."

When they turn the corner I thump my forehead painfully against Saturn's monkey bars. I've been so busy thinking about this stupid Junior situation that I didn't even anticipate half the school playing telephone with the story of what happened yesterday.

And of course they are.

I head toward downtown instinctively, knowing I need to get to the diner, to strategize with my sisters before half the school becomes the whole school.

But the people who stare as I pass the library aren't even kids from my school. They're not kids at all. Mrs. Tate, who runs the desk at the Chamber of Commerce, gives me the side eye as she passes on her lunchtime walk with Mrs. Perkins, the head of the PTA at Meteor Central. They don't even wait until they've passed before they start vilifying me in hissing whispers. It's almost like they want me to hear.

"Now, Nancy, say what you will about the boy's lifestyle, but that family has been through enough this year without having to deal with a bullying incident on top of it all!"

"Oh, you're absolutely right, Susan. You don't have to agree with everything about a political movement to know bullying is just plain wrong. Makes you wonder what the parents are teaching those kids. They work an awful lot, you know . . ."

My limbs start to go numb before Mrs. Perkins trails off. A bullying incident? Lita crashed her bike into Cole because

Royce Bradley is a jerk, but something tells me the bully they're talking about isn't him.

I stand up, my ears ringing slightly. Is it just my imagination, or is everyone downtown staring at me? My palms start to sweat as I walk toward the diner. I need Cereza. Or Fresa. Even Uva will do in a pinch.

When I pass the bench outside the hardware store, Old Vinny and Rick are smoking cigars like they always do on Tuesdays. They're usually nice to me, but today their eyes go wide the moment I'm in view.

"I heard those tough girls rolled up on the skinny boy riding motorcycles! Casting spells, they were, just like in the movies."

"What's that you said? Shells?"

"No, SPELLS! Like MAGIC! Broke his arm clean in half, and that's not the worst of it! They say the girls went after his sister next!"

"A BLISTER, was it?"

I break into a run, my sweat going cold even in 105-degree weather. The back doors of the diner swing open just like normal, but there's no one in the kitchen. Voices drift back from the dining room. My mom's, and a man's. I'm not even sure why, but I creep up to the kitchen door to listen, not making a sound, close enough that their indistinct voices become actual words.

". . . sure you understand," the man's voice is saying, and

my blood suddenly goes colder than my sweat. That's not just a man out there. It's Jack Bradley, Royce's father. "Considering the incident yesterday, the pageant board feels it's more than fair."

"The incident?" my mom asks, incredulous. "It was a couple of teenagers and a bike crash, Jack. You can't seriously be considering this."

"I think you'll find the PTA is calling it more than just a bike crash," Mr. Bradley says, his voice oozing condescension. "Considering the boy's . . . unique situation . . . the charges are more akin to bullying. And as you know, our school board and our pageant committee have expressed a clear zero-tolerance policy for abuse of any kind."

The irony of these words coming from Royce's father's mouth makes me want to launch the entire Bradley bloodline straight into the sun.

"And I'm sure the case will be examined," my mom says, using the no-nonsense voice she usually reserves for the health inspectors. "But I don't see what Selena's has to do with it."

Selena's? I press my ear even closer to the door. Sure, everyone hates us, but what can this possibly have to do with the diner?

"Given that every one of your employees were involved in the incident, the pageant board doesn't feel it would be . . . prudent for any of the official Miss Meteor events to take place in this establishment."

146

"The board doesn't? Or you don't?"

"As chairman, I won't pretend my opinion isn't valued," he says. "After all, the Kendall boy is one of my son's closest friends. You can't imagine how he's suffering today. His friend maimed. His chances at the championship all but ruined . . ."

"Jack, I'm very sorry for the Kendall boy, and for your son's . . . hardships," my mom says. "But the meet and greet is our biggest night of the year."

I can hear it in her voice now. Fear. The kind she's never shown to me.

"You know how tough it is to own a business in this town." I can almost hear my mom's pride disappearing as she swallows it. "We need this."

I know, in this moment, that I will never forgive myself for making my mother admit these things to Jack Bradley. Ever.

"Yes," he says, all fake resignation. "Restaurants. Such a fickle business, Clarita. I always say people will always need cars! That's what keeps the lights on!" He laughs, one of those awful salesman things that sounds like it was made in a plastic mold. "I imagine you can't say the same for . . . noodle casserole con pollo?"

He says pollo like polo. I've never wanted to throw fryer oil on someone so badly, and I work in a kitchen with Fresa three nights a week.

"I'd like to appeal to the board," my mom says, stiff, professional.

"I'm afraid with such short notice, there's no time for an appeal. There's always next year." I can hear his shiny shoes heading for the door, and the words my mom isn't saying. Without this event, without pageant week, we might not make it to next year.

"Where will it be?" she asks. "The meet and greet. Maybe we could . . . cater? Would that appease the board?" I hate that she's asking him this. I hate that he has this power over her. Over all of us.

"Ah, yes, well as I said, short notice. I've offered the local Bradley Dealership as the host and sponsor. We'll be . . . outsourcing the catering. I'm sure you understand."

The bell on the door dings. Jack Bradley is gone.

And my mother is crying.

I should go comfort her, but what can I say? Sorry I literally ruined your life? I can't even look at her until I fix this, so I ease back out the double doors and sprint as fast as I can toward home, hoping like hell someone else has a plan.

When I burst through the front door, the phone is already ringing.

"Lita?" I pant into the receiver.

"Yeah, this is Perez," she says in her most serious detective voice. Or is it buddy cop? I can't tell today, but at least I know she's serious.

"Did you hear?"

"Roger that, Quintanilla, it's all over town. Over."

Buddy cop, then. "What do we do?" I ask, clutching at a stitch in my side.

"We meet at the cactuses. At sundown. Bring all the firepower you've got, do you copy?"

It's absurd, but I do. And I know she doesn't mean guns. "Roger," I say, already heading for the stairs where all the firepower we'll need is waiting in the form of three supremely pissed off Quintanillas.

LITA

IT'S ENTIRELY POSSIBLE that, between the three of them, Chicky's sisters know almost every secret in Meteor. And they're how I know that something happened between Chicky and Junior, even if none of us knows exactly what.

So Chicky would probably threaten me with what's left of Fresa's ribbon wand if she knew I was doing this. But she needs all her friends, whether she knows it or not, and that includes Junior Cortes.

Especially Junior Cortes.

I find him behind the Meteor Meteorite Museum, touching up a board that's a perfect replica of a Rothko No. 61. He's never done with a painting until it's out of his hands.

"Mr. Cortes," I say, "I am here to request your presence at an urgent convening of . . ."

"Before you get through whatever speech from *Henry V*

you memorized," he says, "I'm gonna stop you."

I sigh. "Please?"

He sighs back. "Lita."

"She needs you right now," I say.

"You're either wrong," he says, standing up from inspecting the paint, "or that's news to her."

"I'm right," I say. "I promise."

"Then why are you here instead of her?"

The question steals the words from my mouth.

"I appreciate what you're trying to do," Junior says. "But it's not the best time for me and Chicky to be in the same part of the desert."

The words pinch, but I can't blame him. I know something about Chicky putting distance between her and people she needs.

"Thanks for listening," I say.

He gives me a tired nod.

On the walk over to the Kendalls' house, I keep trying to think of something that might have changed Junior's mind, words I could've said.

But I learned a long time ago that Chicky closes herself off against anything she doesn't want to let in, like desert ground gone hard during a drought.

I breathe in and tap on Cole's window.

It slides up.

"Wow," he says, leaning on the sill. "I can't figure out if

you're brave or have a death wish."

"I've been asking myself the same thing since I entered this pageant," I say.

"Sorry about earlier," he says. "About you having to climb out a window. If it makes you feel any better, my mother tends to have that effect on people."

"Look." I hold my hands up between us, to get him to hear me out. "I know the Quintanilla sisters and I apparently threw a bike at your head . . ."

"Except that didn't actually happen," he says.

"Exactly. So . . . we're . . ." I know I'm not making sense even as I say it, but before I can keep rambling Cole stops me.

"Just let me get my shoes on," he says.

I lead Cole to the stretch of desert with the cactuses I know best. The rainbows. The beehives and king cups. The purple and tulip prickly pear.

For half of the way there, I wonder if we're gonna have to go looking for Chicky. It's been years since she came to one of the cactus birthday parties. She probably doesn't remember the way anymore.

But then I see her, her cropped hair and her tall frame against the post-sunset sky.

She's there, among the cactuses, turning to them one at a time like she's greeting them each by name.

CHICKY

MY SISTERS DON'T believe me when I say I know, without being told, exactly which part of the desert Lita wants to meet us in.

"*The* cactuses?" Fresa says. "We live in New Mexico."

But with the entire town of Meteor likely cursing the day I was born and a literal evil villain trying to destroy my family's livelihood, I don't have the energy to explain what I know about this particular part of the desert, or the way it holds everything remaining of my friendship with Lita like drops of water after a rare desert storm.

Instead of all that, I just say, "I need you guys. Please." And I must look pretty bad, because they just follow without giving me any more grief.

All the way to the little patch of dirt Lita and I staked out as our own when we were eight years old, I wonder why it's always so hard for me to say those words.

When we get there, I panic for a minute. Lita isn't here. Fresa is already rolling her eyes, and I pretend not to see Uva pinch her arm to keep her quiet. I walk a little ways away from them, and—probably also thanks to Uva—no one follows me.

Any uncertainty I felt about this being the right place evaporates when the twilight glow backlights the only friends Lita and I had in elementary school. Hell, they may be the only friends I have now . . . If they'll even have me after all this time.

Then I realize this is my life now. I'm wondering if a group of spined succulents still want to be my friends. "Pull it together, Quintanilla," I say under my breath.

But it's been a hard day, and I can't help laying a hand on the tallest of the bunch, right in the spot where some animal rubbed off her spikes years ago. "Hey, Señorita Opuntia," I say, quiet enough that my sisters won't hear. "And you, too, Señora Strawberry. Sorry I missed your last birthday party."

Her blossoms, their color fading a bit in the lavender glow of a waning desert sunset, seem to glare accusingly at me.

"Fine, fine," I say, chastised. "I guess I've missed more than one."

But as their long shadows melt into the dusk, I realize I've missed a lot more than cactus birthday parties over the past few years. Almost like praying, I walk between them, speaking their names in low voices. Lady Barbara Fig, Violeta Prickly Pear, and her cousins Tortita and Señorita Tulipan. The rake of the bunch, Graham Cholla, was always trying to flirt with the pretty primas until Lita told him it wasn't polite.

When she got it into her head to give them all birthdays, Lita begged me to borrow Cereza's astrology book and figure out their signs.

"They can't tell us who they are," she said. "But don't you think they'll be thrilled if we find out for ourselves? They'll have to stay our friends after that, right?"

So we sat on a striped blanket, with my dad's homemade churros in a paper bag and prickly pear lemonade in a glass bottle, and for many nights just like this one we read their charts and told their stories to each other.

But that seems like a lifetime ago.

I walk back toward my sisters, feeling heavy and sad and slow. There's still so much to do to fix what we broke, and right now, I'm not the least bit sure we can do it.

Lita and Cole's silhouettes are just visible as they walk toward us, shoulders nearly touching. I try to focus on the fact that I have five people on my side tonight, rather than on the fact that a tall, long-haired silhouette is notably missing.

And that I'm not sure if it's his fault or mine.

LITA

I CAN TELL Chicky doesn't want me to catch it, her face falling when she sees Junior isn't with me and Cole.

"He really wanted to come," I blurt out. "But he was mixing the perfect sunset color, and he was at just the moment of finding the right balance between orange and pink." I let out a nervous laugh. "And you know he can't go anywhere in the middle of that, right?"

Chicky gives me a weak smile, and I can tell she appreciates the lie.

But she doesn't believe it.

"Just so you know," Uva says. "Apparently we're all half of *West Side Story*."

"Sharks or Jets?" I ask.

"Not important, Lita," Cereza says at the same moment Fresa says, "Um, Sharks, obviously."

156

"Well, I heard," Chicky says, "that we surrounded Cole with our motorcycles behind Selena's."

"And then cast an evil spell on him?" Uva asks, squinting into the last of the light. "Yeah, I heard that one too."

"I heard we had an evil plan to make sure Meteor Central High has no chance at this year's championship," I say, toeing the dirt.

Cole groans. "This would be funny if it weren't so not funny."

I cringe. "What are we gonna do about Selena's?" I ask. "And the Bradleys, and—"

"Stop," Cereza cuts me off. "That's not for you to worry about."

Uva crosses her arms and shoots Fresa a look. "Well, you were right about one thing. They are gonna be talking about this for years."

"Okay, not helping," Cereza says. "Cole, if we've done anything to . . ."

"Stop it," he says. "This was an accident. I just had the same conversation with this one." He shrugs toward Lita.

Cereza sighs. "But if there's anything we can do . . ."

"If any of you apologizes one more time," Cole says, "I'm signing each of you up for the Christmas pageant decorating committee."

That shuts all of us up. We've each witnessed Mrs. Kendall

berating teenagers and little old ladies alike for putting the wrong kind of tinsel in the holly garlands.

Uva speaks next. "I heard Simon Alter saying Lita set this whole thing up because she knows how close Kendra and Cole are, and she just wanted to rattle Kendra."

"Oh, brother," Cole says under his breath.

"What?" I ask.

Cole runs a hand through his hair. "Kendra."

"What about her?"

Cole takes a breath deep enough for me to see him pulling it in and blowing it out, like he's trying not to get angry. "If there's anyone who's helping to blow this out of proportion, I'm betting it's her."

He starts walking off.

"Are you okay?" Uva asks.

"No, I'm not okay." He turns back. "I'm gonna fix this."

"Cole," Cereza says. "It's not your job to fix anything."

"Maybe no one cares what I have to say about the rumors," he calls back, but doesn't stop. Now he's walking backward. "But I am not letting my sister feed them."

He turns back around.

And with that, with one boy off to squabble with his sister and one boy refusing to come near Chicky, it's just me and the four Quintanilla sisters standing among my cactus friends.

"This isn't over," Cereza says, and I wonder if she's wearing out those words on me.

I try to rise to Cereza's faith. "At least the meet and greet doesn't require a talent. And it's somewhere we all know."

All sisters cringe at once.

"It is at Selena's," I say, "isn't it?"

"Try was," Fresa says.

Uva's look is almost pitying. "The pageant voted to change the location."

"Those fuckers," Fresa says. "It wasn't enough to deny me the crown, now they move the one event we have this week to a car dealership?" She puts disgusted emphasis on those last three words.

My stomach drops.

Our small town has one car dealership, owned by a family with enough power and enough money for countywide ad space.

"No," I say.

"I know," Chicky says.

"NO," I can't help repeating.

"I know," Chicky says. "What are we gonna do?" She's asking her sisters more than she's asking me.

This morning I found the stardust continuing its spread over my stomach and hips. I couldn't wear a two-piece right now even if I wanted to. But right now, with what I've done to the Quintanillas and to Cole, I feel like my bones themselves are turning into stardust. I will crumble at any second.

"We have to figure something out," Chicky says. "I don't care if we have to start catering at the hospital. Fresa, I don't

care if you have to flirt with a skywriter. We have to do something."

Cereza holds up a hand. "One problem at a time." She turns
to Lita. "Yes, the meet and greet is gonna be somewhere you
don't know." She turns to her sisters. "Yes, it is going to be at
the business place of the family who is probably our mortal
enemy now." She looks at all of us. "But we are going to con-
duct ourselves with the elegance and class befitting our places
in Miss Meteor's history."

"Speak for yourself," Chicky says under her breath.

Uva snaps her a look that shuts her up.

Chicky kicks at the dirt in protest. Fresa folds her arms at
her older sister rejecting her dreams of revenge. Uva's weari-
ness is so obvious it makes my own shoulders feel heavy. And
I probably look nauseated at the thought of putting on a pair
of borrowed heels and walking through the freshly Windexed
doors of the Bradley Dealership.

"If they're our enemies"—Uva's stare stays on Chicky—
"what better chance to keep an eye on them?"

CHICKY

MY PARENTS DECIDE to keep the diner open the night of the Fiftieth-Annual Meteor Pageant and Talent Showcase meet and greet, even though there's absolutely no way anyone will be ordering tostada burgers and yucca waffle fries tonight.

"Good luck," my mom tells us as my sisters crimp and curl and apply false lashes and generally transform Lita into something that won't look out of place at the southernmost outpost of Meteor proper: the Bradley Dealership.

Mom still hasn't said anything about the reason for the change of venue, but she knows we know, and we know she knows we know, and it's all really awkward and sad.

No one else hears her say goodbye over Cereza's order-giving and Fresa's backtalk and Lita's occasional yelps of pain, but I hug her for all of us. For the sorry I can't say because we're not talking about it.

She lets go sooner than I do, and it's maybe the worst I've ever felt in my life.

Well, second worst.

When she's gone I try to focus. This is just a step on the road to fixing this, and I have to believe we can. I have one job tonight—even if I know it's just one Uva made up to make me feel better—and I won't rest until I've discovered something about the sleazy Bradleys that will prove useful in the battle ahead.

Sue me, I was watching a Viking show this morning, I'm full of war metaphors tonight.

At loose ends until the beauty portion of the evening is over—I let Cereza put mascara on me, and I'm wearing jeans with no holes in them, but that's as far as I'll go—I wander into the kitchen and engage in my familiar battle of wills with the phone on the wall.

To call, or not to call, I ask it for the hundredth time since my fight with Junior.

The phone still doesn't answer. Because it's still an inanimate object that doesn't know whose fault the fight was or who's supposed to apologize first or if it'll even work.

"Ten minutes!" Cereza shrieks from upstairs, and my nerves start to jangle.

The Bradley Dealership is basically the underworld. Lita will be busy trying to prove she's not some kind of barbarian, my sisters will be watching (and hopefully correcting) her every

162

move, and sure I'll be doing recon but everyone knows that's not a real thing. I'll just be the outcast of an outsider family, walking around completely out of my element.

I pick up the landline, Fresa's the only one of us with a cell, and she pays for it herself. Priorities, she says.

My fingers dial Junior's number by memory, and it only rings twice before I hear the click on the other end.

"Hello?" My stomach sinks. It's Mrs. Cortes.

"Hey, Mrs. Cortes," I say.

"Oh, hi, Chicky. Junior's not here tonight and he left his phone."

I can't tell by her tone whether she's heard what happened between us or not, but I don't press the issue. "Oh, okay. Do you know where he went?"

"I think he said he was going to that pageant meet and greet."

My sinking heart is suddenly afloat. "Thank you," I say, with real relief. "Have a good night, Mrs. Cortes."

When we hang up, I smile bigger than I have all week. Junior and I might be in a fight, or whatever it is, but he would never make me do this alone. I should have known better than to doubt him.

When I climb into the back of Cereza's car, sandwiched between Fresa and Uva with Lita up front, I'm suddenly sure everything is going to be okay.

✳ ✳ ✳ ✳

It only takes seven minutes to drive anywhere in Meteor, so we're in front of the Bradley Dealership before my hopeful bubble has time to deflate.

It's a massive building by Meteor standards, floor-to-ceiling windows, light spilling out of every one into the darkened desert. One of those glass and metal atrocities that reminds you of some fancy bachelor's coffee table, but somehow with a giant fountain right in the middle of it.

Yeah. Inside. It's just as ridiculous as it sounds.

The event is set up in the showroom, and there are three brand-new Corvettes parked in spotlights right there on the floor—an orange one, a blue one, and a silver one. Meteor Central High colors.

I look around for a massive shiny decorative vase to vomit in.

Instead, I see anyone who's anyone in Meteor milling around through the windows while my sisters arrange Lita's outfit by the car. It's casual but classy, according to Fresa. Black pants, tapered at the ankle, a pair of Fresa's suede booties in charcoal gray, with just a little bit of a heel. The top is Cereza's, a deep purple flowy thing with a modest neckline, pinned in the back to account for Lita's height—or lack thereof.

She looks good, as far as I can tell. Well, I mean she looks like someone else. Which I guess is the point.

"Okay, ready!" Cereza says.

"As we'll ever be," Fresa mutters under her breath.

"I don't think we should all walk in together," Lita says,

stopping us. She has her "I'm on a mission" face on, and no one dares to argue with her. "I mean, we are trying to avoid looking like a motorcycle gang, right?"

Fresa snorts, but Cereza agrees.

"I'll go in first," Lita continues, like she's a general in a field tent. "Everyone spread out. Say hello to people who say hello to you, ignore everyone else, and smile. Do one lap, then we'll all meet up at the punch table to go over our next move, understood?"

We all nod, because no one has a better idea, but faced with the actual Bradley Dealership even my fierce-as-hell sisters seem a little cowed.

"Fresa and Cereza, set up camp by the table," Lita goes on. "And Uva, you and Chicky go through the side door."

"Capisce?" she asks me, and I smile.

"Capisce."

They've really gone all out, I think as I follow Uva around the front to the side door. Those jerks. Aside from the stupid cars, there are bunches of orange, blue, and silver balloons bracketing massive banners advertising the pageant.

Well, they would be, if BRADLEY DEALERSHIP, HOST AND SPONSOR wasn't printed bigger on every single banner than the name of the pageant.

I think of Fresa's sabotage idea and imagine one of them on fire.

"No arson," Uva says as we enter, trying to be incognito.

"How did you—"

"It's just a look you get," she says with a long-suffering eye roll. "It's a Fresa look."

I don't know whether to be offended or flattered.

"I need to find Junior," I say, when we've successfully found a corner where no one will hiss or boo at us. "His mom said he's here, and I think he's waiting for me."

"Oh," Uva says, and her face turns a little plum colored right in the hollows of her cheeks. "I don't think he's here yet. Maybe we should get some food instead? You know, check out the competition."

"Why does your voice sound weird?" I ask her.

"It always sounds like that when I'm hungry. Come on."

She takes my arm before I can argue anymore and drags me across the floor toward the food spread.

It's worse than I feared. The Bradleys have gone for the hometown comfort food angle. Barbecue, baked beans, potato salad, little handheld mac and cheese with breadcrumbs made in foil cupcake holders.

Uva takes a mac and cheese cup, and I settle on a withering glare instead of an all-out wrist slap.

"What?" she asks. "I'm hungry!"

"You're despicable."

"Look, there's Lita!"

I turn to look. She's making her way across the super-shiny

166

tile floor of the dealership with . . . determination, if not grace. We'll take it for now. An old lady sucks her teeth at me as she goes by. I wait until she passes to stick my tongue out at her.

From across the showroom, I see Cereza draw a finger across her neck, her eyes locked on mine. I roll my eyes and go back to watching Lita.

Not many people stop her, and I wish I could hear what they say when they do. Whatever it is, she smiles that slightly too-wide smile (a little toned down, since Cereza finally gave up on the Vaseline) and shakes their hands.

So far, so good, I think. But that's where I'm wrong.

Royce Bradley makes his grand entrance at that moment, coming down the massive, curving staircase in the middle of the room. He's in jeans and a blazer, Kendra on his arm in a peachy-goldish sundress that catches every drop of light in the room and dazzles it right back out.

The music changes, the Meteor school song playing over the loudspeakers, and even though donors and board members and judges aren't supposed to play favorites, they literally give Royce and Kendra a round of applause.

Daring Uva to say a word, I shove a whole mac and cheese cup in my mouth.

I'm going to need fuel.

Halfway through chewing the rubbery thing, though, I spot Lita, who's clearly been thrown off by the appearance of

Royce and Kendra. She looks uncertain now, and her clown smile has disappeared, and as I watch her she stumbles on the heels at last. That's when everything shifts to slow motion.

Behind her, someone is carrying a massive flower arrangement to the punch table. I see the heel reach the last moment it can mathematically remain stable, then pass it, taking Lita backward as it topples.

She falls, of course, right into the flowers, which fly absurdly high into the air against the dramatic backdrop of the dark windows, raining down water droplets and foliage on everyone nearby.

Someone actually screams.

I hope whoever it is chokes on this awful mac and cheese. Just a little.

Lita is on the ground. Everyone assembled is stunned. Someone very oblivious or very cruel has cut the music, so there's utter silence in the room.

Cereza and Fresa are already by her side, helping her up. Uva darts off, muttering something about the DJ. I'm about to do something—anything—to cause a distraction, when I see him across the room, his long, glossy hair twisted up into a knot on his head tonight, even though he's told me a thousand times he'll never stoop low enough to rock a man bun.

Even if the girls like it.

Even if I kind of like it.

My heart inflates just a little and then seems to disappear altogether.

Because Junior Cortes did not put his hair up.

He tamed it for the petite blond girl with heels as high as her ponytail.

The girl who is now hanging on his arm, looking incredibly smug.

And even though Lita's plan is falling to pieces around me, I can't look away.

LITA

EVERYONE IS STARING at me.

Not because I injured the star thrower of Meteor Central High's cornhole team.

Not because half of Meteor thinks I'm the sad fifth member of some Quintanilla-sister motorcycle gang.

Not even because my boobs are held up with six strips of duct tape and my nipples are currently reinforced with two halves of a Hot Tamales candy ("Trust me," Fresa said when she made me hoist up my breasts so she could cross the sticky silver under and between them. "Everyone does it, so you'll just look the same as the other contestants.")

No.

They're all staring because I just knocked over an enormous flower arrangement, and between my heels and the wet floor, it takes two Quintanilla sisters to get me steady.

Everyone is staring for a reason that has nothing to do with Cole or Selena's.

So I might as well make it count.

Once Fresa has pushed me back onto my feet, and Cereza has dusted me off, I give a grand curtsy, sweeping my hand in front of me like a princess.

An encouraging laugh rises from one side of the room, followed by the start of applause.

Anyone else might ignore the fact that most of the brown citizens of Meteor in this room are the ones serving the food and the drinks, or staffing the car dealership. They're restocking the buffet table, or circulating with trays, or polishing where oblivious guests leave fingerprints on the windows, because the Bradleys cannot stand a smudge on their establishment—not today, not even for a minute.

These are the Meteor residents Bruja Lupe gives real cures to. Cures for fever, and susto, and the pain of old bone breaks.

These are the Meteor residents who laugh first and applaud first.

Then everyone from out of town, the ones who don't know me as the girl who mowed down Cole Kendall with an antique bicycle, join in. Even the contestants.

With each rise of the clapping, the Meteor residents who hate us, who whisper about us, look a little more uncomfortable.

They realize, with each second, how unfeeling, how stodgy and humorless, they will look if they don't participate.

So, however begrudgingly, they join in.

Even Kendra.

Even Royce.

Even his parents.

They all have to applaud me, or look like spoilsports.

It's sweeter than the strawberry lip gloss Fresa put on top of my lipstick.

It only lasts a few seconds, but that laugh—with me, for once, not at me—and their applause keep me on my feet. They keep me smiling my pageant smile as I shake hands with other contestants (though most of them are not actually shaking, just presenting the upturned backs of their hands like I'm supposed to kiss them). It keeps me standing up straight as Mayor Badii tells me what a nice shade of purple my top is and wishes me luck like she thinks I might actually have a chance. It keeps me as gracious as Cereza when a woman stirring a tiny ramekin of potato salad looks me over and says, "Pants. What an interesting choice."

And it gives me the impulse to catch Junior Cortes topping off his soda, the first minute he's been away from the girl with hair so fine and shiny it looks like she polishes it.

He nods his thanks to Dolores Ramirez, who fills his glass all the way up to the brim. It's the kind of perfect pour Bruja Lupe has been trying to teach me for years, catching it so the fizz just rounds over the top without bubbling over.

Dolores gives me an encouraging smile that I swear looks laced with "get those putas" before she goes back to the caterers' makeshift bar.

"What are you doing?" I ask Junior.

"Taking advantage of eating on the Bradleys' tab." He picks up a foil macaroni cup. "I hope by the time I'm done with them they have to stock their dealership fridge with"—he fake gasps—"generic bottled water."

I can't help laughing. The Bradleys make a big show of their single-use plastic water bottles with their custom dealership labels. Royce even carries them around school, forgoing the reusable bottles Cole has been begging him to switch over to. ("You are single-handedly killing the Earth, man," I have heard Cole lament more than once as they were heading to practice.)

"I meant what are you doing with a girl who's not Chicky?" I can't help glancing over at the blond girl. But I try to give her a smile to show I'm harmless.

Junior groans. "Not this again."

A contestant in a sweater set and flared skirt smiles and nods at me as she goes by. I do the same.

I turn back to Junior. "Why do you want to be one of those guys?"

I try to figure out how to explain, because the next question he's going to ask will be "One of what guys?"

But what he asks instead is, "Why wouldn't I want to be?"

I stick a lime wedge on the rim of his cup. "Because you're not one of those guys."

He looks a little guilty, but more than that, he looks a little sad. He drops the first-date posture he's been wearing since he walked in. His eyes are tracking around the room, and I realize he's not looking where the blond girl just was standing.

He's looking for Chicky.

And he's opening his mouth and taking a breath in to say something, something true, when an almost-yelling voice startles us both.

A member of the pageant board projects over the crowd that it's time for the group photo.

All the contestants shuffle toward the indoor fountain, its tidy shoots of water gurgling at evenly spaced intervals. Dresses rustle against each other. My pants whisk alongside skirts. Royal blue and deep magenta mix with pastels.

Kendra, in her peach sundress that's a perfect lightening of Meteor Central High's orange, edges to the first row. She does it with a genial smile that almost hides how much she's throwing her elbows.

I understand immediately what this game is. We are all trying to seem generous and polite and compliant, unconcerned with our own position, while all wanting to be as front-and-center as possible.

I step off to the side and back. I am too small, and too

174

unsteady on my heels to fight for prime position. And I don't need any more enemies anyway.

A brown hand lands on my shoulder.

"You're in front, pequeña." Another contestant, one of the few with brown skin like mine, shoves me forward. "They're never gonna see you if you hide back here."

I am so shocked by another contestant willingly putting me in front of her that it takes me a second to realize I have landed next to Kendra Kendall.

"Eww," Kendra says, "can you lay off the perfume? I'm literally choking on how cheap you smell."

I sigh and straighten my shoulders as the photographer lines up her camera.

"You might want to turn sideways," Kendra says, preening in advance for the lens. "You're taking up a lot of the frame."

"Say . . . PAGEANT QUEEN!" the photographer yells.

We all obey.

Except me. I just say the "queen" part. Fresa warned me about this. The word "pageant" contorts your mouth into positions unflattering for photography.

"I hope you're happy," Kendra says through smiling teeth. "Cole didn't even want to show up today."

"Say . . . . .PAGEANT QUEEN!"

We all adjust our postures. "PAGEANT QUEEN!"

"Yes," I say through equally smiling teeth. "I'm sure he

couldn't possibly have anything better to do than watch you pose."

"Say . . . PAGEANT QUEEN!"

We put our hands on our hips, trying not to take each other out with our elbows. "PAGEANT QUEEN!"

"He would be practicing," Kendra says. "If you hadn't broken his arm."

"NOW, A FUN ONE!" the photographer yells.

We all drape ourselves into fun positions as forced as Mr. Hamilton's enthusiasm on test days. We shuffle and reconfigure ourselves. Friends cluster even closer and throw their arms around each other. Nervous first-time entrants pull to the sides and stand together.

Cereza's words bite at me.

Elegance and grace and poise.

I remember everything Cereza told me, and I grit my teeth as I gently place an arm over Kendra's shoulder.

I am ready for her to recoil, for another "Eww."

Instead, she throws her arm around me.

It's so familiar, so friendly, my neck in the crook of her shoulder, that I wonder if we're going to declare a ceasefire, even if it's just for the length of this pageant.

Then her arm tightens.

Then it's almost a chokehold.

Kendra grins toward the photographer the whole time.

I try not to squirm.

"You like that?" Kendra asks. "I almost forgot about you and your little lesbo friend."

"Lesbo? Really?" I choke out from under her bony arm. "That's what you do with anyone different from you? You just call them names?" I try to tilt one shoulder back like Uva taught me for posing, wondering if it might work to free myself from what feels like a skinny-girl wrestling grip. And wondering how Cole feels about having a sister who would probably make ruthless fun of him in the halls at school if he weren't her own brother.

Kendra shifts in a way that makes her elbowing me in the ribs seem accidental.

"Get off me, Kendra." I try to wriggle out of her hold.

"But we're smiling now," she says.

"Get off me." I reach into my bra, rip out one of the Hot Tamale halves that is wedged onto the tip of my boob, and throw it at Kendra's face.

She reels back, enough that the other contestants reel back in response. "Did you just throw your nipple at me?"

"Say . . . PAGEANT QUEEN!"

The unison response of "Pageant Queen" is more tentative this time.

Kendra lunges at me.

I shift my weight to dodge.

But on my borrowed high heels, I wobble.

I wobble toward the fountain.

And in that moment a familiar figure comes through the door of the Bradley Dealership.

Bruja Lupe is beaming, looking flushed like she hurried here from her last appointment, glancing around for her little pageant contestant.

Then she finds me, and her expression shifts to horror.

The arc of Kendra's lunge continues. And without the resistance of my standing body to take the force of hers, Kendra goes with me.

Into the fountain.

CHICKY

THE SILVER CORVETTE, loathsome as it is, is angled just right so that if I appear to be admiring it I can see the reflection of Junior Cortes and his date in one of the side mirrors.

By my third root beer float, I've almost convinced myself this is all an elaborate setup, and the five thousand milligrams of sugar coursing through my bloodstream agrees with me enthusiastically.

See, it's like this: the Hair Pony (as I've taken to calling her in my head) is one of Kendra's friends trying to infiltrate our pageant camp and sabotage Lita's chances by . . . seducing Junior to get to us. That makes sense, right? There's no way he could actually like her.

She giggles. He smiles. She reaches out and pushes a glossy strand of hair off his forehead where it's escaped his bun. I can't read lips from this far away, but I'm pretty sure he's not telling her that touching a person of color's hair without permission contributes to the idea that their bodies only exist for the entertainment and consumption of the oppressor.

That consent is dignity, and dignity is humanity.

Objects in mirror are closer than they appear.

Is it weird that I want to high-five this mirror for agreeing with me?

He takes her empty soda, and before he heads back to fill it up she touches his arm too. Like it belongs to her. Suddenly, I feel like I might throw up.

I have to switch to the other mirror, but when Junior approaches the beverage table I really almost do it. Go over there. Tell him that girl with her perky ponytail and her bright yellow strapless dress and her pink lip gloss might be shiny, but that I'm . . .

And that's where I get stuck. Because yes, seeing them together makes me want to paint the very shiny floor of the Bradley Dealership with a half-gallon of partially digested root beer float, but I don't have an alternative. I can't give him any more than I've already given him. I'm not ready. I don't know if I'll ever be ready.

And I shouldn't feel like I have to.

So it's a stalemate. I watch in the side mirror as he fills up her soda. And I watch as Lita walks by him on the way to greet another contestant and stops to squeeze a lime into it—which I hope the Hair Pony will hate, by the way—and I wish it were me squeezing that stupid lime. I wish I was still Junior's best friend.

Or Lita's.

Or anyone's.

"Places for photos, please! All contestants over here by the fountain!"

Lita walks (only a little unsteadily) away from Junior, who watches her go for a long moment. He looks sad, or confused or something, and I know I should be watching Lita, too, but I can't stop watching him. Wondering why he doesn't go back to his *date*.

"It's a fine machine, isn't it?"

Mr. Bradley is next to me. When did that happen? I tear my eyes resentfully from Junior.

"I've driven this one myself. Six hundred and fifty horses of pure American muscle."

"I prefer Mustangs," I say, picking the first car I can think of, my voice as chilly as I can make it with all these Junior feelings still swirling around.

"The Mustang has a tendency to go out of fashion," Mr. Bradley says, his voice all smooth and sleazy like every bad movie car salesman. "But the Corvette is timeless. A classic. It's not going anywhere."

"The Mustang has character." I try to channel Berto last summer as he debated cars with my mom in the yard. "The Mustang has a stubborn charm." I look up at Mr. Bradley. "The Mustang might not look as flashy as the Corvette, or be as expensive, but it's not going anywhere either."

"You're a little spitfire," he says, chuckling. "But it won't do you a bit of good if you don't get a handle on that bad attitude of yours." He looks my outfit up and down. "You could put on a dress, sweetheart. Smile more. Date athletes instead of hospitalizing them. Maybe if you did, that little taco shack wouldn't be empty tonight."

There's half a root beer float left in my glass, and I'm about to throw it in this slimeball's face, consequences be damned, when I hear it. When *everyone* hears it.

"DID YOU JUST THROW YOUR NIPPLE AT ME?"

Mr. Bradley disappears, and so do Junior and the Hair Pony, and it's like there's no one in the room but me, watching Lita and Kendra wrestle back and forth until they both fall backward into Mr. Bradley's timeless, classic indoor fountain.

When the paramedics are done examining Lita and Kendra for concussions, the party is pretty much over.

I see Kendra first, her dress plastered to her, more orange Corvette than tasteful peach now that it's soaked through. It's not a good color on her, even without the stringy, tangled mess on top of her head and the eye makeup running down her face.

Plus, the murderous scowl isn't at all flattering. Fresa would say the crease between her eyebrows is well on its way to permanence.

I'm almost ready to call it worth it for the visual alone until I see Lita, wrapped in one of those tinfoil-looking space blankets even though it's at least eighty degrees in here, looking bedraggled and forlorn.

My sisters are doing their best to do damage control with the sponsors, and Cole is trailing his furious sister and their possibly more furious mother out the door, looking guilty and sad. Junior is with the Hair Pony by the stairs, though he keeps shooting glances at Lita.

I can't decide if it makes me hate him more or less.

The bottom line is, I, Chicky Quintanilla, Lita's pageant manager, don't run away this time. I walk over with a cupcake—sans jalapeños, unfortunately—and sit down beside her.

"Thanks," she says, sniffling a little as she takes it.

"You okay?"

"I'm . . . not even sure how to answer that."

"Yeah, of course. Sorry."

She looks at me, eyes wide. "It's not like you told me to reach down my shirt and throw a Hot Tamale nipple at Kendra Kendall before viciously manhandling her into a fountain. What are you sorry for?"

I laugh, because I think she's trying to be funny, but the question sticks.

What are you sorry for?

She's still waiting for an answer when I realize: I know Lita.

I really know her. I know what she loves and what she's afraid of and what makes her tick. I know who she'd be if she could be anyone—though, to be fair, that someone changes drastically depending on the situation.

And now, when the whole town hates us, and we've already let life push us apart so far it would be so easy to blame each other. To let the pressure push us even farther out of orbit. But instead, we're here. Taking care of each other.

"I'm sorry for never telling you I missed you," I say, before I can overthink it. Her eyes get even bigger somehow, her wet hair and the space blanket reflecting the fluorescent lights of the showroom and making her seem even more sparkly than usual.

"I missed you too," she says, and there's a question in it. An "is this just because I'm soaked and pathetic, or do you mean it" kind of question. An "is this going to end when the pageant does" kind of question.

And right now, call me crazy, but I'm not so sure I want it to. The thought bowls me over, like someone's just told me the sky is green, or Selena's enchilada pot pie is being featured in an elite food magazine.

She smiles, and I can see it. I can see it all. Cactus birthday parties and diner tater tot nachos after school. Maybe we'll go to some of Cole's soccer games. Maybe we'll joyride out to the desert when I get my license.

And I can see it in her eyes, too, in her smile, that she's imagining the same things, and I'm so hopeful I feel like a soap bubble about to burst . . .

But that's when Royce bangs through the double doors— missing the suit jacket Kendra probably demanded he give her to wear home. Everyone else is milling around outside, waiting for rides and gossiping a mile a minute.

And I see it in Lita's eyes just as I feel it in mine. Royce. Kendra. Everything that's happened. All the reasons I pulled away. All the secrets that began our slow drift into opposite corners of space.

My imagining turns darker now, sadder, from tater tot nachos to looking her in the eyes and telling her: I don't just like boys, and I've been afraid of Kendra telling the world since fourth grade.

My stomach knots up. Lita's face closes off. And that little green shoot of renewing friendship is crushed under the heel of everything we've never said. Everything I can't say. Everything I don't know.

"Freaks!" Royce says by way of greeting, his voice echoing through the massive, empty room. "This is private property! Get out!"

And Lita looks at me, her mouth still slightly open, like we'd been in another world before Royce walked in and its debris is still floating around us.

"Did you hear me?" He comes forward in that intimidating way of his that just makes everything in me shrivel up. "Date's over! Go back to your hovels!"

Lita looks at him, and then me, and then him again before she closes her mouth up tight and scampers from the room through the closest door.

I almost call out to her. But what would be the point? Nothing has changed. And this second drifting is even worse, because now we know what it feels like. Not to know each other. We know what we're heading for.

But we go anyway. What choice do we have?

LITA

HOW THE METEOR Regional Pageant and Talent Competition Showcase goes about eliminating contestants is one of the best tourists traps in this town.

The Meteor Regional Pageant and Talent Competition Showcase doesn't cut girls after each event. If they did that, their families, friends, and hometown contingents would check out of their motels and go home the day their girls were eliminated. Instead, to keep everyone here buying our souvenirs and booking up room blocks and eating at our restaurants, the officials stretch out the pageant, one event per day. They never give out scores or call out which contestants will advance.

So I, like every other girl up there, will have no idea how I'm doing until I'm standing in an evening gown on that last night.

But after what's already being called the Meteor catfight of the decade, I have a pretty good idea.

I work at peeling away the six strips of duct tape on my boobs. Oil on my fingertips, rubbing at the edges.

Everyone on this planet, I'm either going to hurt (Cole; the Quintanillas), lose (Chicky), or leave (Bruja Lupe).

I worried at the duct tape, pulling it away from my skin.

A long strip comes away.

Underneath is not the comforting brown of my own skin, but pale stardust, a wide patch under my breasts.

My breath rasps in my throat.

Everything I'm screwing up trying to be Miss Meteor, it's not making me more ready to leave this planet.

It's making the stardust take me faster.

Bruja Lupe's knock rattles my bedroom door. "Lita?"

My breath is too thin to tell her not to come in.

The door opens.

I turn, just enough to catch her eyes.

"Why is this happening?" I ask, my voice trembling.

She presses her lips together. "Because it's what we are."

"Then why aren't you turning with me?"

She lifts her eyes from the floor. "Because it already happened to me."

My hearts opens like a nebula.

"What?" I ask.

"This same thing happened to me." She touches her

shoulder in such an involuntary way, with the lightest shudder, that I know she's telling the truth. I wonder if the Milky Way of silver and white in her black braid is the one mark left on her. It has always shimmered more than made sense, like the light was dancing over the gray.

"Then how are you here?" I ask, with barely enough breath to get it out.

Her smile is sad and beautiful as the collapse of a star. "You."

"What?" I ask. "How?"

Bruja Lupe sinks down onto the bed. "For years, I thought I was just supposed to take care of you so someone would. And when I got my own stardust, all I did was worry about who would take care of you when I was gone. But then"—she looks out the window, at the sky—"I realized I wasn't just taking care of you for you. I was taking care of you for me. I was a mother to you."

I can't tell how quickly the insides of me are turning to stardust, but I swear, in this moment, I can feel my entire heart becoming a shapeless, glimmering thing all at once.

"As soon as I decided I was your mother, even if most of this planet wouldn't agree," Bruja Lupe says, "that's when it vanished."

I have never felt more loved, and more unlovable.

It should make me thank Bruja Lupe, tell her how much she means to me.

Instead I feel ready to bare my teeth like the stray cats in Hubert Humphrey Memorial Park.

"So you could just decide to make it stop?" I ask. "How do I do that?"

"I don't know," Bruja Lupe says, her voice rising.

"If you could decide, there has to be a way for me to."

"Don't you think I would tell you if I knew? Don't you think I wish I knew?"

"So there's something wrong with me that I can't just decide, right?" I throw on jeans and my biggest sweatshirt, not my pajamas. "Like you?"

"Lita," Bruja Lupe says.

I climb out the window I used to climb out of to meet Chicky, because I cannot be in this apartment with a woman whose love for me kept her in her body, on this planet.

And who I, apparently, do not have enough heart for, enough love for, to do the same.

"Lita," Bruja Lupe calls.

But she doesn't stop me.

I run into dimming streets, the sky red at the horizon and deep blue overhead. If I go fast enough, maybe I can get it over with. Maybe I'll melt back into star-stuff. Maybe it'll be easier being ice and dust and fire and far-off shimmer than it is to be a girl anyway.

A hand I know stops me.

"Lita," Cole says.

I hold my hands up between us. "Get away from me."

He pulls back. "What?"

190

"People let me into their lives, and I ruin them. Or they just decide they don't want me. Or I'm just not good enough or strong enough or whatever, okay?"

"You really think you've ruined my life?" he asks.

He takes a slow step toward me, and I feel the gravity of him.

Two people like us don't have the same mass as two planets or stars, not anywhere near. But we are far smaller than planets and stars, so the tiny pull we exert on each other is still one we can both feel.

"Lita," he says. "You're one of my best friends in this town."

The words make me blink, like Cole might dissolve into nighttime and desert dust in front of me. "What?"

"Is that really news to you?"

"Strikers on the soccer team aren't friends with girls like me."

"Then what have we been doing?"

That's when I start crying. Because I don't know what I've been doing. To the Quintanillas, to Cole, to Bruja Lupe, who probably only still has customers because the tourists have failed to make the connection between her and the most disastrous contestant in the history of Miss Meteor.

Cole doesn't pull away. He doesn't reel back.

"You know, I don't mean to brag, and I haven't tried it out yet," he says, glancing at his sling. "But I'm willing to bet I give a really great one-arm hug."

I pull the heel of my hand across my cheek. "You don't have to do that."

191

"I know I don't."

"Boys don't like when girls cry."

"They thought I was a girl when I was born, remember? I'm immune to girl things. It's like a superpower."

"Then why did you used to say I was gonna give you girl-germs?"

"I was eight, okay? Just come here."

With one arm, he pulls me into him. Hard. I don't realize how much I needed it until he does.

Bruja Lupe is always there when I have a fever or a nightmare. Bruja Lupe loves me with a force that kept her on this planet. But she is not a hugger. I can't remember when anyone hugged me like this. Maybe no one ever has.

I never realized it before, but I know what Cole Kendall smells like enough for him to be familiar to me. His scent is as much about absence as a resemblance to something else. It's not detergent or fabric softener (the fragrance doesn't cling to him), or soap (he uses unscented bars from the dollar store), or deodorant (again, unscented), or body spray (he hates it; bus rides back from away games are the worst because they're full of it). The closest thing I can place it to is the desert rock outside Meteor at night.

Yes, the desert outside Meteor smells different at night.

I return his half hug by sliding my arm under his.

"You smell good," I say.

He laughs. "Considering I pretty much never go more than

thirty-six hours without some kind of practice, that's about the best compliment I can think of."

I laugh with him.

Then I start crying again.

"I'm sorry." I set my forehead against his shirt. "I know you don't need this right now."

"Like hell I don't," he says. "When you look at me, I know you see more than the shortstop, or the trans guy, or whatever people call me when they forget my name. Do you know how much I need that? Do you know what it's like to have that when you usually don't get it?"

I pull back just enough that he doesn't have to look quite as far down at me and I don't have to look quite as far up. "Yes," I say without thinking, because I realize right then that maybe he looks at me and sees more than the girl who greets every cactus by name.

"And you wanna know what it's called when people do that for each other?" he asks. "It's called being friends."

"We're really friends?"

His laugh is pained. "Again, ouch."

"No, I mean"—I wipe my eyes on the backs of my hands—"you've always been really nice to me. But I thought that was because you felt sorry for me."

"I don't feel sorry for you," he says. "You have more people on your side in this town than you think. Not just Bruja Lupe."

"Like who?" I ask.

"Okay, in no particular order," he says. "Chicky and her sisters are throwing themselves into trying to make you Miss Meteor."

I don't say anything about how much it hurts, the way Chicky and I drifted apart. For years, I've pretended it didn't matter, that it was just something that happened. But it's like all the hurt I pretended wasn't there is rearing up all at once.

"Then there's Junior," Cole says. "He thinks you're . . . well, he definitely thinks you're entertaining. I'd count him as a friend if I were you."

"Junior," I say, realizing something.

"Yeah . . . ," Cole says slowly.

Chicky and Junior.

If I can't get anything else right before I leave this planet, I can help get them talking again. I can at least get them in the same part of town enough to give them a chance.

It's one thing I can do, something good I can leave behind.

CHICKY

MY PARENTS CLOSE the diner the next day. For the first time in living memory.

So when Junior Cortes knocks on my door, I answer it despite the sick feeling in the pit of my stomach. It's not like things can get worse.

"Hey," I say, looking for evidence of Hair Pony. Glitter, or a scrunchie on his wrist, or a lipstick smear on his cheek. I don't find anything, and I tell myself it doesn't matter.

"Hey," he says, not quite meeting my eyes.

We stand there in awkward silence for a minute that feels like a year.

"So, you came to my house."

"Yeah," he says, rubbing the back of his neck. "So check this out, I worked the early morning shift at the museum and the weirdest guy came in . . ." He looks at me now, looking for permission to tell me the story. To pretend things are normal.

And even though I'm mad, and hurt, I'm also lonely, so I let him. Even though the pit in my stomach doesn't go away.

"What happened?" I ask.

"Well, you always know it's gonna be a weird one when the guy is wearing a tinfoil hat."

"Oh, here we go," I say. More of Junior's stories than you'd think begin with a tinfoil hat. "Was this one for enhancement or blocking?"

"Blocking," he says, laughing. "He didn't want any interference."

"Of course not."

"So he steps up to the door and requests permission to come aboard . . ."

I can't help it. I laugh. And despite everything, it feels good to laugh with him.

"And then I realize he's not just wearing the hat, he's in a full-on *Next Gen* costume, with the *Enterprise* jumpsuit and one of those brutal-looking sash things that Worf wears?"

Junior's dad is really into *Star Trek: Next Generation*, so not only have we seen almost every episode, we had the benefit of his near-constant commentary too.

"Wait, aren't those things like thousands of dollars?"

"Oh yeah," Junior says. "And it was one of the nice ones, too, like the one I tried to sell lemonade to buy before seventh-grade Halloween?"

"I remember," I say, and I do. How we were going to be Worf and Deanna Troi, but then we watched an episode where they kiss and I pretended to be sick to get out of it.

"Anyway he requests a private audience . . . with the rock."

"No!"

"Oh yes. So I get a soda and stand in the other room, close enough to jump in when things get weird."

"Which they always do."

"Right. So this guy pulls out, like, an official-looking scroll of paper, unrolls it, and starts reading from it in Klingon, with pauses for the rock to talk back."

"Oh man, too bad we didn't go to that summer camp at the Klingon Language Institute," I say, getting into it now. "You could have understood every word!"

"Trust that I regretted that decision for every minute this dude was talking," he says, shaking his head. "Especially because he walked out a few minutes later looking super happy, like, just won the lottery happy, and he saluted me before 'departing the bridge.'"

I'm laughing for real now, and so is he, and the feeling in my stomach is almost gone.

"If that guy disappears it's all your fault," I say when I catch my breath.

"Yeah," he says. "Maybe they'll put my picture in the tabloids."

"Isn't that everyone's ultimate goal in life?" I ask.

"Probably not people who don't live in a hotbed of extraterrestrial tourism, honestly."

"Good point."

The silence settles again then, and with it the sick feeling comes back. And suddenly, as quick as a lightning strike, I'm more than sick. I'm mad. I'm mad at him for doing what he did, and for trying to act like everything's normal. I'm mad at myself for letting him.

"Just say it," he says. "Whatever it is. I can't stand this."

"Fine," I say, a Fresa-like flare of recklessness pushing me on. "You're a jerk."

"Is that all?" he asks, trying and failing not to look offended.

"You're a jerk because . . . ," I begin.

"Really?"

". . . because you're my best friend." I say. "And like, the only person in this town who doesn't look at me and think I'm less or different than I should be."

He unfolds his arms, but his eyes stay straight ahead, like he's counting every leaf on Mr. Jacobs's prized corkscrew willow tree across the street.

"I know. I messed up. It's just . . . I look at you and I see . . ." He tugs on his hair, and suddenly I'm remembering her pushing it out of his eyes, and I don't know if I'm ready for what he's gonna say, but I also can't stop him. I don't want to stop him.

Unfortunately, he stops himself.

"What I'm trying to say is I'm sorry. You're *my* best friend, and I pushed you, and I made what I wanted more important than what you needed, and that's not okay. You're enough, just like you are. So don't worry about it. It won't happen again."

He's saying all the right things, offering our friendship back to me without all the complications of growth spurts and puberty and stupid hormones. I should be thrilled, right? And I am. Thrilled. But under it is something just a little sad. Like a star that died millions of years ago finally disappearing from the sky.

"Look," I manage. "I know you have a girlfriend now or whatever, but I don't want to just be some girl you used to watch *Star Trek* with, and . . ."

"I don't have a girlfriend," he blurts out, interrupting me.

"What?" I ask, but in my mind's eye the Hair Pony is prancing into the white-hot center of the sun, and I know. It's not very feminist of me, and I'll unpack that later. But for right now I'm thrilled.

"I kind of asked her out to make you jealous, and I feel terrible about it. It was such a bad idea, and we had a terrible time and had nothing to talk about, and I wanted to tell you like five minutes after I got there."

My eyes get big, it's what Junior calls my judgy face, but I can't help it.

"It's not who I am, okay?" he says. "It's not who I want to be. I just felt so . . . bad. And I did a dumb thing, and I'm sorry."

"Nobody's perfect," I say. "Just . . . don't become one of those guys, okay?" And it hits me then, that it's what I've been most worried about since the day Junior started getting cool-guy looks at school. That he'll change. That he'll leave me behind.

"I won't," he says, and his eyes are so sincere I don't even recognize the guy from last night in them. "I promise."

"Come with me," I say impulsively, before I can chicken out.

"Where?"

"No questions," I say, shoving my feet into my sneakers and striding out the door.

"So what are we doing here?" he asks when we stop in front of Selena's. "I thought the diner was closed today."

"Only if you don't have the keys," I say, dangling them in front of him and opening the door.

Inside, the mood is strange, like it's a relic of a place instead of a living, breathing one. I fight the urge to turn on "Baila Esta Cumbia" just to make it seem less empty.

"I know it's not mac and cheese day, so . . ."

"Shh," I say. "Just trust me."

"Chicky, you're being weird," he says, and it occurs to me that I love the way he says my name. Not like strangers, who think it's a weird thing to be called, not like my parents, who've said it so many times it sounds worn and boring, but like someone who's rediscovering it every time and keeps liking what he finds.

Of course, I would notice this one day after it's too late to notice things like that.

"Sorry, I know, but it's gonna get slightly weirder when I ask you to close your eyes."

The eyes in question widen at the request, and I grab a clean dish towel from a table and hold it up apologetically.

He raises his eyebrows but closes his eyes.

Behind him, I reach up to cover them with the square of fabric, which suddenly seems much more awkward than I anticipated. My fingertips tangle in the sleek strands of his hair, once or twice bumping his ears and brushing the back of his sun-darkened neck as I tie the knot.

My stomach flips more than once, and I silently curse myself for not putting on music, or making him cover his own damn eyes, or letting this idea fade away like a fever dream before saying anything out loud.

"Okay, can you see?" I ask, my voice weird and soft, like I'm breathing too much around every word. The white towel against his skin makes it glow a little, sun behind amber, and I wish I could tell him. Just for a second.

"Can't see a thing," he says, his own voice deep and a little croaky, like when he wakes up from a nap he shouldn't have been taking in class and has to answer a question about geography.

"Okay, walk to the left," I say, and he goes more forward than left. "No, wait, like, straight to the left." This time it's closer, but he's still facing the wrong way, and we're gonna be here all day at this rate, so I sigh and stand behind him again.

"What?"

"Just . . . okay." I put my hands on his shoulders, way too warm through possibly the world's softest green T-shirt, and steer him, pushing when he needs to walk, guiding when he needs to turn. He goes wherever I steer him.

Not that I'm thinking about it what that means. More than a normal amount, anyway.

"Okay," I say at last, letting go, my hands feeling cold without the warmth of his skin beneath them, even though it's easily ninety degrees in the diner. "We made it."

"Can I take this off?" he asks, and maybe I'm terrible, but I do it for him, bumping, brushing fingers and all.

When he's unmasked, we're both facing a blank wall. The paint is peeling along the baseboard, and there's a crack running through the left side from where a pipe burst when I was in seventh grade. Across its surface, squares of discoloration are obvious, sun damage around the borders of magazine articles my dad taped up when we couldn't afford real art.

It's a hideous wall. An ugly wall. A totally unworthy gift. But Junior is looking at it like it's the lost city of Atlantis.

"Chicky . . . ," he says, that heavy deepness still in his voice. "Do you mean it?"

"Look," I say, unable to look at his face. "I'm not always good at this either, but I . . ." I take a deep breath. "No, you. You're the cipher that makes the weird code of high school and this town and just . . . life . . . make sense."

I'm butchering this, but he's looking at me like he looks at that dumb wall, like there's something magic in both of us that he sees clearly even when no one else can.

He bumps my shoulder with his.

"I believe in you, Junior," I say. "And no matter what happens, I never want to not know you."

Is it my imagination, or is there something glinting in one of his eyes?

"If I help you prime it, will you paint this wall, Junior Cortes? Will you show this town and every weird, Klingon-speaking yahoo that you're part of this family, too?"

He steps closer to take the dish towel from my hand, but he doesn't step away once he has it, and there's something magnetic happening in his eyes, there has to be, because I can't look away.

"Why, Chiquita Quintanilla," he says. "I thought you'd never ask."

ĿITA

JUNIOR CORTES IS actively trying not to smile as he unlocks the Meteor Meteorite Museum.

He's smiling in a way that can only be about Chicky. It's brighter than the morning flaring behind him.

"I . . . ," I stammer. I came here to try to convince him to show up somewhere Chicky will be, but from the look on his face, they already figured all that out.

Which makes me feel both happy and even more useless than before.

Junior goes in and holds the door open behind him. "How's your pursuit of the crown going?"

I try to laugh. It comes out hoarse and sad. "Nonexistent. I'm not doing the pageant anymore."

"Why not?"

"Why not?" I ask. "Are you serious? Have you not witnessed the disaster I've made of the last few days?"

"Don't take all the credit." He turns on the overhead lobby lights. "You didn't make a mess of everything alone. You had the help of the Four Sisters of the Apocalypse."

"That's not fair."

"You're right, it's not." He clicks on the ancient air-conditioning unit, which will take a full hour to work up to cooling this place. "You also had the help of possibly the worst human being at Meteor Central High, who managed to take out you, his own teammate, and a priceless artifact of town history." He points to the display case where the sadly dented bicycle now leans against a wall.

This is one more thing I like about Junior Cortes: he thought about the bicycle.

Buzz was too nice to ask, and nobody else even bothered.

"You're really gonna let those jerks scare you off?" Junior asks.

"Um, yeah," I say. "Yeah, I am."

Junior turns on the flickering spotlight over the rock, another part of the museum that needs warming up before open hours.

"What if I have a proposition for you?" he asks in a voice of a 1950s private investigator.

Not fair. He's speaking the language he knows gets to me, the language of Bruja Lupe's old movies.

"What kind of proposition?" I ask. I can't not ask.

"You get back in the pageant"—he pauses, like he's still considering—"I'll try out for the cornhole team."

"What?" I ask. "Why would you do that to yourself? Those guys are jerks. They call you Picasso behind your back."

"I know that. I also know they're too stupid to realize I take it as a compliment."

I appreciate what he's trying to do. Chicky's told me how good he is, from all those bored hours throwing beanbags into his stunningly painted cornhole boards. If he makes the team, Meteor Central High has a shot at the championship again. It might make everyone hate me and the Quintanillas a little less.

But it's not worth Junior having to deal with Royce and the whole team.

"To my knowledge, there's only one guy on the team you can stand, and he's out for the season," I say. "So why would you subject yourself to the rest of them?"

"Why are you subjecting yourself to this pageant?" Junior asks.

"Because I wanted it a long time ago, and I thought I could never have it. Don't try to pretend your dream is sinking a trampoline shot through a bunched target."

"Wow." He laughs. "Somebody's been getting Kendall to school her."

"Honestly, I didn't even try," I say. "You're around him long enough, you just start picking it up. You can't help it."

Junior stands near the tiny gift shop (two postcard racks, plaster models of the rock, a shelf of T-shirts, a few little-green-men stuffed animals).

"Come on," he says. "There's not a little part of you that likes the idea of shaking things up? That's not even a tiny piece of you entering?"

I try not to smile.

I try not to notice the vein of silver winking through the space rock, telling me that yes, of course it is. Of course, even years ago, I loved the thought of being a brown girl with baby fat, taking a crown that almost always goes to thin-limbed blondes with perfect, printer-paper-white teeth.

"If you're back in," Junior says, "then I'm in."

Junior doesn't even know about the stardust. But I do. And I know he's right. If I drop out now, that's how I'll leave this planet, as a girl who got scared off.

"I'm in," I say.

CHICKY

"SELENA'S DINER SHUTDOWN: Day Three." Uva has taken to narrating our lives. It would be so much more irritating if Fresa didn't hate it so much.

"Tense, hopeful, the Quintanilla sisters make their way across town to the Meteor Central High field—the site of the recent town incident between a coven of teen witches and a sad-eyed teen athlete with a heart of gold . . ."

Fresa groans, right on time.

"Is it a paranormal story or a newscast?" Cereza snaps. "Make up your mind!"

"Or, and this is a really out there suggestion: Just stop it. Forever."

"Can we focus, please?" I ask, butterflies in my stomach. Lita wouldn't tell me how she got Junior to agree to try out, just that we all needed to be there. At this point, what could I do but show up? It's not like things can get worse.

Right?

"The field looms in the distance," Uva says, ignoring all of us, her eyes a little manic after an unprecedented three days without cleaning the fryer. "The intrepid young women make their way through the fog. Hopeful . . ."

"You already said hopeful," Cereza cuts in.

"Shut up, all of you," I say. "We're here."

But we do feel a little like an intrepid coven as we approach.

"Well look who it is," says Kendra Kendall as we draw closer to the center of the field. "The misfit squad, here to join the assassin who cut my brother down in his prime." Her ire is directed at Lita, who shrinks a little beneath the weight of her disapproval, but she makes her way over to us nonetheless.

"We're here to . . . ," Lita says, quietly at first, but Junior elbows her and she stands up a little straighter. "I'm here to propose a covenant."

"Which one?" Royce asks with a smirk. "Africa? Antarctica? Europe?" His buddies chuckle, and Kendra tosses her hair.

It takes me a while to understand, but when it clicks I forget to be nervous. Just for a second. "Not *continent*, are you serious? A covenant."

"That's, like, when a relationship is unhealthy because the people can't do things apart," says one of Kendra's sycophants. "I heard about it on *Dr. Phil*."

The only person who laughs is Cole, sitting on the sidelines in his sling. "*Co-ve-nant*," he recites, like he's reading from the dictionary. "An agreement. To agree, especially by lease, deed, or other legal contract." He has to be here, it's part of his Advanced Gym grade, but he doesn't seem to fit in quite as well as he did before he started hanging out with us.

And he doesn't look at Kendra once.

Royce blinks at him, the rest of his face still troublingly blank.

"It means she has a deal to offer you, Royce," Cole says, humor and derision fighting for dominance in his tone. When he thinks no one's looking, he winks at Lita.

"Well, fuck," says Royce. "Why didn't you just say that?"

"The deal is this," Lita says, gesturing Junior forward. "If he can shoot as well as Cole, you guys quit telling people to avoid the diner and let him play with you in the final match."

It's my turn to stand up straighter. We can't go back in time and get my family the meet and greet back, but we can get the social boycott lifted, and that'll be a start.

This time, it's the whole team that laughs.

"What, Picasso over here?" Royce asks. "Sorry, but there are no points awarded for coloring inside the lines in this sport."

My vision goes slightly red, and I object so strongly to the description of cornhole as a *sport* that my knees almost stop shaking, but Junior steps in front of me, which is probably good.

"Laugh all you want," he says. "But I'll be the one laughing when I beat you out for MVP."

210

Something about a broad-shouldered, traditionally hand-some male does what all the reasoning in the world couldn't do coming from Lita. The team stands up, shoulder to shoulder, and honestly, they look way more intimidating than I'd like them to.

"Fine," Royce says, the spokesperson for everyone but Cole, who remains seated. "If you can sink twenty bags without missing, you're in."

It's an absurd number, way more than they'd ever ask during an actual tryout, but Junior clenches his jaw. For the five-hundredth time since they showed up at my door, I wonder how Lita convinced him to participate.

"Why not make it thirty," he says, like he's not worried at all, and I want to dig a hole in the field and climb inside, come out when this has all been over for fifty years.

"Your funeral," says Royce, tossing Junior a mesh bag with ten beanbags inside.

"Or yours," Junior says, throwing his first bag between Royce's legs at the world's most awkward angle and sinking it.

The rest of the team goes quiet, but Royce smirks. "So you're really good at going between a dude's legs," he says. "Hardly something to brag about."

"So, you get that that's an offensive thing to say, right Royce?"

My heart sinks and soars at the same time. Cole seems to have graduated from distraction tactics when it comes to

Royce, and despite the tense shoulders and clenched fists giving away his nervousness, he's steady. Solid. And he's sticking up for Junior.

"Not you, too, Kendall," Royce says with an eye roll. "Can't anyone take a fucking joke anymore? Everyone's so sensitive!"

"I appreciate a good joke as much as anyone," Cole says, his voice still mild. "But most of us have moved on from cruelty as their sole form of humor. Maybe you should try it."

Royce is gaping like a fish, and Kendra is glaring at Cole in a "we're gonna talk about this later" kind of way, and all I can think is that I wish it was me. Defending Junior. Putting Royce in his place. But I'm frozen, and Cole is here, and I feel grateful and guilty all at once.

I look at Cole, trying to communicate all this, and when we lock eyes I nod in solidarity, just a little.

He nods back.

Junior takes his place at the practice line, taking advantage of Royce's shock over being confronted by another jock, and leaving Lita and me standing beside each other. I think if we could bottle how much we want Junior to succeed right now, how much we want Royce put in his place, Bruja Lupe could sell it by the vial.

The first ten shots are no trouble. One of the JV team members gathers the bags and returns the mesh sack to Junior, who's rolling his shoulders, looking a little nervous for the first time.

I wish I could tell him how impressive he looks right now. Even to someone who doesn't understand or care about corn-hole, and probably never will.

The next ten are slower, with Junior pausing between shots to realign his stance. By now, some of the team actually looks curious.

Royce and Kendra, however, look murderous.

Junior stretches before the bag returns, his eyes scanning the crowd that's gathering. I can tell by the way his jaw tenses that he's realizing it for the first time—how different this is from the bags he threw in private at the museum when the tourists had gone home.

He hesitates for too long on his next shot, and it misses the mark, barely sliding in after hitting the board at an awkward angle.

Beanbag two in hand, he freezes, and I can already tell what's next, but for once, I don't just wait to see what's going to happen. I don't let the presence of Royce and all his lackies make me small and silent.

Because Junior deserves a friend right now, and I need this to work for more reasons than I have time to articulate. Even to myself.

"Hey," I say, getting his attention, forcing him to lower his arm.

Keeping his eyes on me, I walk to the business end of the cornhole board, ignoring the stares of several jocks like I can't feel them crawling all over my skin.

"It's just you and me out here," I say to both of us, and he smiles, the kind of smile that sends something warm and fizzy through my bloodstream.

The next three shots go in perfectly, his eyes on me the whole time. The fourth rims in, the fifth nearly bounces back out, but the sixth, seventh, and eighth could be taught in summer camps across the country.

Two beanbags left in his hand, Junior finds my eyes again and holds them. I don't look away.

With one hand, he throws them at the same time. One arcs high, and the other low. They descend for what seems like an hour, the entire field holding its breath, before one drops neatly into the hole, the other following close behind.

The cheers are deafening, and that's just Lita and me.

Junior Cortes has just made the cornhole team.

LITA

SPEAK LOUD, SPEAK *clearly, and trust that you know what to say.* (Cereza's advice just before I go onstage for the first time.)

Breathe, and remember how many of us you have cheering for you. (Uva's)

Annihilate those bitches. (Fresa's)

I run through all three in my head. I'll need them today and the next three days.

Yes, four more days. Not counting the one-day break for the cornhole championship.

To bring in more tourists for the festival, the Meteor Regional Pageant and Talent Competition Showcase only holds one event per day. Question and answer. Swimsuit. Talent. And, on the last day, evening gown.

If we make it that far without them booing me off the stage or throwing lemons at me. (They wouldn't waste their tomatoes, which don't grow as well here).

215

Today is the Q&A, and it's Cereza's advice that rings in my head.

Speak loud.

Speak clearly.

Trust that you know what to say.

But the other contestants, they're all so beautiful. With every shade of hair and skin I've ever seen on this planet. And they all stand up straight. They smell like the perfume samples in Fresa's magazines.

Their teeth all gleam as much as their polished nails, and their eyeshadow catches the sun in perfect rhythm with the translucent sequins on their sundresses.

Now I'm glad Fresa talked me into the glittery teal eyeshadow and blush that was nearly magenta. I know I can't wear the wispy pinks the gringas wear because it doesn't show up on my skin, but . . . magenta? And teal glitter? I was sure pageant week had made Fresa snap, but on this stage, now, I realize she just made me look like everyone else.

We all line up, and the pageant coordinators file us through the opening in the curtain to backstage. Behind there, it's already a mess of makeup bags and extra underwear and the rubbery plastic slices they all call "chicken cutlets." False eyelashes litter the ground like sun-stupored caterpillars. Body and face glitter speckles the concrete like the flecks in granite. Half the contestants are rubbing shimmer powder onto their chests or gluing their underwear to their asses. I adjust my bra (and the duct tape) without trying to hide it.

Any sense of modesty has been glitter-bombed.

The sight of Cole Kendall slipping through the curtain is so strange, so out of place, so distinctly masculine in this flurry of sequined shoes and lipstick cases, that for a second I think I'm dehydrated. Uva warned me about that.

I only know he's there for sure when a girl spots him and calls out, "Hey! No dicks backstage!"

Cole looks right at her. "You have no idea what I do or don't have in my pants."

The girl pales.

"And unless you want to make sure this gets known as the beauty pageant no trans girl will ever feel safe entering, can we just not with talk like that?" Cole is the only boy I've ever met who can sound so angry and so measured at the same time. "Thanks."

The girl steps back, nodding, her stare so wide I can't see her eyeshadow.

"I'll just be a minute," he tells everyone, and they all sweep back into their flurry.

He looks around. "Good. She's not here yet."

"Who?" I ask.

"Kendra. This is the first time I've ever been glad of . . ."

He trails off.

Heat fills my cheeks as I realize Cole Kendall is staring at my boobs that have been duct-taped into defying gravity.

"What?" I ask.

"Sorry." He shakes his head like he just now realized he's been staring at my rack. "I'm sorry."

"No, tell me," I say, gesturing at my chest. "Does it look weird?"

He winces and blushes. "No." His voice sounds strained. "Looks great."

"Good," I say. "For what it's gonna take to get it off later, it better."

He pulls his eyes back up to my face. "Anyone taught you the baby powder trick?"

"What baby powder trick?"

"Exactly what it sounds like, put baby powder on your chest before you tape. It'll help in the heat and later when you want to get the tape off. Kendra does it every time. She likes to pretend she never sweats, but I know better."

Cole Kendall and I are talking about my breasts, and worse than that, we are talking about the possibility that breasts perspire, which I am sure is on the list of things beauty queens cannot think about let alone talk about. I wonder if the judges can sense my thoughts through the curtains and are deducting points before they've even gotten their first look at me.

Kendra Kendall has to tape her breasts too?

Cole knows what baby powder is?

"You know what baby powder is?" I ask.

"Yeah, of course," he says. "Why wouldn't I?"

"You're a guy?"

"I use it when I pack. It helps the silicone slide instead of stick."

"Pack?" I ask. "Are you going on a trip?"

He laughs. Not his usual mild, good-natured laugh. A full-on, I-startled-him-with-something-funny laugh. "So that's the one Trans 101 article you didn't read."

His eyes flash down to his pants and up again so fast no one else would catch it. But it's enough that I feel my face heat. Even though I still don't know what packing is, I can now guess, but I can't think about it too much, because I cannot be thinking about Cole Kendall and his pants when I go out there.

I can't even look at him without my cheeks turning as hot as the pageant stage light bulbs, so instead I scan the other girls.

"What are you even doing back here?" I ask.

"I need to talk to you for a second."

"Now?" I look around. "Kendra's not gonna like seeing you talking to me."

"Kendra's still looking for her shoes."

"Why?"

"Because I hid them."

"Cole!"

"Relax, they're in my mom's car, she'll find them, I was just stalling her."

"I do not need you sabotaging my competition."

219

"Yeah, speaking of that." He pulls me aside, out of earshot of as many contestants as he can. "I know I'm the brother of your competition. I know you probably think I know nothing about this, but believe me, I know more about beauty pageants than I ever wanted to. And I have the advantage of overhearing things because I'm a guy and everyone thinks I don't know what any of the words mean."

"You definitely know what words mean."

"Thanks, but not the point," he says. "Point is: you're about to be set up."

"Set up?" I ask. "This is a beauty pageant, not a 1940s detective movie."

He blinks a few times.

"What?" I ask.

"Nothing, that's just the kind of thing people are usually saying to you."

"I have about ninety seconds, Cole. Can this wait?"

"No. It can't."

"Then make it quick."

He checks the curtain entrance again. "I'm about to ask you for something, and I just need you to trust me."

"Trust you with what?"

He leans down a little to talk to me. "When they give you the question, just say 'world peace.'"

"What?" I ask.

"Look, I don't know what they're gonna ask you, but I

heard enough to know they're gonna go hard on you. So whatever they ask"—he lands hard on each word—"say world peace. It's one of the few things you can answer to just about any pageant question. Believe me, I've been to enough of these things to know."

"But what if the question's about . . ."

"Lita, please, just do this for me."

I back up, my bare shoulder blades brushing the worn velvet of the curtain.

"Just say world peace," he says, quieter this time.

Then he's gone, a few seconds before Kendra strides in, annoyed, with a metal train case.

She walks right past me.

Before I can sort out everything Cole just said, the coordinators herd us onstage.

There's applause as we all walk out for the first time, but I hear it dulled, like it's far away.

Mr. Hamilton, I mean, the emcee, introduces each of us, and I smile more from muscle memory than from meaning to do it.

He asks each girl a question. I barely hear them, these questions about where they would most want to travel in the world ("Europe, the whole thing."), what they would do if they had a week to live ("I would pet every puppy in the world."), if they'd been an animal on Noah's ark which one they would've been ("The dove, because I like to think of myself as a sign of hope to those around me."), what's the first thing they would do as president ("Send everyone a bouquet of daisies and then get right to work fixing things!").

Applause rushes through the air after each girl finishes. Their answers twinkle; I can hear it in their voices even when I can't make out all the words through the fog of the ones Cole left with me.

World peace, no matter what the question is.

Was Cole asking me to throw this competition? So his sister can win? So his family can get current on their bills?

And would I do it for him when the Quintanilla sisters got me this far?

Then it's my turn, and the man grinning into the microphone is standing in front of me.

"Next up is another hometown gal, Estrellita Perez." He rushes upward on the syllables of my name to cue the clapping.

Very scattered applause.

Most don't know me.

The rest hate me.

The emcee continues with as big a smile as if I'd gotten a standing ovation. "Your question comes from Judge Halpern."

The judge nods, one in a line of men and women in pressed business attire, sitting at a shaded table.

"Estrellita, you've lived in this town your whole life," the emcee says.

"Is that the question?" I ask.

This gets a laugh, more from out-of-town visitors than anyone.

It's still a laugh.

I curtsy and smile, my eyes finding Cole in the audience and shooting him a "what exactly were you worried about?" look.

"You're a lifelong resident of this fair town, and we want your take on the real Meteor, New Mexico," the emcee says into the microphone.

Oh no.

Are they about to ask me about the rock in the museum?

Years of the government blocking off the crater site, decades of rumor about whether it holds secrets about life in other worlds, and millions of whispered speculations from both residents and visitors.

Is the emcee about to ask me to settle all of that?

"Estrellita," he says. "What is the most important thing you think is missing from your hometown?"

He holds the microphone in front of me.

My next breath turns hard in my throat.

No girl wins Miss Meteor without a sugar-packet-white smile and a love for her hometown so bright it shines. And now the judges are asking me to criticize it, to pick it apart, to say what Meteor needs that it does not have.

I am a brown-skinned girl. I love this town, but if I say what I really think it's missing, if I say where its sharp places and weak points are, the judges will cast aside my name before we even get to swimsuit.

The emcee and the microphone and the audience and even the craning-forward contestants are waiting for me to say something. But there is no way to answer this question without half the town, and half the judges, counting me as even more of a traitor than they already think I am.

I scan the audience, finding the horrified faces of Bruja Lupe and the Quintanillas.

Bruja Lupe.

She hated the idea of me entering, but she's here anyway, and now she's watching me try to answer an impossible question.

If I say nothing's missing from Meteor, I'm lying. I'm lying about myself, about the Quintanillas, about Junior, about Cole, about everyone who isn't exactly what Meteor thinks we should be.

But if I say the truth, if I pick this town apart the way this town picks us apart, Bruja Lupe will have to watch me get booed off the stage.

My eyes keep moving.

They stop on Cole.

He was right.

They are setting me up.

This town thinks I charged their star cornhole player with an old bicycle. They think I'm a girl who exists to wear down everything they care about.

And now they have me on this stage, where they're trying to get me to admit it.

Because I cannot answer this question without being the girl they already think I am.

He nods slowly, urging me on.

He knew.

He asked me to trust him.

And I have to trust that he gave me that answer to take with me for a reason.

I put my hands on my hips, give my best Rita Hayworth smile, and call out, "World peace."

The audience stares at me.

They look to the emcee.

They look at each other.

Then they start clapping.

They really start clapping, because they take my answer to mean that there's nothing missing from Meteor, that to find something missing from Meteor I have to find something missing from the whole world. They clap because they love the idea that the only thing wrong with Meteor is that the rest of this planet can't be exactly like it. They can't not clap, because they can't not clap for the idea of world peace, especially not at a beauty pageant.

"Cole," I whisper under my breath when the microphone is clear from my mouth. He does know more about beauty pageants than anyone would guess.

He knows the one answer no one can object to.

"Well," the emcee says into the microphone, "I think we all can agree on that, right, ladies and gentlemen?" That cues another round of applause.

Then it's over. My first event in the Fiftieth-Annual Meteor Regional Pageant and Talent Competition Showcase.

"Thank you," I mouth at Cole as I follow the other contestants down the stage steps.

I did it. It may have taken one Kendall and many Quintanillas, but I did it. I managed, for the first time, not to screw up a Miss Meteor event.

My relief only lasts until that night, when I find new patches of stardust covering my thighs.

Less than one day. I had less than one day of what it feels like when this goes right, when I don't let everyone cheering for me down.

Less than one day. That's all the time my body would've had to wait for these new starfields to show up on my skin.

If the stardust had kept up its slow crawl, I would've been fine. The tasteful one-piece Cereza chose for me for the swimsuit competition would have covered it. But now the stardust is crawling up my back and down my thighs.

That tasteful one-piece stares from where it hangs on my closet doorknob, taunting me with every sparkling reason I cannot wear it onstage.

CHICKY

IT'S A PACKED house when we arrive for the swimsuit competition, and my ears are still ringing with the argument Lita and my sisters had about waxing, of all things.

Thankfully, Lita won. No waxing. Fresa is still fuming.

"Just contestants past this point," says Mrs. Kendall, who is, of course, holding a clipboard and looking official. She looks at me like I'm something gross she stepped in, and I bristle.

"I'm Miss Perez's manager," I say, channeling sixth-grade me as I step forward with my arm through Lita's. On her other side she's carrying a strangely bulky bag. I make a note to ask her about this later.

"Contestants only," Mrs. Kendall says more firmly, stepping forward.

My sisters head for their seats, and I'm about to follow when I catch a glimpse of Kendra through the doorway, her golden hair pinned up in an elegant knot.

"Friends and family and . . . little helpers are free to take their seats in the audience."

"Right," I say, feeling Lita shrink a little under her gaze. "Because we wouldn't want anyone's family members being inappropriately involved in pageant business. Might be a conflict of interest, right, Mrs. Kendall?"

Her self-important gaze becomes downright murderous, but Lita giggles, straightening her slumping shoulders.

"I'll be back with the pageant director," Mrs. Kendall says. "Melody Summers? She's a close personal friend of mine."

She disappears, and now I'm laughing too, Lita's and my strange friendship stalemate melting away for the moment. "Close personal friends, right," I mutter. "More like close personal Botox buddies."

"Stop!" Lita says, clamping a hand over her mouth to keep from laughing too loud.

"I should probably sit," I say, unlinking our arms. "But I'll be in the front row if you need anything." I clear my throat. "You know, as your manager."

"Right," Lita says. "Officially."

"Okay," I say, the tension creeping back in. All the unsaid things. "Good luck out there."

"Thanks."

It's only as she flattens her bag to step through the doorway that I realize I forgot to ask her what's inside. But like, how bad can it be? She probably just brought her stuffed Marvin the

Martian to keep her company or something.

I take my seat next to Fresa and command myself to chill.

The lights go down, same as they did last night, and a buzz of anticipation ripples through the crowd. I've told myself since middle school ended that I'm above this pageant and everything it represents, but when Uva grabs my hand and squeezes it, I squeeze back. It's not just about destroying Kendra anymore, or even about the money for the diner.

I want Lita to win because she's Lita, and the world needs a little more of her magic in it.

"And now . . . ," says Mr. Hamilton, who has (of course) volunteered to be this year's Miss Meteor emcee. "May I present your first contestant for the Fiftieth-Annual Miss Meteor Swimsuit Competition!"

The crowd goes wild, and instead of rolling my eyes like I normally do, I clap along with them until my palms sting.

"Miss Aurelia Renee Stevens is a junior at Meteor Central High School," the judge intones as the first girl walks onto the stage, half turning in her blue one-piece and white high heels. I can see the Vaseline on her teeth from here, and I wonder idly how much of it *she's* swallowed.

"Her hobbies include scrapbooking, voice lessons, horse-back riding, and playing with her dog, Spud." Aurelia finishes her strut across the stage and heads back toward the curtain, her smile never faltering, her heels never missing a step.

Three more contestants follow: Jodi, who likes cataloging

whale sounds; Kim, who trains her pet birds to chirp along to pop songs; and Irena, who reads to seniors for the neighboring town's summer library program.

My enthusiasm is decidedly waning when Mr. Hamilton pulls the mic close a fourth time. "And now, a momentary musical interlude while we get ready for hometown . . . resident, Estrellita Perez!"

The "musical interlude," of course, is Meteor Central High's twelve-person marching band. They file onto the stage in their uniforms and launch into what I know will be at least a six-minute-long version of the school fight song.

"I can't just sit here," I mumble, standing up to pace. "I'm so nervous."

"Go with her," Cereza says to Uva. I don't bother to argue.

I'm pacing the aisle with her shadowing me when I hear it: two of the cornhole groupies from the other day, whispering.

"Do you think Kendra did it?" one of them asks, giggling.

"It had to be her. I mean, who decides to wear a scuba suit to a swimsuit competition without a little manipulation?"

"You're sure that's what it was?"

"Hand to God, I went back to give Josie her lip gloss right before! It was . . . kind of hard to miss."

"Oh-em-gee that is wild, I mean I was expecting a kids' one-piece with a unicorn on it or something super tragic, but this is next level . . ."

They go on, but I'm not listening anymore. Because I know

230

there's only one girl behind that curtain who would walk out onstage in a scuba suit.

And she's up next.

I whip around to Uva, who's following at a respectful distance. "Please tell me none of you knew she was switching her costume to a fucking scuba suit."

The look on my sister's face is enough to tell me they had nothing to do with it. "What are you talking about?" she asks.

But I can't even answer. Because of course my sisters didn't have anything to do with it.

"Lita went rogue" is all I can manage to say, and then I'm frozen, my mind's eye awash with ten thousand dollar bills floating down a giant drain. With Kendra's smug face as she waltzes across the stage as the new Miss Meteor, becoming even more invincible.

I did this, I think. I could have just suffered through my last two-and-two-thirds years of high school in silence. I could have saved us all from this.

"We have like one minute before the song is over," Uva says, panic evident in her voice. But Fresa and Cereza are already behind her.

"What's wrong?" Cereza asks, and Uva tells her in hushed tones, that horrified expression still stuck on her face.

"I've got this," Fresa says. "Get up there and stall them, bitches." She slaps a stuttering Uva on the ass before sprinting backstage.

Uva heads for the stage, but I can't let her go alone. I need to be closer. To be doing something. This is my mission, after all.

The marching band bows and leaves the stage to tepid applause, but before the curtain can open to reveal Lita in a scuba suit, Uva and I step up to the microphone.

In the space between the curtains, I see the girl with the headset shrug, but no one runs up to tackle us or anything, which I think is a good sign.

But the bar for good signs is also criminally low right now, so who knows?

"Is this thing on?" Uva's voice is too loud in the room, and I wince along with half the audience.

"I think so!" I say in my best "I don't hate people" voice. The crowd chuckles.

"Well," says Uva's slightly quieter voice as she steps back from the mic. "It's time for a . . . new segment of the Miss Meteor Pageant, which is the local . . . business showcase!"

The crowd, to my utter astonishment, applauds, and Uva goes on, her voice ringing confident and clear through the room as Fresa works what is hopefully magic backstage.

"Selena's Diner is a local favorite," I say, thinking of Mr. Bradley talking down to my mom and standing up straighter. "With a fusion of hometown favorites and cultural flavor, not to mention the atmosphere, it's the perfect place for a pre- or post-event snack!"

232

"And, as a bonus," Uva adds, "we're running special pageant hours—open until ten every night this week."

Uva glances nervously at me, and then at the curtain, which has not yet revealed Lita in her Fresa-approved swimsuit.

"Keep going!" I mouth to Uva, edging closer to the opening, trying to get an idea of how long it'll be. "You can do this!"

"Our menu is . . . one of the longest in town," Uva says, running out of steam quickly. "Beginning with appetizers, which include tater tot nachos, guacamole grilled cheese bites, carnitas sliders . . ."

Slinking to the curtain opening at stage left, I peer into a horrifying scene. One that makes me wish the Selena's menu was about forty items longer.

Backstage, Fresa and Lita are squared off, Fresa brandishing the hip-hugging one-piece they'd agreed on a few days ago, and Lita, zipped into the scuba suit to her chin, looking uncharacteristically determined.

"I can't wear the swimsuit, okay?" Lita is saying, protecting the zipper like it's guarding state secrets. "I'm sorry, but I just . . . don't feel like myself."

Fresa opens her mouth to argue, but I step between them just in time, remembering twelve-year-old Lita huddled at the foot of Señora Strawberry clutching the newspaper full of girls that looked nothing like her.

"Fresa, no," I say. "We're not making her go out there in

233

something she doesn't feel good in. No score from any judge is worth that. We have to come up with something else."

Fresa doesn't speak right away. Lita looks guilty and scared.

Cole Kendall appears beside me, looking just as worried as I feel. The fact that someone else gets it is comforting, but it doesn't make this any less of a disaster.

"I'm just saying if she didn't like the outfit she could have told us yesterday!"

"I didn't know yesterday," Lita says in a small voice, and I wish I could ask what she means, but Uva is already nearing the end of the menu, and we're out of time.

"Focus, Fresa!" I say. "You can accessorize anything! Make it work!"

My most beautiful and terrible sister closes her eyes, holding up a hand for silence. Ten seconds pass, then twenty. Before she gets to thirty, she snaps her eyes open.

"Fine, I can make it work, but I'm gonna need a fuck-ton of rhinestones and something that can stick them to a scuba suit."

"And about a hundred more menu items," I mutter under my breath as Lita discovers a baggie of rhinestones on the dressing table and everyone searches for glue, or tape, or anything.

"You guys, Uva's not doing so good out there," I say, but no one's listening, and I realize it's up to me. I bust back through the curtain, half an idea better than none at all, and take the mic.

"And now, for another new event!" I say, trying to ignore

the eyes of my classmates and the town on me, feeling my palms start to sweat anyway. "A feature from Buzz, curator of the Meteor Meteorite Museum!"

Buzz, in the front row with his wife, looks at me utterly alarmed.

Please, I ask him with my eyes. With every atom of my body. *For Lita*.

He gets up and approaches the stage.

"Thank you! I'll explain later. Thank you," I whisper as I hand off the mic and dart backstage again.

Managing Lita through the cactus field pageants was never this labor intensive.

"Everyone, hello, my name is Buzz, some of you know me from the Meteor Meteorite Museum out on the highway." The crowd applauds, but their enthusiasm is tepid at best. We're on borrowed time.

"There's literally nothing sticky anywhere," Fresa cries.

"I found a Bedazzler?" Uva says.

"Please." Fresa shoots her a withering glare. "I'm good, but even I can't bedazzle an intricate shape on a scuba suit without at least two hours to spare."

All seems lost, but Cole steps forward with purpose, and everyone turns to stare.

"Kendra," he says. "I know you're in there. Come out."

The rack of dresses rustles, and Kendra steps out, somehow looking regal even as she's discovered hiding in the wardrobe.

"You rang," she says, taking in the scene with a condescending sneer.

"The jig is up," Cole says, and for the first time since we came backstage, Lita brightens. "I'm willing to bet you were responsible for this swimsuit catastrophe. As if you hadn't done enough already."

Lita looks a little guilty at this, and I wonder if she's just feeling bad for being so gullible. This really does have Kendra written all over it . . .

Cole pauses dramatically, and through the curtain Buzz discusses the geological surveys that proved too risky for Meteor to be built in the crater left by its namesake.

"Give me the hot glue gun," he says finally, and Fresa gasps, but Kendra's heavily lined eyes dart toward the floor as we all watch the drama unfold, spellbound.

"The what? You think I just *have* a hot glue gun? You're out of your mind."

"You think I just *forgot* about the time you called me crying to bring it to you at the Junior Miss pageant in Albuquerque in sixth grade?" Cole asks her, ice cold. "Or how you said you couldn't compete without knowing it was there just in case?"

"Oh, go read the dictionary."

"GIVE ME THE GLUE GUN!"

Kendra's eyes narrow now, and she clutches her bag to her rhinestoned chest.

"You can pry it from my cold, dead, perfectly manicured fingers, Cole."

But Cole only steps closer, holding out a thumb. "I swear on Grandma Geraldine I will smudge your eyeliner."

Kendra's mouth drops open. "Trust me, baby brother, your little friend here did this all on her own. And you wouldn't dare go near this perfect cat eye." But she doesn't look entirely sure.

Cole steps closer again, mere inches separating his hand from what has to be hours' worth of makeup. "Try me."

In the moment, I believe he'd do worse than smudge her eyeliner for Lita. And I love him for it.

Kendra lets out a frustrated shriek and stomps to her bag, pulling out the glue gun and shoving it into her brother's arms. "Fine, traitor, a fat lot of good it'll do you." She sweeps her eyes down Lita's costumed body and flounces out, but no one notices. Fresa is already at work.

She barks orders, and hisses when the glue burns her skin, and I watch the curtain as Buzz says pointedly, "Now, I'm sure you're all thinking, 'Buzz, it sure would be nice to know how much of Meteor's history we're covering here tonight, now wouldn't it?'" But Fresa has finished. She scribbles something onto a notecard and when she hands it to me I can see the raw tips of her fingers, glue drying painfully, her manicure ruined.

"Give this to the announcer and tell him to read it word for word. Then get that boring old dude off the stage."

I don't dare argue, I just dart out through the curtain and do as she asks, pressing myself against the back wall of the stage to wait, with the crowd, for whatever is going to happen next.

"Well, that was certainly unexpected," says Mr. Hamilton with a chuckle. "But now, please put your hands together for Estrellita Perez!"

Lita parts the curtain and walks out, now mercifully free of flippers. Her full-body wetsuit is unzipped just far enough to show some cleavage, the sparkling one-piece my sisters approved just visible beneath it. On her feet, Fresa's own boots gleam in the stage lights, lending an air of fashion to the ensemble.

The crowd mutters and mumbles, but I get to my feet. "Go, Lita!" I call, and she smiles.

In the booth, our Mr. Hamilton squints at the card and continues.

"Estrellita's hobbies include feeding stray cats, linear . . . algebra? And visiting Meteor's own most infamous attraction—the space rock at the Meteor Meteorite Museum!"

This is almost definitely the strangest list of hobbies ever listed by a contestant in pageant history, but when he reads the part about the space rock, Lita winks and turns around, showing off an almost-perfect replica of the rock in shining gems on the back of her scuba suit.

From confused muttering, the crowd changes tack completely. The hometown pride they feel anytime the rock is mentioned combined with Fresa's—I have to say it, unbelievable—

rhinestone-applying skills, have utterly won them over.

Lita reaches the edge of the stage and winks, blowing a kiss to Buzz in the front row before strutting back toward the curtain in Fresa's borrowed boots.

The cheering goes on for a long time, and my heart, which I've sworn so often not to have at all, feels tender and full and hopeful for the first time in as long as I can remember.

LITA

THE DAY AFTER the swimsuit competition, a woman comes to Bruja Lupe with a headache so deep in her skull she can hardly speak.

"Please," she says, her voice so small and strained that even Bruja Lupe softens.

Bruja Lupe enjoys taking money from those who want to cheat their own fathers, or who want a spell to make their daughters slimmer.

But those who truly need her help, she never turns away.

She doesn't tell the woman to look into my eyes. She doesn't claim I am a child of the stars. She only sits the woman at our kitchen table and gives her the hierbas that let her brain and forehead ease.

"Thank you," the woman says, with the relief of taking her first full breath since the headache came on.

The woman has little money, so Bruja Lupe lets her keep it.

The woman's smile is so grateful and soft that seeing it feels heavy, like it holds everything I'll lose about this planet.

Later, I put on my third application of antibiotic cream—Cereza's orders; I have a constellation of light burns on my back from the glue gun, matching the ones on Fresa's fingers.

The Quintanilla sisters really are the eighth marvel of the world. Because along with Buzz and Cole, they turned an event I just wanted to get through into one that had the whole audience cheering for me.

The stardust on my back catches in the mirror.

Except then it moves, even when I don't.

I look back toward the mirror.

The glass isn't showing my stardust.

It's showing the mobile of shiny paper stars twirling over my bed. They glint and turn, catching the moon outside my window and the light from the hall.

That's the sparkliness in the mirror. Not my own skin.

The stardust on my back has vanished.

Before all of it sinks into my brain, it's fluttering in my chest, and I'm yelling for Bruja Lupe. My voice stumbles to call her.

"What is it, mija?" Bruja Lupe comes through my door. "What's wrong?"

I try to breathe, like Uva told me to onstage.

I pull up my pajama shirt and show her my back.

Her gasp lights the whole room.

"I know," I say, shrugging back into my pajamas, afraid that if I look for one more second, this incredible thing will be gone, like stuff vanishing in the Greek myths the second you look at it too hard.

"How?" Bruja Lupe breathes.

"I don't know."

I start to piece it together.

I told off Kendra, the stardust got smaller.

I took out the star cornhole player, the stardust spread.

The judges gave me an impossible question, I got too rattled to give any other answer than the one Cole had given me, and the stardust spread.

But when we dazzled them in the swimsuit portion, when we showed them part of all of us, the stardust left my back.

In a way I still don't completely understand, something about whether the stardust takes me is getting tethered to Miss Meteor.

It's the smallest chance. But I'm going to grab it in the tightest grip I can get.

"What do I do?" I ask, my voice trembling.

"What do you mean, what do you do?" Bruja Lupe asks, her voice catching with hope. "You keep going. If there's the smallest chance it'll save you, you show up to win."

"Except I still have no talent!" I blurt out.

"What?" she asks.

"I know, I know," I say. "I was gonna do Cereza's monologue

because it has the least chance of me injuring anyone."

"Well, what are you waiting for?" She flaps her hands. "Memorize it!"

"I have memorized it! *Oh happy dagger, this is thy sheath, there rust and let me die.*"

Bruja Lupe cringes at my delivery.

"I know," I groan.

"You sound like you're reading the phone book."

"I know," I say. "I'm terrible!"

Her eyes flash over the room, over the borrowed makeup and high heels scattered alongside my usual clothes and back-pack.

Something is clicking on in Bruja Lupe's brain. I can see it, like a match lighting.

"I have an idea," she says.

I don't know if Bruja Lupe tells the Quintanilla sisters about my new talent, or if they just know. But by the next morning, I am dressed like the woman on a can of Rosarita beans. Ruffle sleeves, green and red ribbons on a white blouse, and a puffy skirt that looks like a cross between a puebla dress and a petti-coat from an old Western.

I shift my weight in Fresa's borrowed cowboy boots, worn for the second time this week.

And it's Fresa who stands with me before I'm pulled backstage.

"I'm scared," I say, a fluffy feeling in my stomach.

Now it's not just everyone watching me.

It's the fact of the stardust on my body. It's the possibility that me surviving and winning Miss Meteor might save me.

"Don't be scared," Fresa says. "You're gonna take these gringas down."

"I think I'm gonna throw up."

She claps my upper arms. "Then you're gonna swallow it and keep smiling."

The fluffy-inside feeling gets worse through all the perfect talents before me. A girl who can gargle the Pledge of Allegiance while tap dancing. Another who twirls a flaming baton. Kendra Kendall singing "Somewhere Over the Space Rock," a performance so moving it brings the audience to standing cheers.

Then it's me, the emcee sweeping a hand toward me as I climb the stage steps.

I say quiet thank-yous to the pageant volunteers who set up everything Bruja Lupe and I brought with us. The little table. The pots and plates and the big clay bowl that holds the empty corn husks. With the little jars of spices, it all looks so pretty, I could be a star on a TV cooking show.

The emcee-solicited applause fades.

Then they're all watching me.

I swallow hard enough that Fresa sees it and nods her approval. I want to tell her I'm okay, I'm not sick. But I can't.

Because they're all watching me.

"So, the holidays are coming up in a few months"—I get closer to the little table—"and the holidays are all about family, and what better way to show your family you care than with a homemade dish?"

A soft *awwww* comes from the audience, and my heartbeat settles.

If I could face the question and answer and the swimsuit, I can do this.

"Also, what better way to keep your second cousin from going on about that boyfriend you can't stand than to make sure she's too busy eating, right?" I say, my voice high and nervous.

But they laugh.

A real laugh, not a they-feel-sorry-for-me laugh.

"Today I'm going to show you how to make tamales." I lay out a corn husk. "I learned how to make the masa from the woman who's been a mother to me my whole life, the woman we all know as Bruja Lupe Perez!" I stretch out a hand to give a showman's call-out to Bruja Lupe, sitting in the audience.

I didn't tell Bruja Lupe I was mentioning this. But she preens, giving a dreamy, mysterious look that matches the witch they all think she is. Her hair looks like the graceful drape of a black scarf.

My nerves knot in my throat.

But I am doing this. Succeeding at this pageant not only means doing something I wanted to do before the sky takes me back.

It might mean the sky doesn't take me at all.

I think of the stardust vanishing from my back, and it makes me brave, and reckless, and I just start talking.

"And just so you know, she is open every day this week, and she can cure anything from insomnia to stage fright," I say, even as my own hands tremble. "Guess I should have thought of that before I came up here, right?"

They laugh again, fuller this time.

"Today's tamale filling comes courtesy of a Quintanilla family recipe that will soon be appearing on the menu at Selena's, right here in town."

The Quintanilla sisters all cock their heads in unison, at the same angle.

They are more alike than they will ever admit.

I set a spoon into the filling bowl. I would usually just do it with clean hands, but a beauty queen never gets filling under her nails.

Probably.

It seems like something Fresa would tell me.

"And I also owe a big thank you to the Quintanilla sisters," I say, "who prepared me for this pageant by giving me perfect posture, a high tolerance for swallowing Vaseline, and a deeper acquaintance with duct tape than I ever wanted."

This laugh is more scattered, less even.

More real.

They did not expect me to make them laugh. I didn't either.

This is it. I can feel it humming along my body, the opposite of the prickling feeling I get before more stardust appears.

This is it, the feeling of when I'm maybe winning. This is what I have to do to save myself.

I have to grab hold of this pageant.

I have to grab hold of this town and make them look at me.

"If I'm walking a little funny, that last part's why," I say.

The laugh this time is so loud I feel it echoing off the sky. I catch Cole laughing, the same kind of sudden, open-mouth surprised laugh as when I asked him what trip he was packing for.

I can't believe it either.

I spoon the filling in. "If this seems hard when you start out, don't worry, you'll get it with enough practice." I spread masa over the corn husk. "After the first five thousand or so, it's a breeze."

The laugh now is almost affectionate, like I'm a strange-but-still-loved daughter.

But out from the laughter, I hear a hard, shouted word.

It's a word that lands me back on the floor of the boys' locker room.

It's the word Royce and his friends shouted at me the Halloween I dared to show up at school dressed up as Miss Meteor, with my cheap tiara and polyester sash and pageant

247

smile, pretending I was a future beauty queen because back then, I still believed I could be.

It's the word that feels like plastic teeth tangling in my hair, like the plastic headband Royce and his friends put in place of the tiara. It had two antennae, the glittery foam balls on the end bouncing in time with how I was shaking.

It's a word Cole didn't hear yelled at me, because he wasn't allowed in the boys' locker room. It's a word I never got to tell Chicky about, because it happened around the time we stopped telling each other big things.

It's a word that means both what everyone thinks of me as a brown-skinned girl, and what they would think of me if they knew how much I was made of the stars.

Alien.

The audience's laughter fades, everyone looking around for the source of the word.

"They think they can come here, live here, take our jobs, and we're just gonna let them?" a man from the back yells. "Go back home."

Every friend I have in the audience rushes toward this man.

He is not a man with a hat made of aluminum foil, or a beard soaked in cheap whiskey from our liquor store.

He wears neat, nice clothes. He is neither young enough nor old enough for everyone to chalk his words up to age or lack of it. He has a head of hair as full and well-styled as the judges'.

248

But he does not wear the judges' smiles.

I do not know this man. He is not from Meteor. But I can tell from looking at him that he is the kind of man everyone listens to.

He is a Jack Bradley kind of man, the kind of man Royce will probably grow up to be.

"She's an alien," he shouts as the town security volunteers escort him out of the pageant grounds, my friends following behind. "You're an alien," he shouts, looking right at me before they shove him toward the exit.

And because every friend I have in Meteor is out of their seat, moving to push him out of this event, there is no one I can look at.

Not Bruja Lupe. Not Chicky. Not the Quintanilla sisters. Not Junior. Not Cole.

The clouds have wisped away, and now the sun is as bright as a spotlight on the outdoor stage. It's too bright to find any of them.

This man, the kind of man people listen to, has just called me an alien in front of the entire Meteor Regional Pageant and Talent Competition Showcase.

But I don't yell after him.

Because he is right.

In the language of this world, I am an alien. The star-stuff in my body makes me not of this planet, even though this planet is where I have lived my whole life as a girl.

And in the language of men like this, I am an alien, his word for brown-skinned girls who may or may not have been born here.

Both ways, the meaning is the same. I am a girl who does not belong in Meteor, New Mexico. I am neither enough of Earth nor enough of this country. *Alien.* A girl as brown as the desert and as odd as fallen stardust.

I lift my hands away from the half-finished tamale.

I can feel new trails of stardust waiting under my skin.

If I stay, it will come to the surface, showing up on my bare legs.

I have already lost.

Spreading my fluffy skirt in both my hands, I curtsy. I curtsy, not for the man who called me an alien. Not for Royce Bradley and his friends, who first burned that word into my brain. Not for the gringos who hate us.

I curtsy for Bruja Lupe, and the Quintanillas, and the Corteses, and Cole, and Buzz and Edna, and Dolores, and everyone else who has ever been on my side.

The crowd stills.

I curtsy, deep as Audrey Hepburn in *My Fair Lady*. Because losing Miss Meteor will probably be my last act on this planet, and I am at least going to make it a good exit.

I leave the little table and the corn husks behind, my petticoat fluffing up as I descend the steps from the stage.

250

When I get to the Meteor Meteorite Museum, Buzz is already there to let me in, like he knew I was coming. Like he knew where I'd go.

I stand in front of the rock that brought me and Bruja Lupe here in the first place.

Can I? I ask without speaking.

A vein of iron winks through the rock, its way of saying yes.

I put my arms around it, my cheek against its rough surface.

In the air-conditioned chill of the Meteor Meteorite Museum, the grain of the rock is almost warm. I close my eyes and understand that maybe this is how human beings feel when they greet old friends.

Maybe I have lost the Meteor Regional Pageant and Talent Competition Showcase.

Maybe I lost it the moment that man threw a word at me that will stick to my body.

But this—not that word, but this, my brown arms around this piece of the sky—is who I am.

This is mine.

A ribbon of light flashes bright enough that I can see it behind my eyelids.

I open my eyes to streams of silver and gold.

The light swirls and pulses within the rock, brightening and darkening like the rhythm of a heartbeat.

All the star-stuff held in this rock is coming to life, just for this one moment. Even as it dulls and fades, I hold on, because this rock is as much my family as Bruja Lupe.

It glows to tell me that I still have light in me.

It is reminding me of everything I am made of as I say goodbye.

CHICKY

AT THE FIFTIETH-ANNUAL Cornhole Championship, the stands fill by noon. I've been here for two hours already, too restless and nervous to stay home, and too reviled by this town to wander its streets.

My sisters shove their way in beside me just as the church bells chime, to the spaces I saved for them with my bag and sweatshirt.

"Lita?" I ask, and Uva shakes her head.

"We stopped by Bruja Lupe's to see if she needed a ride, but she wasn't home."

"Dammit," I say. I was counting on her being here. Counting on having a chance to tell her how useless that man and his xenophobic shouting were.

But now it's going to have to wait. Because moments later—at 12:30 on the dot—the match officially begins.

And I know Junior only entered to keep Lita from quitting

the pageant. And I tell myself cornhole is stupid and everyone who plays it is stupid, and it doesn't matter in the grand scheme of the pageant or the mission, and I'm only here because my parents want people to see our Selena's T-shirts, etc.

But if it doesn't matter, why do I bite my nails every time Junior steps up to the board?

There are multiple elimination rounds, teams of two competing against players from around the state as the crowd cheers and groans.

Of course, Junior is paired up with Royce Bradley.

Of course, they make it to the final round.

The sun is high in the sky as they finally face off with a team from Cloudcroft, twin meatheads that look like they were carved from stone, in matching red tracksuits. They probably have a coach at their school, not just Mr. Bradley with a clipboard doing what my mom likes to call "reliving his glory days" in a tone she usually reserves for Fresa.

The twins' movements are so precise, so synchronized, that even the best Meteor has to offer looks a little ragtag by comparison.

Royce approaches the board with his usual swagger, but Junior looks nervous, and I stand up before I realize I'm doing it.

"Where are you going?" Cereza asks, and I'm about to make an excuse when Fresa says, "Like you don't know." And that's all there is to it.

Climbing down from the bleachers, my butt numb from sitting on metal for so long, I wonder what I'm doing. I'm not Junior's girlfriend. We settled all that in front of the holy (and holey) Selena's Diner wall.

But Kendra Kendall is standing across from Royce in the spectator area, blowing him kisses in this ridiculous cheerleader outfit, and as much as I hate this, and her, I stand a few feet away where I know Junior will be able to see me. Because even if I'm not his girlfriend, I'm his . . . someone.. And he deserves to have someone in his corner.

When he sees me, he smiles, and I swear some of the tension leaves his shoulders.

"What are you doing here, freak?" Kendra asks, the titters of the girls around her making my face heat up. "Come to cheer for your little friend? Don't worry, he's mostly ornamental. Everyone knows my Roycey is the real hero."

I look at Kendra, bracing myself for the fear I've always felt when I look at her. But in this moment, I have more important things to worry about, and it makes her look a little smaller than I remembered.

"Gentlemen," says the town radio broadcaster, here to call the match. "To your marks."

Royce and Junior step up, three hundred pounds of high school boy with everything to prove. The fluttering feeling is back in my stomach, and I give Junior a weak thumbs-up, which he returns as Royce readies his first bag.

To quell my nerves, I look at the boards. The swirls of *Starry Night*, like Van Gogh himself came back to Earth just to paint cornhole boards, and the cover of Nirvana's *Nevermind*, with the baby swimming for a dollar bill.

Even if they don't win this match, I think Junior is going places, while Royce has a one-way ticket to a job slinging used cars with a beer belly. A future where he spends his nights at the Meteor Saloon in his too-small MCH jacket telling stories to the ladies about his own glory days.

If we're very lucky, he'll be telling them about today.

The thought cheers me up just enough to stand beside Kendra as he takes his first shot.

It goes right in, and the roar from the crowd is deafening.

For the next eighteen minutes, I barely breathe. Junior and Royce are good, but the other team didn't make it to the finals for nothing.

"When is it over?" I ask Kendra as they sink another bag in the Nirvana board.

She spares me a withering glare. "You actually don't know cornhole is played until someone gets twenty-one points?" she asks. "Do you actually live under a rock?"

"I *actually* do," I retort, before I can overthink it. "I find it's a good way to beat the desert heat."

She doesn't speak to me again, but now at least I know what I'm waiting for. Junior and Royce have fourteen points, and the twins have twelve.

The one with the slightly wider shoulders makes his next shot.

Fifteen.

Junior's next shot slides across the board, stopping just short of going in, and there's a collective groan from the spectators.

Fifteen.

Royce and the other twin sink their next two respective shots.

"Three points?" I ask, without looking at Kendra.

"Duh," she replies.

So they're tied at eighteen.

Junior is spiraling after missing his last shot. I can tell. His shoulders are too high, his chin ducked to his chest. I wish I could call out to him like I did at tryouts, tell him it's just us on the field, but it would be a lie, and more than that it would be violating the treaty we made to get our friendship back, so I stay quiet, picturing ribbons of light like the ones that trail meteors extending from my chest to his.

Maybe he feels them, because he looks up at me and smiles a little.

If he makes this shot, Meteor will have twenty-one points, and the match will be over. If he misses, the twins will have a chance to win it.

I'm a little angry about the fact that I know all this.

"I can't believe it's him making the last shot," Kendra pouts. "When did he even join the team, yesterday?"

"I think it was after your boyfriend's bullying caused the bike crash that maimed your brother," I say, mock thoughtfully.

"Oh, suck it, rug-muncher," she says.

I freeze for just a second, starting to shrink, looking for the quickest exit, wondering if anyone heard. But then I think about Junior, up there about to decide the outcome of the cornhole championship.

And Lita. Without her bravery, none of us would even be here.

And me, too, if I'm being honest. Haven't I been brave, too?

"Which is it, Kendra?" I ask, my voice only wobbling a little. "Munch or suck? You can't do both at once, you know."

Her horrified face is just enough to get me through the endless moment before Junior takes the match's final shot.

The final shot. Because it goes in.

It goes in.

Junior Cortes has just won the cornhole championship, and Kendra's shriek almost bursts my eardrum. Before I know it, we're hugging, and I might be crying, and there's so much noise everywhere that I feel like nothing is real, and that's okay.

Disgusted, Kendra drops her arms the moment the din dies down. "That never happened," she says. "So, like, don't get any weird lesbian ideas."

This time, I don't shrink. In fact, before I know it I'm saying, "Oh, Kendra, I'm so sorry . . . you're just really not my type!"

"Oh my God, gross!" she whines, running off toward Royce.

Once I stop laughing, I almost follow, but that's when I notice that Junior is surrounded. The team, the crowd that's pouring in from the bleachers, the radio announcer that's asking for an interview. His face is flushed, and he's smiling, and I think it's not fair that he's been hiding himself from the world all these years.

But there are the girls from tryouts, with their tiny tank tops and their long hair and their perfectly applied lipstick, and it doesn't matter that things didn't work out with the Hair Pony, because there's a stable full of them out here, and one of them is touching his arm, and there's something alive and clawing in my chest, there must be, because I can barely breathe.

It hits me then, as I stand on the side of the field, as everyone else takes their turn congratulating the boy who has made my life livable for the past five years:

I lost my best friend all those years ago because I was hiding. Because I didn't think there was another way.

And I'm about to lose Junior too.

I don't think any more after that, I just charge into the crowd, pushing aside shoulders and backs and arms until I reach him. One of the guys from the team is approaching, too, but I don't care. I grab Junior's elbow, and I turn him toward me, and his eyes widen a little as I throw myself into his arms, hugging him like I never want to let go.

259

After a moment of shock, he hugs me back. Hard. Like he doesn't want to let go either.

"Don't go with them," I say, as Royce jumps up on top of the *Starry Night* board to accept the adulation of the masses.

"Go where?" he asks, his lips twitching upward.

"To whatever meatheads and waifs party they're about to invite you to."

"Why not?" he asks, and I can't quite tell if he's being sarcastic. "It sounds so fun."

I take a deep breath. "Because I don't want you to."

His eyes get more focused somehow, like he's just tuned out everything besides the answer to this question. No pressure. "Why not?"

"Because I have an idea?" I say, and it's true. One is just occurring to me, in the wide-open space where my fear is fleeing the scene. But it's a not good enough reason, and I knew it wouldn't be. "Because," I clarify. "I want you to come with me instead."

His smile is ten winning cornhole shots. It's tacos al pastor with just the right amount of lime juice squeezed on top. It's everything.

"You got it," he says, and when he takes my hand I don't let go.

"There's just one thing," I say, and his smile gets more familiar.

"Of course," he says. "We'll pick up Lita on the way."

"Did I hear someone planning an adventure?" comes a voice from behind us.

It's Cole Kendall, his arm in a sling, and he's smiling too.

"Don't you have plans?" I ask, and we all turn as one to see Royce stage dive off the cornhole board into a crowd not quite big enough to catch him.

"Oh, all this?" he asks with a smirk. "I think I can handle missing one night."

Leaving behind the crowd, now chanting Royce's name like *he* made the winning shot, the three of us walk back to the parking lot, to the root-beer-brown Pontiac Junior's mom let him borrow for the game. As Cole slides into the back seat and I get in beside Junior, I get that weird fluttery feeling again.

The kind that tells me this is gonna be quite a night.

LITA

THE DAY AFTER the talent competition, I ask Bruja Lupe
to tell my friends I'm not home, or that I'm sick, or anything to
make them hang up or go away.

I don't think any of them will try talking to me, not after
what happened, but just in case.

That night, the sun is barely down when I put on my
favorite pajamas, one more thing I'll miss (along with the
hundred-washes-soft tank top I have on underneath). They're
patterned with shooting stars arcing across a cotton-candy-
pink background like they're comets, rainbows in place of
their tails.

I think about missing them, because it's too big to think
about everything else I'll miss, everyone else I'll miss.

The stardust hasn't burst onto my arms. Not yet. But it's all
over my legs. From my thighs to my ankles it looks as silvery
and glimmery as a mermaid's tail.

My arms are next. I can already feel the buzzing feeling under my skin.

Alien. Alien. Alien.

The word spreads out in my brain like a coyote's call through the desert.

When I come back to my room after brushing my teeth, Cole Kendall is leaning against my open window.

"Why are you in my room?" I yell.

He must catch that I'm more startled than annoyed, because he smiles.

I look at his sling. "How did you even get in here?"

"First-story window?" Cole asks. "Easy. Do you know how many times Kendra and I have snuck in at two a.m. after a party? If I can get my drunk, belligerent sister in a window, I can get myself in with one hand tied behind my back." He glances down at the sling. "So to speak."

"Belligerent," I say. "Nice word."

"Adjective," he says as though reciting from a dictionary. "Definition: My sister after her third Jell-O shot."

I laugh. "What are you doing here?"

"You just kinda bolted after the talent thing," he says. "I thought I'd give you space, but when none of us heard from you, I got worried. Then when you didn't show up for the championship, I really got worried."

Junior. I say a little prayer that God let the stars in the sky give Junior a little extra luck today.

Missing it gave me a sad, hollow feeling that still hasn't gone away. But showing my face at the championship right after I bailed on the talent portion, for no reason the audience could see, felt as impossible as Chicky and me being friends again.

"Did he win?" I ask.

"If you wanna know that," Cole says. "You're coming out with me."

I cross my arms, pajama flannel scritching over pajama flannel. "What do you mean?"

"I'm not letting you mope in here all night."

"I'm not moping. I am brooding."

"You can brood any other night. But sorry, not tonight."

"Why are you even here?" I ask. "Did you not see the fiasco I was onstage?"

Fiasco. That's another good word. I wish I could take more joy in it right now.

"I don't remember any fiasco," Cole says.

"Are you kidding?" I ask. "If Miss Meteor pageant had a talentless competition, I'd take first place."

"You handled an asshole as well as anyone could've."

I stare up at my star mobile as though there is not a boy standing in my room. "Thanks for checking on me, but I'm staying in tonight."

"Fine," Cole says. "But your friends are gonna be really disappointed."

Friends?

Plural?

Cole lifts his hand, showing me his palm. "I can tell you no more. I am merely a messenger."

He's given me just enough to make me curious.

And he knows it.

I call out to Bruja Lupe in the living room.

"Yes?" she answers back.

"Cole Kendall's in my room, and I'm gonna go out the window with him."

"Why don't you both just use the door?"

When we get outside, Junior is standing in front of his mother's car.

I can tell how everything turned out from the look on his face.

"You won?" I ask.

Junior doesn't bother to answer; his proud smile says everything. And I don't wait for an answer before I jump up and down shrieking, because this, at least this, has gone right.

Chicky steps out from the other side of the car.

The sight of her stops me cold.

Chicky, the friend who became a not-friend, is here at my house. In front of Cole Kendall, the boy this town loves so much I cannot believe he'll even be seen with me. In front of Junior, Meteor town hero of tonight and probably forever. There will be years of stories about the brilliant artist whose long-secret talent for cornhole saved Meteor's chance at the championship title.

"We are going on a caper," Chicky says, a note of intrigue in her voice.

I bristle at the word. This is not us.

We don't do this anymore.

"I'm not in the mood," I say.

"You haven't even heard about the caper."

"I don't want to go on a caper."

"Will you let me at least describe the caper?"

"Stop saying caper!"

"You just said it too!"

The sound of our bickering, how ridiculous we are, makes us both crack a smile.

I can't help it.

She can't help it.

If the amount of unstardusted skin I have left is any indication, if how it's speeding down my legs is any indication, I probably only have a handful of nights left in my girl body.

I don't want to spend this one putting distance between me and Chicky Quintanilla.

"Fine." I cross my arms. "What kind of caper?"

Chicky looks at the three of us. "We're gonna make sure all those tourists and conspiracy theorists really have something to talk about."

Junior pulls a yellow legal pad out of the front seat. "I've already drawn up a design."

He shows me a page of intricate flower-like arcs and curves.

It's a pattern I recognize.

It's one I flashed at Kendra Kendall and half the town.

"Is that . . . from my bra?" I ask.

Junior points a thumb at Cole. "He remembered it perfectly. He described it in detail."

Cole looks down at his shoes. "Thanks for that."

"Anytime," Junior says.

"We've decided to give everyone definitive proof of life elsewhere in the universe," Chicky says. "For once, we decide what the rumor mill says."

I look at Chicky, searching for some sign that she feels obligated to be nice to me. I search her face for some pinch in her smile that tells me she wishes she weren't with me in front of two of the boys who matter most in this town.

"So what's it gonna be?" Chicky asks in her best mafia don voice. "You in or out?"

The impression is so perfect, such a precise copy of a fine-suited man in a 1940s restaurant corner booth, that I say, "I'm in," before I can think about it.

All of us climb into the car, and Junior drives away from the lights of Meteor, New Mexico.

I'm glad I'm in the back seat. It gives me a better view of Junior as he drives and Chicky as she sits in the front passenger seat next to him, both of them laughing as they argue about which static-fuzzed radio station to tune into.

They're both realizing something their hearts have known for a long time.

I'm still thinking about them, what it must feel like to discover that feeling between you and someone else. Which is why I'm not expecting it when Junior glances in the rearview, catches my eye, and says, "So what's with all the glitter?"

"Junior!" Chicky and Cole both say at the same time.

"What?" He shrugs at them both, without apology. "Like you both weren't wondering too."

I sink down in the seat thinking about how often they've noticed bands of stardust winking between my shirt and my jeans. Or if they can see it now, through my pajamas.

Chicky and Cole are actively trying not to look at me. So actively that it somehow feels more intense than if they were staring.

Junior keeps driving, patient that I'll answer eventually.

So I do the only kind of lying I know how to do.

Lying without really lying.

"It's been in me forever," I say. "I just used to be better at hiding it."

"Does it mean something bad?" Chicky asks.

Junior glances over at her. "Can we rephrase that to sound less judgmental?"

"Can you forget your mom's articles about communication for one minute?" Even saying this, she sounds like she's

268

flirting with him. For a second, it lets me think about them again instead of the stardust.

But only for a second.

Now Cole looks at me. "Are you okay?"

My heart contracts. My skin feels hot, like the stardust on me wants me to explain it. But I can't. Not right now. Because Junior has just won the Cornhole Championship for Meteor. Because Chicky and I are almost friends. Because whenever Chicky looks at Junior she can't help smiling. Because Cole seems like he can actually be himself around the three of us, instead of whoever Royce and his friends and this whole town decide he has to be.

There is something perfect about the four of us in this car together, right now, on this night. And maybe it's selfish, but I want to take it with me, exactly like it is. I don't want to ruin it with explaining.

I look at Cole, knowing I have to tell the biggest lie I'll ever tell this boy.

And I have to say it in front of my once best friend and the boy she's just figuring out has her heart.

"Yeah," I say. "I'm okay. Just weird."

I don't know if I'm talking about me or the stardust, but before I can figure it out, Junior says, "We like you weird."

"And you're in a car with some of the weirdest residents of Meteor," Chicky says. "Except maybe Cole."

"Yeah," Cole says, "picture of Meteor normalcy, right here."

Junior merges onto the highway.

"Where are we going?" I ask.

"To where Meteor would've been founded if it weren't for uncertainty about geological integrity," Cole says.

"And if the government hadn't cordoned it off for a decade of investigation," Junior says.

I lean forward to Chicky in the front seat. "We're going to the crater?"

The crater. The place where the stuff I'm made of first touched this planet.

Junior turns off the highway onto a dark dirt road and parks the car as close as he can get it to that hollow the meteor left in the Earth.

Then we're off in the night air, the stars thick above us. They're distant as dreams and close as relatives. They're as much mine as I am theirs. They're mirrors of my body and heart.

I breathe in the almost-midnight chill of the desert. We all do. We run down into the bowl of the crater, laughing and clutching at each other to keep one another from sliding down the dirt slope.

And we do it, that caper Chicky has us all out on. We throw a flashlight onto Junior's drawing, and we pull small rocks from the edges of the crater.

When Cole reaches for a bigger one, I reach out to stop him. "You can't do that. You're hurt."

"They're rocks, not boulders," he says. "And you really think I'm gonna miss this?"

So we all do it.

We move rocks, a few at a time, into arcing paths that reach out from the crater's center. I thought it would look like petals, that everyone would recognize it as a flower pattern. But as we add more stones, it starts to look like a galaxy made of rocks.

That's when I realize how much genius is in this caper.

The stones look like the whirls of galaxy arms.

Exactly the kind of sign that people on this planet would expect from otherworldly visitors.

After we set down the last handfuls of rock, Chicky and Junior flop down on the slope of the crater. They laugh and shove each other's shoulders in a way that would look brotherly and sisterly if I didn't know better.

I settle onto the ground a little ways away, far enough to let them feel alone, close enough that I can still wave to them like I'm sending greetings across a lake.

Cole stands over me. "Mind if I join you?"

"Yeah," I say. "Sure."

I am still getting used to having friends beyond cactuses and neighborhood pets.

Cole looks toward Chicky and Junior, who are nudging sand onto each other's shoes.

"Giving them a minute alone?" he asks.

"That obvious?"

"To me, maybe. But not to them. I don't think anything's obvious to them at the moment."

271

"Not even how they feel?"

"People are slow about that sometimes, even when they're quick about everything else."

He sits down next to me. I can feel the warmth of him on my left side, a break in the night air's chill.

Cole looks out into the crater opening in front of us. "Don't give up yet, okay?"

I try to place what he's saying.

"The pageant," he says.

After the swimsuit competition, I had a shot. But I ran out of the talent portion.

Now I have no chance.

"It's gonna be Kendra or it's gonna be that girl from Quemado," I say.

"The blond chick in the American flag bikini?" Cole draws back. "No way. Fresa wore that exact same one, and better if you ask me." He traces his hand through the fine dirt between us. "No, I think we really need to worry about"—he considers it—"tasteful green one-piece, Lady Macbeth monologue."

"Oh please don't tell Cereza that," I say. "She was set on me doing Shakespeare."

"Well, you kinda did."

"You mean while hurtling toward you on a bike I could barely ride?"

"Most original staging of the death of Juliet in the history of

New Mexico." He puts his right hand to his chest. "It brought tears to my eyes."

"It brought tears to your eyes because I gave you a concussion," I say. "Okay, fine. What about the girl with the really bright-blue eyes?"

"Eh." He shrugs. "She's okay."

"Okay? Her skin looks like it was poured out of the full-fat cream Mrs. Quintanilla stocks at the diner. Except she doesn't have any fat on her."

He looks at me. "Overrated."

Overrated?

A blond white boy with this much height on me is calling a milk-skinned girl with that kind of body overrated?

"You know who I think has gotta be on the judges' radar?" Cole asks. "Vintage two-piece with matching swim skirt."

"The girl from Magdalena?" I ask. "Oh yeah, she's good."

"She could win this."

"I hope so." I'd like to see her win. Especially after hearing she borrowed the swimsuit from her aunt, who she calls her favorite person in the world. "But do girls that nice ever win?"

"Lita. She was dancing on pointe shoes while playing the violin. If she doesn't place in the top five, the taste of the judges is beyond hope." He picks up a handful of fine dirt and slowly lets the wind take it, like gravity stripping away stardust. "Don't count yourself out either. The rhinestone Space Rock? I've got to hand it to Chicky's sisters. Genius."

"Girls like me don't win."

He brushes his hand on his jeans. "Girls like you?"

It's not even just my height, or my baby fat, or my mediocre posture.

"Girls who don't even call their mothers 'mom,'" I say. "You and Kendra and your mom and your dad, you're the kind of family this town wants. Not me and Bruja Lupe."

Cole looks out onto the crater. He's not watching Chicky and Junior try to stick little bits of sagebrush under each other's shoelaces.

He's looking into the dark in front of us.

His laugh is as light as the whisper of the stars, and almost as sad.

"My dad's gone, Lita," he says.

I stare at him, trying to get him to turn his head.

"What?"

"He left," Cole says. "He's not traveling for work in Helena or Phoenix or Albany. He left."

The words drop and pull me down, like I'm falling into the crater.

It all falls together.

How Cole's father can never seem to make his games.

How Cole sometimes mixes up what city his father is in on any given business trip.

The overdue bills stuffed into a drawer.

"So there's your perfect family," Cole says. "No one else in this town knows that except you, me, my sister, and my mom. And probably our pastor, but I don't know. So in case you were still wondering if we were friends."

"You didn't have to tell me that for me to know we're friends."

"I know," he says. "But I really had to tell someone, and I wanted it to be you."

Friends. The word is still its own kind of music, and I let it cycle through my head until it makes a song.

I will miss this boy in a way that's breaking through me, fast as a shooting star.

So I decide to say it, because why hold back now, when I don't know how much more time I get on this tiny little planet?

"I'm gonna miss you, Cole," I say.

He gives me a weird look, part question, part smile. "You're not getting rid of me after graduation. You know that."

I change the subject before I start thinking about it too hard.

"I see what you're doing, by the way," I say, and then nod toward Chicky and Junior. "So do they."

"What am I doing?" he asks.

"Not letting your sister get away with it anymore."

He doesn't ask what *it* is. He knows. Everything he's tried to give Kendra a pass for. Everything he's let slide because she's his sister. But he's been slowly calling her on it, the way he's been trying to with Royce for years.

He looks into the crater. "I'm starting to wonder if maybe I could make things a little better around here for someone else like me."

"You definitely can," I say. I think of everyone he's already made it better for around here. Daniel Llamas and Beth Cox and Oliver Hedlesky. Chicky and me. "You've been sticking up for everyone but you for a really long time."

He nods like maybe he knows I'm right.

"I'm serious," I say. "Since your brother graduated, you've been the only reason half the school doesn't wish for another meteor to fall on the cornhole team."

He laughs. "Weirdest compliment ever."

I want so much for this boy. I want so much for all of us. I want Cole to get the chance to love this town forever even if he doesn't stay here. I want him to find a place where he can be who he is without feeling like he has to earn it. And I want that same choice for Chicky, and for Junior, and for me. I want places on this earth where Cole is seen for everything he is. I want places where the only insults Chicky ever gets are the ones from her sisters. I want places where Junior's art is seen for how beautiful and brilliant it is, instead of something the Royces of the world can make fun of.

I want places on this earth where I am a girl made of stardust, not one crumbling back into it.

Just then, a meteor drags a thread of light across the sky. I wonder where it's been, what stars it has seen, what might become of the star-stuff it's carrying.

Where it might fall, what wonder it might seed into the ground where it lands.

Cole shuts his eyes like he's making a wish, so I do too.

"What'd you wish for?" I ask.

He smiles. "I'm not telling you that."

"Because then it won't come true?"

He laughs. "Because I'm not telling you."

The woven-together sounds of Chicky and Junior's distant laughs is soft enough that I could fall asleep to it.

Being in the hollow of this crater where I first touched this planet, the inside of me feels like streams of light, like my veins are becoming the same glowing ribbons that shined off the rock.

I am so lit up with that feeling of glowing that when Cole's fingers and mine brush between us, I think I might burn him.

But he doesn't pull back.

We stay.

My eyes are still shut when the laughter fades, when it turns to the growing sound of footsteps.

I open them when Cole pulls me to my feet.

"What—"

Chicky claps a hand over my mouth before I can say anything else.

Junior leads us all into a shadowed patch of the crater, unlit by the moon.

"What is going on?" I whisper when Chicky's hand gives.

Cole silently flicks his head toward the opposite edge of the crater.

Figures cluster along the rim of the basin.

"Do you come in peace?" one of them calls out.

"Do you bring greetings from your world?" another shouts.

"Have you come to destroy our planet?" a third asks.

We should have known this week would bring out the tourists not just to Meteor, but to where the meteor hit.

"Come on." The boys hurry us toward the edge that will get us close to the road.

"Wait!" Chicky whisper-shouts.

We all stop.

Chicky raises an eyebrow at me. "These tourists want a show. What do you say we give them a real beaut?"

"A what now?" Cole asks.

"Gentlemen," Chicky puts on her mafia don voice to address Junior and Cole. "If you've got the stomach, we could use a couple of guys with good brains and fast wheels."

"Who even talks like that?" Junior asks, but he can't hide his own smile.

"You two gonna stand there"—Chicky keeps on with the voice—"or you two gonna get the getaway car ready?"

She sounds so sure, and her Vito Corleone is so convincing, that the boys sneak off through the shadows like they've been dispatched on a mission by M herself.

Chicky pulls me onto the ground. "Stay down."

My heart is beating so hard I can feel it in my neck.

"Gym roof, fourth grade?" she whispers.

I almost tell her that this is where I leave her, that I can't do this. Not with the years we lost.

Not with why we lost them.

Then I feel the stardust snaking down to my knees. And the feeling of it glimmering across my skin leaves me with a question:

This whole time, I've been thinking about what I've wanted to take with me from Meteor, what I've wanted to take with me from this planet.

But now I'm starting to wonder: What do I want to leave behind?

"You're not serious," I say. "That took months of planning,"

Her eyes are flashing, thinking. "How about Maddie Bascom's birthday party?"

I think back on how we hid and made enough ghost noises that everyone thought the bowling alley was haunted. The right sounds, at the right time. "Simultaneous approach?"

"You got it," Chicky says.

We crawl into a hollow where they won't see us.

"Ready?" Chicky asks, holding my forearms.

I nod.

We've both picked up from Cereza how to be loud.

But this is not shouting an order across Selena's or

proclaiming Juliet's last words.

These are the strangest, most otherworldly sounds our voice boxes can make, like we are our own spaceship. Buzzing and whirring like we are the little green men people so often imagine. Pitching high and low as though we are part machine and part living things from other planets. Even a few robotic, nasal yells of "Greetings, Earthlings!"

This is us. This is how we acted out movies when we were little. It's how we came up with note-passing schemes so elaborate we were sure we could sell the plans to MI6. This is how we convinced half the girls in our class that we once saw a spaceship deliver the mail.

The tourists reward us with wondering gasps that fill the crater's basin.

They lean forward, like they're considering coming down to greet us.

Chicky and I grab each other's hands, and we run, staying low enough and deep enough in the crater edge's shadow that the onlookers can't see us. We fly up the far slope, pitch ourselves over the edge, and race toward the road.

Junior is driving, and Cole is in the front passenger side, and they've left the back door open for us to throw ourselves in. Between that and how they've stayed out of the tourists' view, they're the best getaway men two girls could ask for.

"Go, go, go," Chicky yells, so Junior's already rolling out of park by the time we reach the car.

Chicky shoves me in front of her, forcing me in before her. I grab her arm and pull her halfway in, then grab the loop on her jean shorts to tug her the rest of the way into the car, and we're a heap of limbs by the time we get the door closed.

"Seat belts, ladies," Junior says, trying to sound patient.

But he loves this. He loves that Chicky is both stranger and more of a leader than she realized.

Chicky and I buckle up like he asks. But as he gets up to sixty-five, we lean out the windows and yell "Greetings, Earthlings!" over the rush of the highway.

Chicky doesn't hesitate. She doesn't look embarrassed to have done any of this in front of Junior, the friend she loves, and the Meteor cornhole hero. She keeps smiling over at me every mile or so.

She looks not just humoring or kind.

She looks almost proud.

In that moment, all four of us are meteors. We outrun the headlights going by in the distance on the highway. We outrun anyone who could see us. Only the gaze of the stars and the setting moon catches us.

Junior stops the car a mile or two from the edge of town. We're still blanketed in the star-dusted dark, Meteor's lights in the distance before us. There's a bubbly feeling in the car. Our bodies are humming from breathing the chilled desert air outside town, and none of us is ready for this night to be over.

I'm not ready for this night to be over. Because I don't know how many I have left on this tiny, imperfect planet.

"So," Cole says.

We all look at him.

"You wanna go to a party?"

CHICKY

WHEN WE PULL up in front of the Bradleys', my first thought is that this is more kids than even *go* to MCH.

This might be more kids than live in the state of New Mexico.

Only a mile or so from the dealership, on a piece of land that's small enough for the neighbors to see the place but big enough that they can't hear it, Royce's house is the perfect place for a party, I have to admit.

For a while, we just sit in the car and watch. It's barely midnight and there's already someone passed out in a lawn chair, two people making out like they're alone in a bedroom, and— yep, two girls Jell-O wrestling in a kiddie pool.

"I'm not so sure about this . . . ," I say, but Junior has already opened his door.

"We've already been to one other world tonight," he says, grinning back at Lita who looks just as freaked out as I do.

"Why not make it an intergalactic caper?"

"KENDALL!" Royce screams in a beer-soaked voice from the doorway. "GET YOUR ASS IN HERE. MISTY'S ABOUT TO DO A KEG STAND!"

"Wait," I say. Maybe it's the stardust. Or how worried I was until she said she was okay. Maybe it's everything about this night, and everything that will happen tomorrow. But whatever it is, I'm ready. Now. Finally. "You guys go." I take a deep breath. "I need to talk to Lita alone for a minute."

I'm not sure which set of eyebrows goes up higher, but Cole is the first to respectfully leave the car. Lita looks at him like she wishes he wouldn't.

"Don't take too long," Junior whispers, hugging me in that awkward side-by-side seats way. "I'm in enemy territory here."

"Offended!" Cole calls from just outside the door.

We all laugh, but then I look outside, and then back at Junior. "Not anymore, Champ."

"Shut up," he mumbles. "The Dark Side can't take me that easily."

"Leave a trail of breadcrumbs just in case you get lost. I'll find you."

His eyes sparkle at me. I mean, they really do. It might just be Chelsea Gardener's taillights in front of us, but I choose to believe we brought some space magic back with us from the crater instead.

When Junior finally gets out, he takes a little of my

impulsive bravery with him. Lita is still in the back seat, and I turn around.

"Come sit with me?" I ask, hoping it sounds winning and not awkward. But she hesitates.

"I don't want to ruin tonight," she says. "Maybe we should just go to the party."

I take a deep breath, because there's only one thing I can say to change her mind, but once I say it, I know there's no turning back.

"We need to talk about seventh grade."

Lita climbs into the front seat, her eyes wide as dinner plates. Chelsea and her taillights are gone, but Lita's eyes still sparkle.

Magic, I tell myself, hoping there's enough of it to bring us through this in one piece. Because she's right. Tonight has been perfect. Which means I have even more to lose.

"I wasn't ready," I say, and she opens her mouth, but I hold up a hand. "You'll get a turn, I swear, but I have to get this out."

She closes her mouth again, but she doesn't look away.

"I wasn't ready. But I think . . . I finally am. I mean, I stood next to Kendra Kendall today and wasn't even scared. I told Junior not to go with the Hair Ponies. I can do this, I think. I think I can finally do it."

True to her word, Lita doesn't interrupt, even though I'm talking more to myself than her at this point. She lets me have a moment to gather my scattered thoughts.

"Allison Davis," I say finally. "Fourth grade. You probably

285

know this, but Royce called us lesbos on the bus and Allison wouldn't talk to me anymore. That's why Kendra calls me Ring Pop."

The words are this horrible, painful, cathartic mess, but Lita just lets them come. She doesn't even say whether or not she knew, whether her interest in snails on the ground and cactus birthdays over the gossip of her peers protected her from it or not.

"It got worse and worse," I say, my voice catching, pushing past it. "People were so mean, and they weren't letting it go, and I knew you were supposed to tell your best friend how you felt when stuff like that was happening, but I couldn't. I just couldn't. I wasn't ready, and I wasn't okay, and I couldn't talk to you, and it made me feel like something was broken in me."

Lita's eyes are so wide, and I TAKE a big, shaky breath.

"Like I couldn't be your best friend," I say. "Because I was so afraid. Because . . . I think they were right. I mean, I like boys . . . but I think I like girls too."

Have you ever come up from the bottom of the ocean in scuba gear after ditching your weight belt? Okay, neither have I, but I think it probably feels like this.

"Chicky," Lita says, her eyes shining. "I never would have asked you to talk about that before you were ready. Never, ever, ever." It's her turn to take a deep breath. "And I'm so glad you told me that, but I would have waited a million years for you to be ready. A hundred million."

I'm crying for real now, what Fresa calls "ugly crying." I take Lita's hand on the center console, and I don't cover my face. I want her to see me right now. She's earned it a hundred million times over.

"I know," I say. "But I felt like such a bad friend keeping it from you and—"

"Royce and his friends called me alien," Lita says, like it just burst out of her. "They . . . pushed me down . . . they yelled it over and over. I can't . . ." The tears spill over here, and she wipes them away. "I still can't talk about it all the way. So I know about secrets. And not being ready." She stops, because she's crying too. Only on her I'd never call it ugly crying. It's more like her sadness has reached terminal velocity.

"I didn't know," I say, a whisper between us in the car as the windows around us fog up with our laughing and crying and confessions. "Lita, I'm so sorry. I never would have . . . I didn't . . ."

She hugs me. I mean, really hugs me. Squeezing me as tight as she can, her cheek pressed against mine, her shooting star pjs smelling like the peppermint tea Bruja Lupe makes when Lita has a stomachache.

There's a glint in her eye that's not just tears, or taillights, or magic now. It's something a little sharper. It's the kind of look that got us out of bed one night to TP the Hudson family's house because Lita heard they gave their cat away when they moved.

Animals are part of the family, she'd said as she threw roll after roll.

That look used to terrify me, but tonight I'm not even sure it's enough.

"I'm going to win this pageant," she says. "For the scared girls we used to be."

The scared girls we used to be. It's the perfect thing to say.

"But first we have to go to a party," I say.

"Right." The Pontiac Space Station touches down. "The party."

When we open the doors, the boys are still standing there waiting for us, and it feels like it's been a hundred years, but it's only been about ten minutes. And everything is different, but it's better. It's so much better.

"Everyone okay?" Junior asks, and I think about how we must look ridiculous, tear streaked and smiling and glinting with determination all at once.

I look at Lita. She looks at me.

"We're at a party," she answers, and it's perfect.

"I say," says Cole. "No turning back now."

So we don't.

The four of us stand shoulder to shoulder, like explorers about to discover a new territory and claim it in the name of weird misfits everywhere.

"One small step for man . . . ," Junior says, and we walk across the lawn together.

Inside, my first thought is that I need to find somewhere to hide. These are the people I've been running from my whole life. But I'm with the recently crowned regional cornhole king, a jock who has been high-fived three times since we got through the door, and a girl who just might be the most talked about Miss Meteor contestant in fifty years.

Maybe things are changing.

"Okay," Lita says, rubbing her hands together, eyes narrowed like she's about to attempt a gymnastic floor routine. "What do we do?"

"It's just a party," Cole says with a shrug, slinging his good arm around her shoulder. "Just do whatever you'd . . ." He trails off then, as we look at him with identically blank expressions.

"Oh, wow, none of you have ever been to a party, have you?"

The blank looks persist.

"Okay come on, let's do a lap."

We follow Cole like very determined ducklings, getting the lay of the land. He gives us casual tips as we go, and I like him even more for not being condescending about it. I collect them like items for the lost and found at Selena's.

Don't stay in one place too long.

Always have something in your hand.

It's okay to pretend to see someone you know to get out of an annoying conversation.

But when Lita stops for the fifth time (this time to look at the Bradley family photo album) I can tell Cole is torn, and I pull him aside. He's not the only one with tips to hand out tonight.

"Mostly, you just go with it," I tell him.

"Sorry?"

I nod at Lita. "She's never gonna stay where you put her, she's never gonna do what you expect. You're never, ever gonna be able to predict what's next."

The way he smiles, like I'm instructing him on the care of something precious, tells me I'm right about him. The way he feels about her. The way he probably always has.

"But there's something about just going with it," I say, smiling at her affectionately as she shows Royce's naked baby photos to Amy Perkins. "You usually end up somewhere even better than you thought you would."

"Thanks, Chicky," he says, and we both flinch as Lita leans in close to an enormous decorative vase.

"Go ahead," I say, patting him on the arm in a way I hope isn't as awkward as it feels. He surprises me by taking my arm and pulling me into a hug that, even with only one arm, is warm and safe in a way that tells me I can do this, I can trust him with my favorite person in this world.

Besides, with the air finally clear between us, I can give Lita and Cole this night. Lita and I will have a billion more.

"Looks like you won't be bored, either," Cole says with a

meaningful eyebrow raise at Junior, who's trying not to look like he's waiting for me.

"Shut up," I mutter, but I can't help the smile that spreads slow like honey across my face. It's not a small thing, this camaraderie between Cole and me. It's just a little something more I always let Royce and Kendra keep me from. A little something more I'm taking back.

"Come on, Champ," I say, leaving Cole behind to slap Junior on the back. "Let's get into some trouble."

In the kitchen, there are a few people hanging around the beer pong table, and it gives me an idea. When you're on an alien planet, it's polite to show appreciation for their customs, right? And telling Lita everything, finally, has made me bold in a way I didn't think I'd ever be.

Bold enough for this. Maybe bold enough for anything.

"What are you doing?" Junior asks, as I grab two empty beer bottles and take them to the sink, filling them with water.

"Something I learned from Fresa," I say, which makes his eyebrows shoot up in alarm. "Here." I hand him one of the bottles, ignoring his utterly puzzled expression and turning back toward the game table.

"Hey, can I get in on this?" I ask, and two girls with long blond ponytails laugh.

"You?" one of them asks, and I shrug off my jacket.

"You?" Junior asks.

"Me."

They get out of the way, leaving me to face one of the lesser jocks. He's visibly drunk, swaying from foot to foot, his gaze hazy and unfocused on my face.

"Fill 'em up," I say, brandishing my beer bottle and giving Junior a shadow of a wink.

He's looking at me like he's never seen me before, and I kind of like it.

Just like Fresa said, no one notices I'm using water. They're all too drunk. So I throw three balls, getting more precise as I get a feel for the distance while my opponent loses coordination by the second. The blond girls are looking at me differently too.

"Last cup," I say, with four still sitting in front of me.

My final shot is a dagger, and Junior cheers the loudest of all.

The drunk jock stumbles off, swearing at his shoes. I stand on the chair one of the blond girls has just vacated and say in a voice that would make Cereza proud:

"And now! As the reigning queen of this table!" People are starting to stare. "I, Chicky Quintanilla, challenge hometown hero Junior Cortes to a game of no limits beer pong." I look at him, and my stomach flips over when he smiles. "Right here, right now," I say, only to him.

The room is quiet, like it's holding its breath. They're all waiting to see what's going to happen next. I'm on a chair, in the middle of a popular kids' rager, everyone is looking at me, and I'm okay. In fact, I'm better than okay.

"I accept your challenge," he says formally, reaching up to help me down off the chair. I ignore his hand, hopping down to land hard on both feet in front of him.

"Fill 'em up."

LITA

IT IS THE happiest and saddest thing all at once, Chicky and I having each other back. It's like the perfect fall weather day in Meteor, the one we only get once or twice in October, the one you have to make the most of because it never lasts before it gets hot again or cold for the winter.

Only worse. About one-thousand, eight-hundred, twenty-five times worse.

Because I've missed her in a way I had to ignore for every cactus birthday party, every time I've avoided Selena's when she was on shift, every time I saw her in the hallways, towering over me and half the girls in our grade.

I've missed her, and she's missed me, and we have each other back just in time for me to turn back into the stardust I used to be.

I push away the thought of my glimmering stomach and back. Tonight we are friends, and tonight I am on this Earth, and tonight Chicky told me something she's been working up to for so long. Something that's part of her, something that's hers.

Everything I noticed but didn't ask her about when we were younger. Her checking out a girl's jean skirt or a guy's hair. She's claimed it. Even if people like Kendra have made it unsafe to declare it, she has claimed it.

It dulls the places in me that ache when I think about the years we lost.

So does seeing Chicky with Junior, pretending to focus on throwing a ball into red plastic cups.

Even when Meteor lets me go, she will have Junior. She will have the friendship that's held between them for years, and the new thing growing out of it.

And she'll have Cole, who will probably understand the things she just told me better than any other straight guy in Meteor.

My eyelids feel damp and scratchy thinking about asking him to do this for me, to be a brother to Chicky, because I won't be here to be her fourth sister.

I should tell him about the stardust, about the sky taking me back. About how I had a chance if I had really done Miss Meteor right, but I lost it.

But as soon as I think of telling him about me vanishing into the night sky, my heart deflates, like the sad foil balloons they keep replacing around town, stars and Saturns and comets losing their helium and slumping toward the dirt.

I can feel him behind me, and I reach back for his hand. This feels like a world I will get lost in if I don't hold onto him.

Then a breath of flowery perfume hits me at the same time a French-manicured hand grabs my arm.

Sara, the pageant contestant who wore her aunt's vintage swimsuit.

She greets me with, "There you are!"

"Why are you talking to me?" I ask. "I'm the embarrassment of the Fiftieth-Anniversary Pageant."

"What are you talking about?" she asks.

"Did you not hear about my talent?"

She blows air through her lips, a *pfft* sound. "I would watch that ten more times over bleach-blond Dorothy Gale over there."

Her making fun of Kendra is so unexpected that I let her pull me out of the crowd in the living room and toward the hall.

We pass two boys from school yelling into each other's faces.

"It's Meteorite," one says. "Just ask my dad."

Even the festival signs don't agree. Half say Meteor, half Meteorite. And nobody but me ever wants to talk about the science behind the debate. No one can agree whether the town is named for the meteor as it streaked through the sky, or the meteorite it became when it struck the Earth.

Even the census paperwork here is inconsistent; we have to combine the recorded populations of "Meteor, New Mexico" and "Meteorite, New Mexico" to figure out how many people actually live here.

Should I bring up the science with these two? Break up a fight, make conversation, and maybe even impress a fellow contestant all at once?

"Your dad just wants a run at mayor," the second one says. "He'd call the town Hershey Bar if it helped him suck up to the city council."

"There's already a town called Hershey Bar, you dolt."

"Dolt? Did you get that one from your dad too?"

Yeah, the science may be beyond these two and their blood alcohol levels. They look like they're about to throw pretzel sticks at each other.

"Come on." Sara pulls me along. "We're late."

"Late to what?" I ask.

She opens the second door on the left. "Nobody told you?" She leads me into a bedroom that smells like perfume and Aqua Net and newly varnished nails.

Seven or eight pageant girls sit on the jacket-covered bed and sofa cushions thrown on the floor. The light from the bedside lamp shows the glitter in their hair and on their eyelids.

"Is this some kind of a secret pageant event?" I ask.

"You could say that," a girl with her hair in a messy bun says. She's pouring from dark-glass bottles into shot glasses, so slowly that the different-color layers stay separate.

"Secret from the ringers, anyway," another girl says, this

one with nails painted like the night sky, silver glitter on deep-blue polish.

"What are you wearing?" a girl with hair bright as pennies asks. "Did someone bring you here against your will?"

"No, I wanted to." I pull my pajama top closed over my tank top. "He just came in my bedroom window."

"He?" Sara nudges my shoulder.

"You have a he?" another girl asks.

"The guy with the broken arm," the one with the outer-space fingernails asks. "You all need to pay attention."

"Wait," I say. "After the talent competition, you all don't think I'm . . ."

They blink at me.

"A loser?" I ask.

They chime in with a chorus of *hell no* and *so you had stage fright, it happens to all of us* and *I bet the judges thought you were adorable.*

"And now," the redhead says, "we have a quorum."

"A quorum for what?" I ask as she pulls me down onto a sofa cushion next to her.

"Ladies"—the redhead hands us each a shot—"I call to order this year's gathering of the First Timers' Club!"

"What?" I look at Sara.

"We're making a new Miss Meteor tradition," she says. "This pageant is so crowded with girls whose mothers or sisters

298

or aunts ruled the competition that those of us who are the first in our families to enter are gathering together for a little liquid courage."

"Now, you do not have to drink." The girl with outer-space nails holds up an outer-space-polished finger. "Your participation is not mandatory. But your presence here is. You are hereby part of the sisterhood of unlikelies."

A flutter inside me tells me that beauty queens doing shots in a borrowed bedroom is something forbidden, against the rules, like sneaking off school grounds at lunchtime to visit the rock.

But like sneaking off school grounds at lunchtime, it feels like a rule worth breaking. Between all of us contestants, this is so much like a spell that it lures me. It's as magic as the sound of the few falling-leaf trees each November.

I tip back the shot with them, and everyone cheers.

It goes down hot, like accidentally swallowing mouthwash.

"How much alcohol is in this?" I ask. I've had little bits of wine and mezcal before, but nothing like these layered liqueurs.

"Don't worry," the redhead says. "Five shots or less and you'll still wake up pretty as Sleeping Beauty, three or less if you're a lightweight."

"And let's call you a lightweight just to be safe," Sara tells me.

Three or less.

So I take the next one with them, and it tastes not just like mouthwash but like chocolate and mint.

And the next one, sweet as vanilla and raspberries.

I slump across the sofa cushion.

Sara laughs. "Okay, we're cutting you off."

The room turns fuzzy, like seeing pool lights underwater. Or Christmas tree lights through a rain-blurred window on the few nights it rains in Meteor, New Mexico.

CHICKY

AT LEAST FIFTY people watch as I beat Junior Cortes at beer pong. I take the last shot with my eyes closed, because it's going to go in. It's just that kind of night.

Everything slows down after he drinks his last cup of "beer" and there are people jumping up and down and drunkenly shouting, ribbing him and congratulating me, but it's all just noise. The only real thing in the room is the way he's looking at me.

The way I'm looking back.

And I feel like maybe finally, finally coming clean—coming out—to Lita has unlocked something in me, something that's been building for a long time. And that something starts to crystalize, and I feel, in this moment, like maybe I do know Junior. Maybe I've finally figured out what I have.

Maybe it's time to decide what comes after knowing.

Even after liking . . .

"I got next!" shouts one of the twins from the final match, his red jacket unzipped, his hair disheveled. His cheeks are flushed, and he's drunk, and sure, it would be fun to beat him, but Junior already took care of that.

"Why would I play you when I already beat him?" I ask, a hand on my hip. "Seems like kind of a step down, doesn't it?"

"Oooooh!" goes the crowd, and two high fives are bestowed upon me by people I don't even know.

"Wanna get out of here?" I ask Junior, and his new smile has none of the suave, newly popular Junior in it. This one is just for me, and I feel the pull of it, tugging at all the places we've tied ourselves together these past five years.

"For sure," he says, and I slip my arm into his as we leave the noisy kitchen and all my new fans behind.

There's nowhere quiet in the entire Bradley house, and I don't see Lita and Cole anywhere, but I'm not worried. This is Cole's turf, and I trust him. And even the knowledge that Lita is here, and she knows who I am, and she's my friend, makes me feel safe in a way I've been missing for five years.

That safety is what makes me follow when Junior gestures to a sliding-glass door and the dark, velvety night beyond it. It's a little scary, another new world, but this time I think I'm ready for it.

There's a bite of fall in the air out here, and my sweatshirt is still on the kitchen chair. Junior notices before I even react, sliding off his own hoodie and holding it out like one of those guys in movies helping some fancy lady into her coat.

I let him, and his fingers brush my collarbones as he's drawing it around me, and it's nice, the feeling of him being close to me. It's more than nice.

"So," he asks, his smirk on full display even though its edges are softer tonight. "What's no limit beer pong?"

"Shut up!" I say. "Like I have any idea! I was just trying to sound cool."

"Well, you did," he says, his smile turning tender.

"Whatever," I say, but I'm smiling too.

"No, I'm serious," he says, something shifting as he moves a little closer. "You were kind of incredible in there." We're in the side yard, and I'm leaning against the house. The only light is coming from inside, and it feels like we're on our own little planet out here, just the two of us.

"Had to stop hiding eventually," I say, feeling suddenly shy at the thought of myself on that chair, shouting without fear like a true Quintanilla sister.

"I never got why you were hiding in the first place," he says, and it's quieter.

"Maybe the world wasn't ready for the real Chicky Quintanilla," I say, like it's a joke, but he doesn't laugh.

"Maybe it was. Maybe it is."

I want to want to, kiss him so much, and I swear I almost do, but it feels like everything is moving too fast all of a sudden, and I break eye contact, snuggling deeper into the sweatshirt that smells like him.

"Junior?" I ask, like there's anyone else out here.

"Yeah?"

"Who would you be, if you could be anyone?"

He smiles now, and instead of moving closer again, into that space that makes my heart beat funny and my hands get a little shaky, he leans against the wall beside me, our shoulders touching.

He's not pushing. He's keeping his promise.

The panicky feeling recedes, and I think this is perfect for now. Just this. But maybe I won't be afraid of what's next for very much longer.

While he's thinking, I notice his shoulders, and the line of his jaw, and the way there's still a little bit of that awkward middle school boy left in his cheeks. I notice the way he catches every speck of light, how it reflects off the sleek crow-black of his hair until he glows like he can't possibly be real.

I've never looked at him like this before, and he must feel it, because he looks back—really looks, like he wants to memorize my slightly crooked teeth and the blunt line of my kitchen-scissor haircut and the freckles just a single shade darker than my cinnamon skin.

"I think," he begins, not looking away. His breath smells clean and sharp, like I imagine snow on pine trees might. "If I could be absolutely anyone . . ."

Inside, something—or someone—crashes loudly into something or someone else. The door slides open, and three people run out, giggling into the dark yard.

The spell we've woven in this little quiet corner breaks, but it breaks softly, like there's something left of it. Our shoulders are still touching.

"You tell me first," he says, and in the light from the doorway I think he might be blushing.

LITA

FIVE SHOTS IN—well, three for me, since I skipped two rounds on Sara's advice—the First Timers' Club spills into the hall and back into the party. We hug each other goodbye until tomorrow, and as Sara calls after me, "Do you want somebody to walk around with? I'm a little worried about you," I'm already weaving into the crowd.

First I look for a sink. Bathroom, kitchen, laundry room, I don't care, I just need to splash some water onto my face to make the world less blurry.

I wander through a door that I think might be the laundry room.

It is.

But a blond girl stands between me and the sink, her shoulders heaving.

She spins around.

"Kendra?" I ask.

Within a second, she recovers, and in the dark room I see her crossing her arms and straightening up.

"What do you want?" she asks.

I take a step into the room. "Are you okay?"

She shakes her head, which I know is supposed to be her clearing away the crying, but it looks like a no.

"You know, I was actually kind of impressed," she says. "How you decided that jackass just wasn't worth a response."

I wobble in the space of the words.

I am officially drunk.

Well, check that off the list of Earth experiences.

I must be drunk.

Because it sounds like Kendra Kendall just complimented me.

Just in case I'm right, I say, "Thank you."

"People are jerks," she says, and even under her careless laugh I hear what's left of her crying. "You know that."

I can't help laughing with her. "Yeah. I do."

The laugh drains out of her. "Then why do you want Cole to be like you and Chicky?" she asks.

Her saying Chicky's name the way she does, like a brand of clothing she would never be caught wearing, makes me want a throw a capful of detergent on Kendra's dress. Sure, it wouldn't do anything but pretreat any drink stains, but the thought of the sticky mess on that pretty patterned fabric is too satisfying not to revel in for a minute. For me. For Chicky. For everyone like us.

"Think about if you really want him to be the same kind of loser as you," Kendra says.

I'm not drunk enough not to get it.

Hanging around with a girl like me makes things harder for a guy like Cole.

That word rings back through my head.

Alien. Alien. Alien . . .

Kendra eyes me in a way that makes me feel as small as a postage stamp. "Drink some water." She pushes me out the laundry room door. "You look awful."

The world is still blurry and shiny and wobbly as I wander back toward the living room.

"You seem . . . happy," Royce Bradley's voice says.

I turn around to find the rest of Royce Bradley.

Royce Bradley, who drove Chicky further into the closet, and me into curling up in a ball on a locker room floor.

And the guy who, at this moment, thinks I look . . . happy?

"So you and Kendall, huh?" Royce asks.

"Huh?" I ask. I don't mean to echo his last word, but I do.

"I'm just saying," Royce says. "If you ever want a real man."

A beer bottle rolls across the floor. I try to kick it at Royce's feet but end up stumbling over it.

"Excuse me?" I ask.

"What, do I need to give you an anatomy lesson?" Royce says.

I know where this is going, and I hate it already. Royce

Bradley may the last person on this planet I would ever want an anatomy lesson from.

Royce puts his hand on my arm. It's the exact place Cole has touched me probably twenty times. It's the spot on my arm Chicky grabbed when we were scrambling into the back seat of Junior's car. I want her grasp, and Cole's touch, on that spot, not Royce's.

But Royce's grip is hard enough to bury the feeling of their hands.

My stomach tightens.

Alien.

Alien.

Alien.

Royce Bradley has no business with my body, and no business commenting on anyone else's.

This body I'm in, this short, brown-skinned body, is mine. It's mine the same way Cole's body is his.

I live here, on this planet. Maybe it's just for now. And maybe I'm made of star-stuff that flew here from light-years away, but I am a girl who stands in this space.

I am a girl with a body of my own, and three friends who showed me their hearts in the hollow of a crater.

And I am not letting Royce Bradley talk about any of them like this.

Whatever I had left in me to withstand being close to Royce, it's burning up with every second his hand stays on me.

And in this moment, I am done. With Royce and his friends thinking they can push around Chicky and Junior and me and everyone like us. With them thinking they can make the kind of jokes they make about Cole and still say they're his friends.

"Let go of me, Royce," I say, my voice steadier than it's ever been with him.

Royce gives a grinning nod. "You know I have equipment Kendall doesn't have."

I grab his arm for leverage, as hard as he once grabbed mine, and I knee him right in his equipment.

The sound Royce makes is the same sound Bruja Lupe's vacuum cleaner makes when I accidentally trip over the cord and cut the power.

He stumbles into a side table, but I don't stay around to watch.

When I look up, Cole's in the hallway between the door and the kitchen. He looks like he got there a second earlier, a what-just-happened look on his face. I sink into the relief of knowing he didn't hear Royce talking.

On the way to the doorway, I trip, because the world is still blurry and nothing quite stays where it is. I don't so much fall as melt toward the ground. First I try to stay up and then I don't; the carpet looks nice, and I think I'd like to lie down on it to see how it feels.

From here, the lights set into the ceiling look like tiny suns. My classmates stepping around me are giants, and I am a tiny mushroom person looking up at them. I laugh at all of it, light-bulb suns and giants and a mushroom girl growing out of the carpet, and Royce still doubled over, which right now feels like the funniest thing in the world.

Just as I'm considering whether to flail my limbs and make a carpet angel—I've always wanted to make a snow angel, but we don't get any snow here—I feel Cole's hand on my arm. The light way his grip lands, the warmth of it, blots out the memory of Royce grabbing onto me.

"Are you okay?" Cole crouches next to me. "I was looking around for you."

"Just beauty queens and beauty shots," I say. "Or something like that."

He laughs, running a hand over his face like he's trying to wake himself up. "Oh, they're gonna kill me. They're actually gonna kill me."

"The beauty queens?" I ask.

"Chicky's sisters."

"No, they won't, they're nice," I say. "They're nicer than everyone thinks."

"Nice goes out the window during pageant week." Cole offers me his hand. "You know that by now."

I'm not done with my carpet angel, but I let him help me up before my classmates trip over my wings.

I'm still stumbling, so Cole gets me to lean on him.

"We have got to stop meeting like this," he says.

311

I may be blurry with those three shots, but I still laugh, catching the joke, the memory of me and Cereza pulling him up after I crashed into him.

Kendra pauses next to us. "Wow."

Cole sighs. "Can we forgo your running commentary for once?"

"Just saying"—she raises her cup like she's toasting us—"classy girl you've got there."

Whatever moment of understanding we had a few minutes ago, apparently Kendra threw it down the laundry room sink.

"You know what?" Cole holds onto me tighter, but I don't think he knows he's doing it.

It feels good for him to hold me that tight. Or it would feel good if I wasn't so worried about how Kendra is still a giant like everyone else and I'm still a mushroom.

"You lost your right to review my life a long time ago," Cole says. "But if you had it, you gave it up the minute you messed with a family's business. That's how they make a living, Kendra. I'd think you of all people . . ."

He stops. Another slow breath. And even though I don't know what words he almost just said, I think of the red-lettered bills in the Kendalls' kitchen drawer.

Kendra should know better.

"Small towns talk." Kendra gives a delicate shrug. "I might have said a few things. What everyone did with them isn't my fault."

"You got in everyone's head. It's what you do."

Kendra tosses her curling-iron curls, and I can see the gesture covering up a flinch.

A flinch that makes her and Cole into a sister and brother who look more alike than I've ever noticed.

"I have done nothing but support you, Cole," she says.

"Your medal's in the mail," Cole says. "You don't get a free pass on all the other shit you do to try to make everyone around you smaller than you."

Smaller than you.

I wonder if he's ever been on the floor, too, feeling as small as a mushroom.

"You can't keep using me, Kendra," Cole says. "I'm not some prop to make your point. I'm not here to make your life a better story."

The feeling of Cole's arm around my waist drifts, like we are touching each other underwater.

"You have no idea what I do for you," Kendra says. "Do you know how many times I've explained who you are to anyone who asks? For like three years I was the Cole encyclopedia. And any time anyone asked, I always answered so you didn't have to."

"Yeah, you answered in the same breath you were calling someone else a dyke," Cole said. "Why am I the exception, Kendra? How the hell would you treat me if I wasn't your brother?"

I couldn't talk right now if I wanted to.

313

He just said it. He actually said the thing I've been wondering about Kendra and Cole for years.

How would you treat me if I wasn't your brother?

Kendra looks away, pursing her lips. I wish I didn't see the shininess in her eyes, but I do.

"You wanna talk to everyone about me so I won't," Cole says.

"Because every time you make a joke about the kind of stuff you do, it just makes people uncomfortable," Kendra says.

"The kind of stuff I do?" he asks. "You mean like packing?" He hits the last word as loudly as if he were making an announcement to the room. "Everybody hear that?" Now he really is. "Packing. We're talking about packing."

He almost sings out the word, and I try not to laugh. Especially not now that I know what it means.

It has nothing to do with going on a trip.

Looking it up left my cheeks flushed enough that Bruja Lupe asked what I was doing. I made something up about a school project on desert moths and then went to take a shower.

"You don't have to do this," Kendra says, still flinching. "No one would know. You look normal."

Cole tenses. "Normal."

"It's like you want everyone to know."

"Maybe I do!" He's almost yelling now. If it weren't for the fact that everyone has to yell their conversations at a party this loud, everyone would be staring. "Maybe I'm sick of trying to be exactly what this town wants me to be." Then he sighs, and his voice gets softer. "Maybe I even want to help make it easier for someone else to be who they are too."

Kendra's mouth pauses half open, not shocked, but thinking, like she hasn't decided whether she's gonna say anything back.

Then she does, her voice a whisper. "But why do you want to throw it in everyone's face?"

"Why do you care if I do?" Cole asks, matching her whisper.

"Because you're my brother, and I don't want the world messing with you, okay?" Kendra says.

Not whispering. Like the words got loose and broke out of her.

"And your new friends aren't helping." Kendra's eyes flash to mine, just for a second, before going back to her brother. "Is this what you want? For people to think you're nothing? Because that's what they will think if you spend all your time with the rejects."

Even in the noise of the party, the silence between Cole and Kendra is so sharp I feel like if I reached between them I'd cut my hand on it.

"My friends are only rejects because people like you and your friends decided you get to do the rejecting," Cole says.

In the second stretch of silence I see a glint of something in Kendra's meanness. What I saw a little of in the laundry room gets clearer.

Kendra was never as awful to me as she was to Chicky, not before this week. And it's not because I am one more pageant contestant she has to step over to claim her title.

Kendra Kendall hates me because she thinks I am dragging her brother down. And now that I've been putting all my strangeness and otherness on display, now that Cole has become just as much Team Quintanilla-Perez as he is Team Kendall, she's afraid it will come off on him like glitter.

Royce's voice breaks in.

"Kendall," he calls after Cole. The vacuum-cleaner undertone is mostly but not all gone.

Cole tips his head back and groans, like you do when the bell at the end of the day rings but the teacher wants you to stay put for just a few minutes until you get through this section.

"You're really gonna blow us all off?" Royce catches up, and I realize it's not just me and Cole. Chicky and Junior are here now too. Royce looks at them. "For Picasso and Ring Pop"—then at me—"and this bitch?"

"I'm not a bitch," I say.

Everyone looks at me.

Cole pauses, mouth open, like he was about to say something before I did.

The words I couldn't say on the floor of the locker room are stuck in my throat.

Royce and his friends ripped my fake crown off my head, some of my hair coming with it.

316

They put those stupid antennae on me.

They yelled "Alien, alien, alien" at me because of how weird, how brown, how other, I was to them. Because they thought it was funny, and because they thought it would break me down.

But I won't wear any of it tonight.

Maybe Cole and Chicky and Junior weren't there the day it happened. But they're here now, and having them here means that whatever words I say now, I'm not saying them alone on a locker room floor.

I look right at Royce. "I'm not an alien either," I say. "Or whatever you wanna call me. And my friends are not whatever you wanna call them."

"Oh, I'm sorry. I forgot your full title, didn't I?" Royce fake bows, stumbling from all the beer. "Forgive me. Queen Alien Bitch."

Cole shakes his head, almost smiling down at the carpet. And that look tells me he's had it. He's done. I don't know if that just happened or he just now realized it, but he's had enough.

I understand this about a half second before Cole throws a punch into Royce Bradley's face.

CHICKY

I DON'T GET the chance to tell Junior the sort of embarrassing truth: that if I could be anyone, I'd be the real Selena Quintanilla.

Not the part where she was tragically murdered before her time, obviously, but the talent, and the true love, and the adoration, and the perfect, shiny confidence.

I don't get the chance to tell him, because at that moment two jocks push through the doorway talking loudly to each other like we're not even here.

"Did you see that? That spacey scuba suit girl kneed Royce in the balls!"

"I know! She is so wasted!"

"It looked like Cole and Royce were about to get into it too. What, is Kendall dating that freak?"

"I don't know, man, but we better get outta here before the cops show up. What a party!" They literally high-five.

"Excuse me?" I say, my voice sliding up about four octaves over those two words alone. There's no way I'm letting these idiots leave without an explanation.

"Oh, hey, Beer Pong," says the other one.

"Shut up, ugh. Lita's drunk? What's going on?" Even as I'm brushing off the new nickname, I can't deny it's a hell of a lot better than Ring Pop.

"Go see for yourself," the guy says with a laugh, gesturing through the screen door at a writhing mass of bodies gathering around the violence like vultures.

"Oh my God," I groan as they walk away, still laughing. "My sisters are going to kill me."

We barely make it inside in time to hear Royce use our charming nicknames in the same sentence. Lita is clearly drunk, giggling and swaying a little in my peripheral vision as we all watch Cole's good fist meet Royce's face. From beside them, Kendra screams, exposing the electric Jell-O blue of the inside of her mouth.

"Lita!" I yell, worried she's gonna fall and get trampled, but unable to look away from Royce, who's clutching his rapidly purpling face.

I have the immediate and intense desire to high-five Cole—a desire only made stronger when he gets to Lita, steadying her on her feet.

"I'll help him," Junior says before I ask, smiling and shaking his head as he runs up to take Lita's other arm.

I mean to follow, but Royce is clutching his face, and I'm so annoyed that I can't enjoy this moment. How long have I been wanting someone to punch Royce in the face?

"Dude!" he calls after Cole. "You don't have to slum it like this! *You're* not a freak!"

But Cole doesn't even turn. Clearly Royce's bruising jaw was the last remark he had to make on the subject. He and Junior are helping Lita toward the door, and I should follow them. I should. But there's something swelling in my chest, and I've never felt more like a Quintanilla than I do when I get between Royce and my friends, blocking his way.

"Fuck you, Royce," I say, too quietly, and to his shoes instead of his face, but still, people around us go quiet to listen.

"Oh good, Ring Pop, here to avenge her girlfriend the crazy alien. What do you want, loser? Because I know it ain't this." He reaches for his junk in a familiar gesture, and when he winces from the pain I let myself laugh.

On their way to the door, Junior, Cole, and Lita pause, watching.

"You're pathetic, you know that, right?" I ask him, my voice a little louder now, trying to channel Fresa during her marathon porch fights with Berto. "High school is gonna be over in a year for you, Royce, and then what? No one to pick on, no one to humiliate. How are you gonna make yourself feel better about being a jerk who thinks a covenant is a land mass?"

"Oh, so you're a dyke and a bitch!" he says, looking around for the high fives that usually materialize every time he speaks.

This time though, they don't come. Everyone's looking at me, but I'm finally—finally—looking at Royce. Not his shoes, or his left knee, or the space over his right shoulder, but right square in his mean little eyes.

"Bashing people for who they like is so sad it's barely even insulting," I say, every time I didn't say these words adding up, giving weight to what I'm saying now.

"Oh! So you admit it, huh? Lesbo?"

He's drunk, and his face is sweaty and shiny. His breath is bad, I can smell it from here. Beer and something sour. The look in his eyes is desperate, and I wish I would have looked into them like this a long time ago. Maybe then I would have known there was nothing to be afraid of.

It's so obvious now, with everything that's happened. Royce and Kendra were never the real obstacle. They're jerks, but they never had that power. It was always me. Me, figuring out who I am, and how not to be afraid to let them, or anyone else, see it.

But I don't feel afraid now.

Everyone is still staring at me, waiting for me to answer. It's like an out-of-body experience. My realization prickles on my skin, and I glance over to meet Lita's eyes. They're a little blurry and unfocused, but she smiles at me from between Junior and Cole. No matter what happens tonight, I have my best friend back, and a boy who might be more, and another boy who really gets it.

I'm a Quintanilla, and my friends are here. I can do anything.

And so, I do.

"Yeah, Royce, when we were in fourth grade I gave Allison Davis a Ring Pop. That's not the weird part, though. What's weird is how long you guys have been obsessing over it. Maybe you're jealous, is that it? That I had game when I was nine and you still don't?"

"She fucking admitted it!" he says, spit flying from his mouth as he laughs like a braying donkey. "Ring Pop the dyke and her lesbo lover the alien bit—"

"Lita isn't a lesbian," I say, finally facing my fear head on, once and for all. "And I'm not a dyke." I pause, taking a steadying breath. Am I really gonna do this?

Hell yeah I am. But first, I turn to look Kendra in the eye.

"I'm pansexual, okay? And I don't care who knows, so both of you, get some new material."

The room is silent, like the entire sophomore and junior classes—most of whom were there on the bus in fourth grade— have turned briefly to stone. Which makes me the snake-haired, coming-out Medusa. And I've never been so happy to be anything.

I did it, I think over and over. *I did it, I did it, I did it.*

"You're what?" Royce asks, with that look on his face that

says he's confused and pissed off about it. "What kind of freak-ass thing . . ."

Around him, most of the rest of them seem equally confused, but more curious than angry. I'm trying to figure out how to explain it through my haze of relief, but Cole is calling out from across the room, a proud smile playing around the corners of his mouth even as he hangs on to Lita for dear life.

"Pansexual," he recites. "Of, relating to, or characterized by sexual desire or attraction that is not limited to people of a particular gender identity or sexual orientation."

I just shrug, my own smile spreading slow like honey as I turn back to Royce. "You heard him."

Royce seems to have been robbed of words, and beside him Kendra is slack-jawed, equally mute. By my reveal, or by her brother sticking up for me, I don't know. And I don't really care. Because for the first time ever, I realize: My secret was always their strength. Now that I have nothing to hide, they have no power. And so I don't have to wait for the rest of them to react. For the first time, I don't care what they think.

"I'd kick you in the balls right now, or punch you," I say. "But my *friends* already took care of that."

With a hair flip that would make Cereza proud, I cross the room to join said friends, who look more than ready to leave this alien landscape and head for home.

"Come on, babe," Royce says to Kendra, who's perched on the counter, her eyes darting from Cole to Royce and back again. "We're champions. We don't need this shit."

I want to say Royce isn't the real champion, but enough people's eyes slide Junior's way that I realize I don't have to. That legend is already making itself.

And Kendra still hasn't moved.

"Babe, come on," Royce says, louder now, his face going purple and splotchy.

But Kendra doesn't obey the command. She sets down her red cup on the counter and pushes past us into the night alone, without even looking at him.

"You okay?" Cole asks her back, and she waves a hand. One of her girlfriends—the one who inadvertently told me about Lita's scuba suit, I think—follows her out, and Cole grabs her arm.

"She doesn't drive, got it?"

"Duh," the girl says with an eye roll, and disappears after Kendra yelling, "Bitch, wait up!" as her heels sink into the Bradley lawn.

We all laugh, even Cole, as we turn the other way, supporting Lita as we head for our space shuttle, and home.

When we get there, Lita is still giggling, but she reaches for my hand and squeezes, letting Junior's arm fall. "You okay?" she asks, and it's so cute that she sounds just like Cole.

"Actually, yeah." I smile and squeeze her hand back.

When she lets go, Cole nods in that calm way of his, extending his bruised fist, which I bump lightly with my own.

I take a breath before turning to Junior, whose eyes are wide, and I wonder for half a second if this changes anything for him, if it'll make him feel differently about me.

About us.

But before the feeling can even take root, he grabs me in a hug so tight my feet actually come off the ground.

"I am so proud of you," he says into my hair. I'm glad no one can see my face, because I honestly tear up a little.

When we break apart, Lita is unbuttoning the rainbow buttons of her pajama top to reveal a matching tank top, and bands of shifting, shining sparkle wrapping around her arms.

It looks like part of her, otherworldly and somehow still grounded to Earth. They look like her eyes when a comet streaks by, or the rock when it reflects her rainbow shoelaces. And I'm remembering so many things, so many little things adding up over a lifetime. Things I didn't look too closely at because I was afraid to make us bigger freaks than this town already thought we were.

But maybe I've known for a long time that there was more to that story of a meteor hitting the Earth fifty years ago than just history. That Lita wasn't just a prop in Bruja Lupe's curas. Maybe if I'd let myself understand us sooner, let myself believe in us, we could have had one less secret between us.

Tonight, though, we're done with secrets. Lita isn't hiding any more than I am. She's trusting us with this. With her. With all of her.

"Does anyone actually know how she got drunk?" I ask, coming back to earth.

Because tomorrow is the biggest day of this pageant—maybe of our lives—and Lita is going to be as hungover as Uva after Fresa gave her strawberry wine on a camping trip last year. We're not all triumph and starshine. We're also in very big trouble.

And even though Royce and Kendra are (figuratively and literally) in the rearview mirror, I have never wanted to win this pageant more. It's time to move past the secrets and the fear. It's time to let this town see who we really are.

Cole sticks his head out the window from where he's climbed in beside Lita and is carefully brushing her disheveled hair off her face. "All she'll say is that telling me would be betraying a sacred covenant."

"Of course," I mumble, wondering if we'll ever get the real story. "Covenants seem to be a theme of the evening."

I wonder if we should get her coffee, or water, or one of the greasy things Cereza eats with her sunglasses on after a night out with her nursing school friends, but it's no use. What she really needs is about twenty-four straight hours of water and sleep—which, considering she needs to be in an evening gown on a stage in about fifteen hours from right now, doesn't seem likely.

"Take us to my house," I say, smiling at her. "Bruja Lupe's probably still awake, and if you think my sisters are scary . . ."

Sitting shotgun as Junior starts the car, I feel different. Lita is my friend again, my real friend. The kind we should have been to each other all along. Junior is smiling at me, his hand inches away from mine, and even though I don't grab it, I could. And I think I'll be ready to soon.

More than that, this town knows who the real Chicky Quintanilla is at last, and my friends know, and I'm okay with whatever comes next.

Lita sticks her rainbow pajama top out the window as we drive away, past the party and all the kids still drinking on the lawn. As it catches the wind, she waves it like a flag, the orange streetlights of South Meteor reflecting and refracting off her star-stuff as she shouts *love is love is love is love* over and over until it starts to sound like a song.

I'm not sure, because I don't have a ton of experience with protracted bouts of smiling, but I think my smile is actually big enough to get stuck like this.

LITA

MY EYELASHES HURT.

I feel it before I open my eyes, like a thousand tiny lightning strikes stabbing into my brain. But it's an ache I can revel in, because it means I'm still here, a girl on this planet.

And it means last night happened. Even if the sky takes me back, last night happened.

I shift my weight and feel the poke of Chicky's knee. We're in her and Uva's bedroom, sharing her bed like we used to during sleepovers. She'd show me Junior's latest drawings. We'd make microwave popcorn, then make it better with chili powder and garlic. We'd eat too much of the Halloween candy we stockpiled each October.

But the sugar headaches Chicky and I got after eating too much sour candy didn't even come close to this.

My whole forehead throbs as I open my eyes.

It throbs worse when I realize all three of Chicky's sisters are standing over us.

I gently elbow Chicky. She groans halfway awake.

She opens her eyes, sees Cereza, Uva, and Fresa craned over us with their hands on their hips, and she startles the rest of the way awake.

Fresa almost wrings her hands. "What have you done?"

Uva studies me, concerned. "Has she ever had a drink before?"

"Did you get enough water into her last night?" Cereza pulls on my eyelids to get a better look at my eyes.

I whimper.

"Both of you"—Fresa pulls us out of bed—"shower. Lita first. We need all the time with her we can get."

"It's six in the morning." Chicky double-checks the orange-and-yellow sunrise in the window. "Do you really need all day to get her ready?"

"You tell me." Fresa points at me, and I can feel in the roots of my hair how I must look. Hair fluffed out not from teasing but from being slept on. Lips and teeth that haven't seen Vaseline in thirty-six hours (I think I even have a toothpaste smudge on my cheek from sloppily brushing my teeth last night). And wrinkled pajamas; even the shooting stars probably look a little sleepy.

"Drink up." Uva shoves cups of coffee at both me and Chicky. "Even stronger than we make it at Selena's."

I locate one shoe (under Chicky's bed) and then the other (next to Uva's dresser).

"I'm sorry, are you under the impression you're leaving?" Fresa asks. "You need a lifetime of tweezing, curling, and highlighting. Not to mention some serious moisturizing to undo last night."

"I'll be right back, I promise. And it'll be worth it, I promise."

"That doesn't sound good," Uva mutters.

I look at Chicky. "Could I borrow . . ."

She's already throwing a pair of jeans at me.

I grab them out of the air. "Thanks."

She grins at me.

She grins again when I notice they're already cuffed up enough for me that they won't drag.

I wanna tell her that watching her declare who she is, as sure as if she was shouting her own name, made me prouder than when we ran through the desert making spaceship sounds.

I wanna tell her that the reason Kendra calls her any name she can think of is the same reason she flinches when Cole makes jokes about what's in his jeans. Their fierce pride, their fearlessness, the way they own everything they are, scares her. It's true and frightening in its beauty, flaring bright as the sun over Meteor.

If I have to leave this planet, I want to do it while being like my friends.

I'm going to make everything I can of it.

The jeans Chicky lends me are loose on me, and no doubt baggy on her. Probably the only ones she owns that fit the way I'm bigger in the hips and thighs and butt than she is. She knew, in the split-second before I even asked.

I'm still buttoning the fly as I run out of the Quintanilla house.

I run through town, catching little whispers. Even though my forehead feels both too heavy and too empty, and even though my body feels no more coordinated than the spinning stars on my mobile, I have to try not to smile. Meteor is already chattering about the mysterious appearing of otherworldly visitors and the rock formation they left behind as their coded message. (Score one for our rock formations and buzzing flying saucer sounds.) Any motel rooms that were open have booked up. The souvenir shops and the Meteor Meteorite Museum gift counter are scrambling to restock. Tourists are complaining about lack of parking because of a new crowd driving out here to see for themselves.

And they'll all have to eat somewhere tonight. Hopefully the chrome marvel that is Selena's Diner.

I keep running, knowing that Fresa is waiting with her tweezers. This morning, I may have new stardust climbing down my arms—I can feel it under my pajama shirt—but I'm finishing this pageant. That means getting the evening gown I borrowed from Bruja Lupe's closet.

331

Bruja Lupe doesn't even know I took it, a long-sleeved, floor-length number that, yes, kinda drags on me, but that will hide my stardust. And it means I'll have a little of Bruja Lupe with me up on that stage.

Fresa is actually tapping her foot when I get back, out of breath, hair fluffed around my face.

I present the dry-cleaning-bag-covered hanger. "Voilà!"

Fresa shrieks like she's seen a spider.

"What"—Cereza is staring in horror—"is this?"

I slump a little. "My evening gown. For tonight."

Chicky is trying not to laugh.

Uva takes the bag. Through the clear plastic, the dress's sateen flashes. Tone-on-tone embroidery thickens the deep olive, and thin, cylindrical gold beads speckle the skirt. The dress Bruja Lupe wore to officiate Clover Flores's wedding ten years ago.

"What?" I ask. "It tells the judges I'm sophisticated."

"It tells the judges you want to be the girlfriend of a lounge singer!" Fresa says.

"Fresa!" Cereza says.

"What I think Fresa means is"—Uva cuts Fresa a look of *this better be what you mean*—"it doesn't exactly suit you. It doesn't seem like something you'd really wear."

"Oh, come on," I say. "It is not that bad."

"Yeah, if you're forty-five," Chicky says. "But on you?"

My stomach sinks.

I study the crisp line of the dress's shoulders, the pencil skirt, the matching shrug jacket. It's a piece Bruja Lupe made look as glamorous as an old magazine page. But Uva's right. It would never have a home among my blue skirts and pink sneakers and cat-ear sweatshirt. It would never look at home on my soft, rounded body.

I hadn't thought of that until now. All I'd thought about is whether it might belong on a stage.

I'd just considered the dress. I hadn't so much thought of me in it.

"You are not putting the miracle we're about to work on you today"—Fresa gestures at my hair and face—"into that." She points at the dress. "How are we gonna get her something else in an hour?"

"Do you have anything that might work?" Uva asks Fresa and Cereza.

"Do you *think* we have anything that'll work? She's like four feet tall but also almost as uncoordinated as Chicky! She'll trip off the stage."

"Hey!" Chicky and I say in unison.

"Is Goodwill even open?" Uva asks.

"Do you think Mom has something she can borrow?" Cereza asks.

"Mom's taller than you," Fresa says. "Good luck."

Uva picks up a phone.

"Who are you calling?" Fresa almost shrieks it.

"Our spy," Uva says.

"Who?" Fresa says.

Cereza nods. "Put him on speaker."

"WHO?" Fresa asks.

Uva doesn't answer. She just lets the call go through.

Chicky seems to be enjoying Fresa's annoyance. I just watch them.

"Hey, Cole," she says. "It's Uva."

"Oh, hell no," Fresa says. "He's a boy! He doesn't know about this stuff!"

"Fresa," Cole's voice says through the fuzzy speakerphone, in a voice that means business enough that Fresa goes quiet. "I once had to help my sister spray-glue her swimsuit to her ass."

All three remaining Quintanilla sisters tilt their faces to Fresa.

Fresa purses her lips. "Yeah, he's good."

Uva looks back at the phone. "Do you have anyone short in your family?" she asks.

"Uh, why?" Cole asks.

"Our girl is planning on wearing the worst evening dress to ever grace the Miss Meteor stage," Uva says.

"Hey!" I object. "Bruja Lupe wore it!"

"Bruja Lupe is half a foot taller and decades older than you," Cereza says.

"We'd lend her something," Uva goes on, "but she'd trip on it, and we can't hem anything in time."

"Yeah, I can probably find something," Cole says. "Mid-shin length was big in my grandmother's time, that might work on her."

"You can't ask him to do that," I tell Uva.

"Too late," Cole says. "I'm already doing it."

CHICKY

DID YOU EVER hear the one about the girl who woke up after two hours of sleep, already surrounded by three angry, curling-iron-bearing harpies?

Me either. But I hear it doesn't end well.

"Look," I say, but Cereza holds up a hand.

"Don't even," she says. "It doesn't matter."

"Do you think there's any chance she's coming back?" Uva asks.

"She'll be back," I say confidently. We've come this far, and after last night I know she wouldn't abandon this. "Just . . . I'm not sure when . . . or in what state?" I try to smile. Fresa grabs my hand and pulls me, my boy boxers, and last night's tank top to my feet.

"Before we start torturing you," Cereza says. "We heard about your performance at the party last night. What you said to Royce and Kendra and everyone."

336

I take a deep breath. "And?"

"And we're proud of you, hermanita."

"We hate you for *this*," Fresa clarifies, gesturing around at the current state of things. "But *that* was pretty rad."

Uva steps forward and hugs me, and I honestly think this must be a dream until Mom and Dad walk in.

"Oh, are we talking about your sister schooling the town bully and planting a rainbow flag in the nearly barren soil of rural New Mexico?"

"Dad, don't say 'schooling' please." Fresa rolls her eyes. "But yes," she adds.

I look at my parents with something between terror and hopefulness, but the terror doesn't turn out to be necessary. "We love you, Mija," my mom says, pulling me into a hug. While I'm there, Dad ruffles my already-beyond-hope hair.

"You guys aren't, like, mad? You don't think I'm a weirdo?"

"Honey, we're not even surprised," Dad says, and Mom lets go of me to whack his arm. "I mean, at first I didn't know what the word meant. I thought maybe we'd left you alone in the kitchen to wash the skillets too many times and . . ."

"Dad!" Cereza yelps, horrified, but I'm laughing. One of those deep, belly things that starts low and builds and lasts for an hour. It's relief and it's love and it's everything I couldn't admit to myself I needed.

"Chicky," my mom is saying now, tears in her eyes, "you've never been one to truly hide how you feel, no matter how hard you try. You've just been getting braver, and you finally felt ready to trust yourself. That's an important thing, and you should be so proud."

"Plus," says Fresa, "being pan was never what made you a weirdo."

She smiles, though, and we're all together, and they're looking at me with all their different kinds of love, and I remember Lita shouting *love is love is love* out the window last night, and I think things probably couldn't get any better.

Except maybe if Cereza would wear less perfume, because the smell of it is making my head hurt.

It's a mark of our first family moment in ages that I don't tell her this.

"Anyway," Mom says, wiping at her eyes. "No work today. Your father and I have some things to get ready for tonight, but here . . ." She pulls three twenty-dollar bills out of her wallet and hands them to me. "This is for you girls. Go down to the street fair and have some fun today, just be at the diner by six for the dinner rush. I think it's gonna be a little hectic tonight . . ." She smiles in an enigmatic way before she and Dad leave the room together.

"Oh, and stick together," Dad clarifies. "Or we're taking the money back."

We all pretend to be annoyed, but I know my sisters well enough to know they're not dreading this. And surprisingly, neither am I.

338

"Wait," I say as we leave the house. "What did she mean it's gonna be a little hectic tonight?"

"Oh, you'll see . . . ," Cereza says, and her smile looks exactly like Mom's.

And I do.

The streets of downtown Meteor are absolutely packed, like, way more than I would have expected even for the final day of the pageant. "What's going on?" I ask, wide-eyed gawking at the news crews, and the crowds, and yes, *all* the tinfoil hats.

"Oh right, you were sleeping it off," Cereza says with a smirk.

"Yes," I interrupt. "Sleeping off my water. For two hours. Until six o'clock in the morning."

"Anyway," she says, waving a hand to stop me. "A ridiculous rock formation showed up in the crater last night. They're calling it the Second Miracle of Meteor."

Something jolts in my stomach as I remember the four of us, Junior's design that we burned with a Bic lighter as soon as we finished it, Lita and I making otherworldly sounds until the tourists believed in the beyond and all its inhabitants.

"What?" I say, hoping my fake surprise isn't too overdone. "When?"

"Probably around the time your best friend was getting drunk enough to ruin our pageant hopes, and you were playing beer pong with the cornhole champion," Uva says. "Or thereabouts."

"Right," I say, a little sheepish. "So, what's up with all this?"

"A local news station picked it up this morning when someone who lives out there called in a tip, and it's just sort of snowballed from there," Cereza says, shaking her head.

"Probably just some bored idiots who weren't invited to the party," Fresa says, yawning.

"But what if it wasn't?" I ask. "What if it's for real?"

"What, like you think actual aliens showed up last night and gave us a little geological heads up that they were here?" Uva asks.

"Yeah," I say, shrugging. "Why not?"

But regardless of what anyone believes or doesn't, there's one cold, hard fact that can't be refuted: There are hundreds of new tourists in Meteor, and they're all gonna need somewhere to eat tonight. And even though our parents gave us pageant award day off for the first time in history, after an hour of pretending otherwise we know there's nowhere we'd rather be.

A feeling that's only magnified when we show up at Selena's around lunchtime to see a line out the door.

"We need to find Lita, get her dressed," Cereza says. "But you guys stay?" She's looking at me and Fresa. "Help Mom and Dad out?"

"I'm her manager!" I say, indignant. "I should be there!"

"You're her best friend," Uva says, smiling. "And I want you to be surprised. Trust us, just this once."

And that's how I, Chicky Quintanilla, pageant manager, end up in an apron on the day of the evening gown competition.

But just when I think the day can't surprise me any more, I see a familiar tall, long-haired figure approaching the kitchen door just after the dinnertime rush.

"Got a second?" Junior catches me leaning against the back dining room's wall between tickets, things slowing down now that the evening gown competition is fast approaching.

"Exactly one," I say, smiling.

He takes my hand, and it doesn't even feel strange anymore, just good. Like coming home. A feeling that only intensifies when he stands me in front of the sheet-covered wall I gave him as a make-up present when I thought I had lost him for good.

The sheet has been up for days, Junior refusing to let anyone near it. But apparently tonight, at last, is the night.

"I wanted you to see it first," he says, ducking his head and smiling.

He's nervous, I realize, and it makes my heart flutter. "What, no dish towel blindfold?"

"Sorry, no time," he says. "Are you ready?"

I feel like I'm answering two questions when I say: "So ready."

He pulls a corner of the sheet, and it falls to the ground as if in slow motion, revealing Junior's masterpiece inch by inch.

This time, I can't help it, my eyes fill with tears that spill over, and I'm sniffling into my apron. It's Selena, of course, in her iconic purple, glittery jumpsuit. But in Junior's rendition, she's astride a rocket ship like it's a bull. Above her hang planets close enough to pluck from the sky, swirls of stars and galaxies that remind me of the rock pattern we left in the crater. Below is the New Mexico desert at sunset, almost just as it looks outside the window right now.

Selena's Diner, it says across the top, and along the bottom: *Welcome Home.*

"So, you hate it, right? It's too kitschy, too cheesy, too . . ."

"Too perfect," I interrupt, snaking an arm around his waist and pulling him into a half hug. "Junior. It's . . . everything. Thank you."

"Chicky," he says, turning me to face him. "You know what else would be perfect?"

"What?" I ask, sniffing as the last of my summer storm of tears dry up.

"If you'd let me take you to the post-pageant party tonight." He clears his throat. "Like, as a date."

"I wish I could," I say, that pang from earlier back with a vengeance. Because I do wish I could go with him. I honestly do. "But I should come back after the announcement. Help out. My family needs—"

"Go," says a voice from behind me, and Fresa is standing there with her order booklet, looking flushed but exhilarated, her familiar scowl missing for once.

"I can't," I say. "There's so much to do."

"I'll cover for you," Fresa says, and my jaw drops. "What, bitch?" she says. "Go before I change my mind."

"You heard the boss lady," Dad says, and Mom smiles.

"We're doing this?" I ask Junior, and he smiles too. Brighter than every star that inspired his mural. His perfect, perfect mural.

"We're doing this."

I shrug off my apron but leave the hat to cover my sweaty hair.

"Thanks, guys," I say. "I guess we're going."

"Wait, not like that you're not!" Fresa says, horrified by my shorts and Converse without socks and the grease-splattered Selena's cap.

"It's okay," Junior says. "I took the liberty of bringing an accessory."

Jewelry? I wonder, my heart sinking just a little. I'm not really a jewelry kind of girl, and I thought he knew that. I thought he knew everything about me. I was kind of betting on it.

What if I was wrong?

But Junior's eyes sparkle with mischief as he digs into his pocket to pull out a crinkling plastic wrapper, and I'm already laughing, my heart right back in my throat, all dipping forgotten.

"I figured it was about time to take back the Ring Pop," he says, opening the package to reveal the biggest one I've ever seen, in every color of the rainbow. "We've deprived ourselves long enough."

My family clearly doesn't know what's going on, but they can tell it's a moment, because they're as quiet as they've ever been while Junior slides the plastic ring onto my middle finger. "There," he says, surveying my outfit with satisfaction. "Perfect."

"That's adorable," Fresa says, like it's anything but. "And you're still not going to the evening gown competition like . . ."

Mom and Dad clap their hands over her mouth at the same time, smiling at me as she flails between them.

Junior takes my hand, and I've never cared less about what I'm wearing. I'm Chicky Quintanilla, reigning beer pong queen, the first openly pansexual girl in Meteor's history. So what if I'm not wearing the right costume? I'm dressed as myself.

The boy with his hand in mine thinks that girl is pretty great, and better than that, so do I.

"Watch me," I say to my silenced sister, throwing a wink at the lot of them before pulling Junior out the door into the purple dusk.

LITA

I DON'T HAVE the nerve to ask if Cole is actually doing what I think he's doing, if he's really considering raiding his family's old dresses.

If Kendra catches him, I'll be lucky if I ever see him again, because Kendra might actually kill him.

And then me.

"Maybe we should have gone over there?" I ask Uva.

"Behind enemy lines?" Uva says. "Have you no self-preservation instinct?"

Like with all the Quintanilla sisters, there's more warmth behind the words than the words themselves suggest.

They talk to me a little like they talk to each other.

"Uva?" I ask as we walk to the pageant grounds.

"Lita?"

I think about the things Cole was trying to tell me the night he held me in the middle of the road.

"Are we friends?" I ask Uva.

She laughs. "Honey, I have helped in a plot to rhinestone-adorn your ass. I think we can safely say yes, we are friends."

It's a feeling like drinking Bruja Lupe's manzanilla tea on the coldest nights in Meteor.

Cole was right.

I have him.

I have Junior.

I have Uva and Cereza and Fresa.

I have Chicky.

Chicky and I have each other, in a way we maybe never did before.

I will have them, a little bit, even when the sky takes me. I will take a little of them with me.

No matter what happens tonight, there's still a chance for me to walk off that stage less lonely than when I first walked onto it.

Cole is waiting for us at the outer edge of the curtain.

"I'm gonna keep watch." Uva looks around, ready to guard us from prying contestants, especially the one contestant who would probably get me out there in the Meteor Central High mascot suit if she could. (The Fighting Space Rocks, an inexplicable mascot considering there is only one Space Rock, and that rock wouldn't fight anyone.)

Cole crouches, setting down an old dress box, the kind lined with tissue paper. I kneel across from him.

"It'll probably go down to your shoes, but I think it'll work." He opens the lid and pulls out the dress.

Strapless. Blue. A fabric that's the thinnest velvet I could ever imagine.

"First question," Cole asks. "Do you like it? Or at least like it enough to wear it for the next few hours?"

I can't answer him. This dress is spinning its own spell, even deeper than the ring of fellow contestants in that borrowed bedroom.

Because this dress looks like the sky. The bodice is the blue of almost-night over Meteor. The color darkens as it runs down the skirt, to the deep blue of the midnight sky above the crater.

"It's the most beautiful thing I've ever seen," I manage to tell him.

As Cole unfolds it, the last of the sun winks off it. It's speckled with translucent gold sequins that begin sparse on the bodice and thicken toward the bottom of the skirt. It's like the stars coming out as the sky deepens.

"Where did this come from?" I ask.

Cole looks down at the dress, a little sad. "It was my grand-mother's."

I try to catch his eye. "Cole."

His grandmother. The first Miss Meteor, decades ago.

He's lending me something that's part of his family's history, passed down and priceless.

Kendra really is going to kill him.

"You're gonna need all of us to protect you once your sister finds out about this," I say.

"It's not Kendra's." He lifts his eyes to my face. "It's mine."

The sadness in him deepens.

"What?" I ask.

"My grandmother," he says, "she died before she ever really got to know me. She thought maybe I'd grow out of being a boy and start being a girl. She even thought maybe I'd be Miss Meteor one day." He tries to laugh, but it's pained. "So she left this to me."

The Cole in front of me is so much the Cole I've always known, that I wonder how anyone could have missed it.

"I'm sorry you lost her before she really saw you," I say.

"Thanks." He smiles like he's shaking it off.

"Cole."

He meets my eyes again.

"I can't wear this." I fold the dress back into the box. "It's beautiful. What if I mess it up?"

"I don't care." He sets the fabric back in my hands. "It's yours now."

For a second, the sparkle off the dress leaves me dizzy.

"What?" I ask.

"I want you to have it," he says. "Do you know how long this has been in my closet? And it doesn't belong there. It's part of a life I never belonged in."

"Doesn't Kendra want it?"

His laugh is slight and bitter. "She says it's too old-fashioned."

Too old-fashioned?

This is the kind of dress Grace Kelly would wear to a ball. It's a gown Libertad Lamarque would wear while sitting on a flower-adorned swing.

"How is your family gonna take me going out there in this?" I ask.

"That's not for them to say," he says. "I'm giving it to you, and it's yours now."

I don't know if it's the light, but for the first time I catch the gloss on his eyes, the flicker of shine at the corners.

"But won't seeing it"—I imagine him watching part of a past that was never his cross the stage on my body—"hurt you?"

"I think if I see it on you, it won't feel like it was ever supposed to be mine." He shakes his head at the box. "It'll be a different dress. Because it'll be on you."

He is giving me part of a life he did not want.

I kiss him on the cheek, like I've done for years. "Thank you."

"You're gonna be great out there," he says.

"What?" I ask. "No last-minute advice?"

As he gets back to standing, he nods to Uva. "I think you've got plenty."

"Didn't I say this whole time you should be in blue?" Uva asks.

I see her already thinking about how to style my soft curls, and which shade of rose-gold lip gloss to put on me.

Uva stops Cole as he leaves. "You did good, kid."

Cole smiles. And it's still a little sad, or maybe just tired. But there's a peace, a kind of slow breath in it, that he didn't have when he was still holding that box in his hands. "Thanks."

A minute after Cole leaves, I notice for the first time how small the waist is cut.

It was made for Cole's grandmother, who—I know from the photos—was both a tall woman and one with a full chest. But in all other respects, my body is softer, with more to it. The fact that I have smaller breasts will not make enough room for the way I do not have a slender, willowy rib cage or a waist that looks as though it's been gathered tight with drawstrings.

There is a reason Bruja Lupe's curandera friends call me little, but never skinny.

"Uva." I lean close into the only Quintanilla sister I have right now. "I am never gonna fit in this."

"You really think that didn't occur to me?" Uva asks, "You think I didn't plan for the fact that the Kendalls' legacy of bony asses is a little different than ours?"

"Uva," I say her name slower this time. "I will never fit into this dress."

Or I will, and the zipper will crumble onstage, live in front of a crowd of cheering, blood-thirsty pageant enthusiasts.

They will be cheering on the zipper rather than me.

Uva reaches into her bag and holds up something that looks like a cross between a corset and a leotard. "Oh, ye of little faith."

Uva looks around for where we can squeeze me into it, away from the other contestants.

I lift the dress out of its box again.

Strapless.

This fact sinks into my chest.

Strapless, as in, the shimmering patches covering my arms and crawling onto my collarbone will show.

"May I suggest an addition?"

A voice I've known my whole life on this planet warms me.

Like a fairy godmother, Bruja Lupe appears. I wonder how long she's been watching.

Her ubiquitous bolsa isn't on her shoulder. My guess is it's on a chair in the audience, holding her place.

Even the tourists know better than to take a bruja's purse.

Bruja Lupe takes the white lace mantilla from around her shoulders.

She sweeps it onto mine, the fine weave fluttering in the wind.

When it lands on me, it feels like her blessing for this whole stupid, messy thing I wanted to do before I left this planet.

Tears prick the corners of my eyes and well in my throat.

"What if I can't win?" I ask, my voice breaking. "What if I can't stay?"

Water glints at the corners of her eyes, and I see it, all the grief she's been holding back because she didn't want to set its weight on me.

Bruja Lupe sets her hands on my shoulders, the mantilla between her palms and my sleeves. "Then leave the way you want to leave."

CHICKY

I SMELL LIKE chilies and garlic, and Junior's shirt is flecked with paint—of course this is our first real date.

The streets are strangely quiet as we move toward the town square—the site of the final pageant event. I'm strangely nervous when I think of wishing Lita luck. For better or worse, tonight is the night.

Junior and I pick through the debris of the street fair, and we're quiet, but we don't let go of each other's hands. Not even when people pass and look.

"Isn't that the one that just told the whole town she's gay?" old Mrs. Leary, owner of Meteor's only pet store, asks her daughter as she helps her up the street. "What's she doing hold-ing hands with a boy?"

"Pansexual!" we shout at the same time, Junior's deeper voice carrying mine even farther, and we walk away laughing, but we still don't drop our hands.

Normally, the final event of the Miss Meteor pageant is held in the school auditorium like the others, but with the massive influx of new tourists our little rock stunt pulled in, the planning committee worked fast to move it outside just to accommodate everyone.

It comes into view now, at the end of Main Street, a massive stage standing in the middle of town square, strings of lights connecting signposts to trees to the gazebo roof and back, crisscrossing like a web of smaller stars opening for the main event.

"There they are," I say, pausing to take it in from a distance.

The giant, rocket-shaped clock on the front of city hall is about ready to chime seven. The evening gown competition will begin in just a few minutes.

And then I spot Lita, standing on the side of the stage, and I'm running.

She looks beautiful, her dress a soft blue that deepens as it moves down her body, dotted with golden sequins that look just like stars. Her curls perfectly frame her face, her lips shining rose-gold in the twinkle lights above.

She has one arm tucked behind her back, a beautiful white lace shawl across her shoulders, the stardust just peeking through for those of us who know. Lita—and Cole—decided to show this town exactly who Lita is tonight, and I'm so proud of her I think my heart just might bust right out of my chest.

She looks like an old-Hollywood movie star. She looks like a beauty queen.

She looks right at home.

"Lita!" I catch her right before they call the contestants onto the stage, and she smiles like she's been waiting for me. "I'm sorry! The diner got slammed, and—"

"They told me!" she says. "It's okay!"

As if to prove it, she pulls her arm around to the front. In her hand is a gold headband with antennae attached, springs with sparkly gold balls like the kind you'd find in the Halloween aisle at Meteor Mart.

She's taking it back. The word Royce threw at her like a weapon. The word that man used to try to make her feel like she deserved this less. She's folding it into her shimmering, shining self like a streak of stardust, and I was wrong before.

Now she looks right at home.

"I'm so . . ." But I don't know what I am, except that I'm tearing up, because we're here. And not just for some shallow revenge plan against our middle school bullies, but to show this town we belong. That we deserve to shine as much as anyone.

I try to tell her all this with my eyes, because my throat seems to have closed completely.

"Chicky?" Lita asks, as the girls all shuffle toward the stairs.

"Yeah?"

"You're my best friend in the world. My favorite thing about this planet. Just don't forget that, okay?"

"Lita . . . I . . ."

"We'll talk after. At the party. Over cupcakes. I just wanted you to know."

"It might not have gone like we planned," I say, taking her lead. "But . . ."

"Nothing ever does?" she asks, and her voice is a little proud and a little sad and I wish we had the last five years back. I wish it so much I feel like it's visible on my skin.

"Contestants to your places!"

"Chicky, I'm going to hug you now if that's all right."

"Yeah," I say, laughing a little. "It's all right."

The hug is one of those little kid affairs, like when you don't want to leave your best friend's house but your parents say you have to, and the hours between now and the next time you'll be able to count all the sticky pennies in your piggy bank, or eat old Halloween candy, or play marbles, just seem endless.

"Good luck," I say into her hair, and then she's marching up the stairs. Ready to shine.

Junior must have been close by, because he finds me as they begin judging the gowns, each contestant displaying her choice as the judges confer.

"Do you think she'll win?" I ask Junior.

"In a way, maybe she already did," he says in that son-of-a-psychologist way. But he squeezes my hand, so I can't even tease him.

Though it probably feels like an eternity to Lita, it's more like a second to me before Mr. Hamilton takes the mic.

"And now, with the results of our evening gown competition in, here's the moment you've all been waiting for! The announcement of the winner of the Fiftieth-Annual Meteor Regional Pageant and Talent Competition Showcase!"

It's hard to tell which I'm holding harder, my breath or Junior's hand.

"Just to remind you what's at stake here, folks: The winner tonight will spend the year as Miss Meteor, sit on the planning committee of next year's pageant, and of course, in honor of Meteor's fiftieth anniversary, walk away with ten thousand dollars in prize money."

"GO, LITA!" I yell, before I can stop myself, and Junior laughs with me as scandalized eyes dart our way in the crowd.

"So, without further ado, the second runner-up in the Meteor Regional Pageant and Talent Competition Showcase, and the winner of the five-hundred-dollar cash prize is . . ."

With every breath trapped in my body, I silently plead for them to not call Lita's name right now.

"Sara Rodriguez!"

I'm so relieved I almost pass out, but I'm even more surprised when this girl—who is absolutely gorgeous, her dark-brown skin setting off the magenta of her strapless gown flawlessly— runs straight up to Lita and hugs her.

"What?" I say, laughing. "Since when . . . ?"

"Think this has anything to do with the mysterious drunken

covenant?" Junior asks, and I laugh again, so loud people around us turn to hush me.

When I settle down, I feel it in my somersaulting stomach that there are only two more spots to go. Runner-up, and the crown. Before I know what I'm doing, I'm pulling Junior through the crowd, realizing I'm too far away, that she won't see me when they decide her fate up there.

Our fate.

People grumble and shout as Junior and I push through the crowd, two underdressed kids who are there and gone before they can lecture us about the sanctity of this moment. Like we don't know better than any of them.

We burst into the open air, a darkened area to the side of the stage where no one is standing, and I can tell we're both holding our breath now.

"The first runner-up, and the winner of the thousand-dollar cash prize is . . ."

Has an envelope ever taken so long to open?

"Estrellita Perez!"

Something like an implosion is happening in my chest. She lost. But there's a beaming smile on her face, a kind of acceptance, and her eyes are wide open as she hugs Sara again, and waves from the stage as the town claps around us, and it looks like she's trying to take in everything she's seeing all at once. Like she's holding on to it.

And I'm sad that we lost, but I'm so glad for everything

we've gained, and Junior pulls me to his side as if he sees all that and wants to help me bear it until I can untangle it all, and I think:

I could get used to this. To not holding it up all alone.

"And that makes our first-place winner—no surprises here, folks—Miss Kendra Kendall of Meteor, New Mexico!"

Kendra bursts into tears that almost look real as the entire line of girls collapses around her, and her mother rushes onto the stage, and the applause around us is so thunderous that it feels inevitable. Of course she's the one sliding into the sash, the one taking the crown, the one holding the ridiculous scepter and looking like she just stepped out of a formal dress catalog.

We may have opened a few eyes this week, but Meteor is still Meteor. Beauty pageants are still beauty pageants. Maybe this is enough, though, for our first attempt at changing the world.

"Here she comes," Junior warns, as Lita comes drifting through the crowd we just fought our way to the front of, looking strangely untethered to the Earth. The gold antennae bob up and down, joyful and mourning all at once as she accepts congratulations, handshakes, even a hug or two, but there's no doubt she's heading straight for us.

And then she stops, halfway there, and clutches her stomach with both shimmering arms, the spaces where her skin shines through, disappearing as the stardust reaches for itself across the suddenly fragile brown.

Lita looks at me, once, her eyes startled open like she's been hit, even though she's all alone, and I'm already moving toward her when she turns and, fast as the *Enterprise* switching on the Warp Core, disappears into the crowd.

"Hey!" Cole says, running up behind us, his eyes tired. "Did you see where Lita went? I wanted to say . . ." He stops cold at the look on my face. "Which way did she go?"

I'm about to tell Junior we need to go after her, the cold goodbye feeling from before back with a vengeance, spreading through my chest, but he's the one running ahead, urging us to hurry, leading us because Cole and I are too scared to do anything but grab each other's hands and follow.

"Chicky!" It's Bruja Lupe, and I slow but don't stop, hoping she'll see the panic on my face. That she'll know what to do.

"I don't know where she is!" I call, and I see something settling on her face.

"I'll check home," she says. "Find her. Please."

As we try, I look to the stars just peeking out, asking them to keep Lita safe just a little while longer.

LITA

FIRST RUNNER-UP.

It's far, far more than I thought I'd get.

But as I feel the stardust prickling over my body, claiming the rest of me, I know it's not enough.

I walk out into the desert dusk as the sky turns the blue of my dress bodice. Then it deepens until it matches the skirt hem.

The cactuses greet me as I walk deeper into the desert. I bid farewell to Monsieur Cereus, Señora Strawberry, Herr Rainbow. I nod at each of them, my gold antennae bobbing on my head. And before I can help it, I am gasp-sobbing, because my fingers are covered in stardust, and my heart is so full it feels like it's holding a whole galaxy.

I feel the stardust crawling up my neck. When I pat my fingers to my cheeks, my tears come away like the shimmer of desert rock.

My heart says goodbye to Meteor. To Buzz and Edna and the space rock that brought me here.

To Dolores Ramirez, and everyone who clapped for me when I got to my feet in front of people who hated me.

To Junior, and the Cortes family.

To the Quintanillas.

To Cole, the boy who gave me my first and only bike, and himself as a friend.

To Chicky, and movie-star voices, and making spaceship sounds in craters, and everything we had and everything we missed.

To Bruja Lupe, the closest I have to a mother.

Bruja Lupe, my mother.

I am emptied out, and crying so hard that I'm dripping shimmer onto my dress, but I am so proud of these people who are my family and so grateful I had them for my time on this tiny, spinning planet.

I feel the inside of me going soft and flickery, not just my skin but my bones and heart turning to stardust. I crouch down, layers of skirt fluffing around me. I dig my nail into the fine desert dirt, and I start writing.

Tonight or tomorrow, someone will probably find this dress out here, in the shadows of my cactus friends.

I want them to know who to return it to.

Not Cole. He doesn't need it back in his closet.

Bruja Lupe, because I could not look her in the face tonight and tell her goodbye.

I could not let her watch this happen.

"I found her," a boy's far-off voice sounds through the desert.

I place it.

Cole's.

"She's over here," calls another one.

Junior's.

I hide behind Señorita Opuntia.

I peer between Señorita Opuntia's arms and spot the silhouettes of those two boys.

Then the shape of Chicky on her lightning-storm-fast giraffe legs. She rushes forward between them, running.

No.

No.

They cannot see this.

It's bad enough losing them.

They can't watch as I do.

Chicky races toward Señorita Opuntia, the boys not far behind her.

I try to make myself small enough to disappear behind Señorita Opuntia, but even if I could, my skirt sweeps out on either side.

Chicky slows, and I know she's seen me.

Or at least my skirt.

"Chicky, what are you doing here?" I keep ducking behind Señorita Opuntia, hoping she, and the dark, will hide me. "Shouldn't you be at the diner?" It's gonna be their busiest night of the year.

"I'm exactly where I should be right now," she says.

The boys catch up to Chicky.

"Uh, Lita?" Junior says. "Why are you hiding behind a cactus?"

Three sets of eyes in the dark look at Señorita Opuntia so intently, I'm afraid they're going to burn through her.

I carefully lift my skirt off the ground and cringe out from behind Señorita Opuntia.

Every part of me I can see, every part not covered by the dress, wavers with light.

I am glowing, and sparkling, and falling apart.

Their faces are half terror, half wonder.

"I can't stay," I say, sniffling, my voice barely audible.

As if by instinct, Cole takes off his jacket and drapes it on me as best he can with one arm.

Chicky lets out a nervous laugh. "Yeah, Cole, she's a little chilly, that's clearly the problem here."

"Any other ideas?" Cole says. "The floor is yours."

Then I can't help laughing, even though I'm still sniffling, and trembling.

"I'm sorry," I rasp out. "I didn't know how to tell you." I

look at all of them, their shapes set against the darkening blue. I am glowing so much that it almost shows me the features on their faces. "And I didn't want to make everything worse for you than I already have."

"Make things worse?" Junior asks. "Are you kidding?"

"You helped me be ready to come out," Chicky says.

"You got me to finally give that dress away," Cole says.

"You convinced me to try out for the cornhole team," Junior says, "and if that's not a Meteor miracle, then what is?"

With the way they look at me, something in me shifts. Like two planets colliding. Like a star becoming part of another star. Like a supernova bursting into a world of light.

Maybe my bones and my heart are already stardust, but at this moment, it is holding together.

It hasn't just been one way. I haven't just needed Bruja Lupe, and Chicky, and Cole, and Junior, and the Quintanilla sisters.

Maybe, maybe, they've needed me.

"I'm you," I say out loud without meaning to, "but for you."

"What?" they all say at once.

I shake my head to try to keep the thoughts from rattling around too much. "What you are for me, I'm a little of that for all of you." My heart feels like the burst of light off a planetary nebula. "You need me. I don't just need you."

They all stare at me, at me, not just at the stardust, giving me a look like they're saying, *Obviously.*

In the next moment, I feel heavier and lighter at once, like a new gravity is holding me to the Earth, and like the weight of all the stars is lifting off me at the same time.

It's the pull of everyone I can't let go of, and the knowledge that maybe they can't let go of me either. Not just Bruja Lupe, but these three best friends in front of me.

They are holding me here, like a star they don't want to lose.

When the stardust shrank on my body, it wasn't because of things going right with the pageant.

It was things going right with everyone I love.

It was them helping me remember that there's space on this planet for me.

The tears in my eyes are so thick, I almost don't see the stardust's glow softening.

The brown of my skin starts at my fingertips. It spreads up to my wrists and then my arms, my collarbone, my neck.

The terror on their faces fades, leaving more room for the wonder.

The color of my skin settles, and then there's just a faint shimmery dusting on the brown.

My gasp, my own wonder, echoes off the wide sky.

I lift my skirt, and the tulle and satin fluff in every direction.

Junior laughs, shielding his eyes like a brother who's just walked in on his sister changing. It almost starts me laughing.

But I can't. I can barely find the air to gasp again when I look at my legs.

Brown. My legs are brown again, no stardust. Just that

slight glimmer, barely a sheen.

I let go of my skirt and a second later I am crying into my hands, as hard as I cried on the floor of the locker room, except this time I am also laughing. I am laughing and crying as hard as I ever have, but all at the same time.

Because I am a girl worth the space I take up. I am a girl this world, this town, and most of all, the people who love me, will not let go of. Because I am a star they won't let the sky take back.

I hold out my brown, unstardusted arms to my three best friends in the world.

Even though I can never know for certain, I am pretty sure what happens next is the best group hug that has ever happened in the history of this planet. And I, a girl with brown skin and a stardust heart, am part of it.

CHICKY

WHEN WE GET back to the town square, we are different. And no one notices.

That we've been to another world and back. That we've experienced something I'll never, ever forget.

As we pass the statue of Hubert Humphrey, Lita extricates herself from our protective, joyous circle, and I want to snatch her back into it just in case. But she's smiling, and reaching for her headband, and before we know it Vice President Humphrey is just a little sparklier.

"One small step for man," says Junior, and Lita bumps him with her hip before letting us encircle her again.

"Thank you all for being part of our pageant," the emcee is saying. "We hope you'll join us for refreshments and games and dancing to follow in the town square! Good night!"

He hits a button, and above us a thousand twinkling lights

blaze to life, music swelling from speakers placed somewhere in the trees.

We're alone in the center of it for now, Lita, Cole, Junior, and me, and Lita laughs and spins in a circle, and I try to see her like she is, and not huddled in on herself, bright white around the edges and about to come undone, about to shed what makes her human—what makes her ours—and let the sky take her back.

"Come on," she says. "Let's dance!"

I'm still just looking, remembering it all, my knees a little shaky, but Lita is so human in front of me. So small and round and brown and full of contagious joy.

"You're really back?" I ask her, even though I saw it with my own eyes. I saw the sky take the star-stuff back and leave Lita with us. With the people who love her.

"Chicky," she says, planting herself right in front of me and looking up into my eyes. "I'm not going anywhere." And then she laughs, a laugh so perfectly of a human girl it convinces me like nothing else has.

Royce couldn't take her from me. The sky itself couldn't take her from us.

And now, we really do have all the time in the world.

She grabs my arm, and Junior's, and I grab Cole's, and we sway back and forth in a strange but perfect rectangle for a few minutes, laughing and nearly falling over, hearts lighter than they've been in longer than I can remember.

369

My friends, I think as Cole's elbow bumps my ribs and Junior sneakily shifts himself closer to me, his side pressed up against mine.

Lita's eyes snap to us then, like she can somehow feel it, the way my skin is fizzing like Coca-Cola in a glass bottle wherever he's touching me. Like her finally cementing herself to this world, choosing us instead of the sky as her home, made it okay for me to feel all the rest of it too.

"Cole, I think I just remembered I need cotton candy," she says with an exaggerated wink, pulling him out of our tangle of limbs.

"Lita, wait!" I say, because I want to be alone with Junior so, so much—this wild, otherworldly emotional rollercoaster was supposed to be our first date, after all—but I don't want to let Lita out of my sight.

"We'll see you guys in a few minutes," she says to both of us, and then quietly, just to me, "I promise."

Junior laughs, still standing with his arm around me as she leads Cole into the crowd. "That was subtle," he says.

"I don't know if you've noticed, but subtlety is Lita's specialty."

"We can go with them," Junior says, just a tiny bit of reluctance in his voice despite his obvious and heroic attempt to keep it out. "If you don't want to stay . . ."

"You heard the lady," I say, letting the fear go, letting myself be here in this moment. "She'll see us in a few minutes." And this time, I think I really believe it.

Junior tightens his hold on me, and I'm ready to see what this first date stuff is really about, when I hear the last voice in Meteor—in the world, in the galaxy—that I want to hear right now.

"Oh, I get it," says Royce Bradley. "Pansexualism is like a weird orgy of freaks." He's smirking, watching Lita and Cole walk away in a way that tells me he saw every moment of our four-way dance.

Junior stiffens beside me, and I know he's worried I'm going to let Royce ruin this moment. But I've never cared less what Royce Bradley thinks. My friends and I conquered the will of the stars tonight. Royce is barely an ant under my shoe compared to that.

I squeeze Junior's hand before dropping it, bringing my rainbow Ring Pop to my mouth slowly, making sure Royce sees.

"Yup, you found us out," I say, offering a lick to Junior. "Now that the whole town knows I'm pan, I'm dating every-one."

Royce's dull eyes widen, confusion warring with anger at the fact that I've confused him. He has no idea if I'm serious or not, and it feels so good to see behind the curtain, to see how small he is without the power our fear gave him.

"And I should say thank you," I say, leaning toward him with a wink. "For being so pathetic that your girlfriend dumped you. I finally have a shot with Kendra now, and you know I have a thing for champions." Kendra Kendall is nowhere in sight, but I wink and wave over his shoulder anyway, causing him to turn in circles like a dog.

"Have fun tonight," Junior says, clearly dismissing him. "And Bradley? Stay away from my friends. Seems like I'm the only one who hasn't had a chance to get a hit in, and I'm starting to feel left out."

"Fuck you guys," Royce says halfheartedly, and then, at long last, he leaves us alone.

Junior shifts in front of me, pulling me close. "Dance with me?" he asks, just as the song shifts to something slow and dreamy.

"Why, Junior Cortes," I say. "I thought you'd never ask."

LITA

"SUBTLE," COLE SAYS as we walk away.

"When people are your friends, you don't always need to be subtle," I say.

"Then how about it?" Cole holds out his hand to me.

I notice the diamond white of his sister's column dress.

"Just a minute." I clasp his hand to tell him I'll be right back.

"Kendra," I call out.

She turns, her curls sweeping her shoulders.

"Congratulations," I say.

"Thank you," she says with a small, regal bow of her head.

I'm grateful she doesn't add "you too." Kendra isn't one for polite gestures, at least not with girls like me. Everything she says to me, she means, so at least I know she means the "thank you" part.

There is meanness in Kendra. So much of it. But there is fear there too. I think about all the things she did to me, and somehow I cannot unhitch them from the memory of those red letters in that kitchen drawer.

Now the Kendalls can get their bills current, and Selena's will still survive.

More than survive. With all the traffic coming to see the extraterrestrial rock formations, Selena's has a new wave of tourists discovering their tostada burgers.

"Oh," I say, "and congratulations again."

Confusion spreads over Kendra's face. "What?"

"On dumping a Royce-Bradley-worth of dead weight."

It might be the first real smile I have ever seen out of Kendra Kendall. More than when she's laughing at me. Even more than when she was crowned the newest Miss Meteor.

I decide not to press my luck. So I nod my goodbye and turn to leave Kendra to her public.

"You know, my grandmother would have been proud," Kendra says.

I turn around and give her a smile I mean, for Cole if not for her.

"Yeah," I say. "She would."

"No, I mean of you." Her eyes stay on me, flashing to Cole a few paces behind me just for a second. "You did her dress justice."

The words flood into me, almost as warm as Sara's perfume, or sitting on couch cushions with the other first-time girls.

I am not like the Kendall women. I am not cream or snow in this dress. In this dress, I am desert rock against the sky.

But I guess I wear it well enough for Kendra to look at me without shuddering.

With a little help from Uva and the corselette she pulled me into.

"Thanks," I say.

Kendra tugs up the strapless top of the dress. "Just try not to show everyone your boobs again."

She pulls me into a hug.

Why is Kendra Kendall hugging me?

She pats my back, smiling so that, to anyone else, she looks like she's congratulating me. "If you break my brother's heart, I will make sure they never find your short-ass little body, okay?"

Then she's gone.

I turn back to Cole, breathing in the smell of the stars.

This night is the best kind of strange and wondrous, and I want to remember how it tastes.

I hold out my hand to Cole. "Where were we?"

It's nothing particularly graceful, a girl in borrowed high heels dancing with a boy who can't use one arm. But it's us. And we are in front of this whole town and so many people from outside it, that it's proof Cole has no fear of being seen with me.

Or close to me.

I slide my arm across his back, easing us a little closer. I wonder if I can get away with it without him noticing.

The same bubbly feeling I get about how beautiful polar equations are floods into me.

I feel my lips part, and I am too surprised to press them back together.

If you break my brother's heart . . .

Even Kendra saw it before I did.

A boy giving me a bike meant for the girl he never was.

Me bringing him the only kind of galleta I knew how to bake right every time, because I wanted to say thank you for the bike that brought me to school each day.

Me kissing him on the cheek.

Him wiping it off with the back of his hand and then, one day, not.

Me climbing in the window of the Kendalls' kitchen.

Cole coming in my bedroom window.

Him holding me against him with one arm and telling me I have friends on this planet.

Him holding me against him now.

"Oh." I hear the sound in my own voice, more realizing than surprised.

I look up at Cole, who's studying my face like he's trying to follow what I'm thinking.

I will marry this boy one day. It's not a wish. It's something

I know, the same way I know that, no matter how far I ever go from Meteor, New Mexico, I will carry around a heart made of stardust.

The way I know that I now have enough people who care about me and let me care about them to hold me to this planet.

"I love you too," I say, the words filled with my own surprise. Not because I realize they're true. But because I realize I've always known them.

Cole's shock makes him completely still for a second.

But then the smile that comes is the bright, glowing rain of every meteor shower.

"Yeah?" he asks.

"Yeah," I say, laughing as I repeat his word.

And I kiss him on the cheek, closer to his mouth than I've ever done it.

But this time I pull away slowly enough to let him stop me.

This time, he catches my mouth with his, and I am every shower of light that has rained through the night sky.

My mouth against Cole's is a soft brush of light across the sky. It's a meteor blazing through the night.

And when we pull away, when we look at each other in that way that is both stillness and wonder, we are still lit up. We are light against the sky.

The first sound between us is the faint start of my laugh.

I've left a rose-gold lipstick mark on him.

He ducks his head a little.

"I've never seen you blush before," I say.

"Then you haven't been paying very close attention."

I settle into the feeling of him holding me, of everyone who loves me holding on to me, keeping me here, giving me the space on this planet I never thought I was allowed.

And with that last thought, I have an idea.

CHICKY

I LEARN, IN the next fifteen minutes, how much two people can say without words.

Junior and I don't talk much, but that's because the rest of our bodies are busy. Arms learning the weight of arms, feet learning the rhythm of stepping together, faces learning how little space can be between them before both people combust.

I know what I want, but knowing isn't the same as doing, and I'm a little afraid I won't be able to. That maybe the scared feeling I used to have will come back when I least expect it and ruin everything.

But what I find in my heart, as he casually brushes a tiny desert beetle off the back of my shirt, isn't something new and uncertain. It isn't something that makes me afraid. It's like all the while our friendship has been this plant in full leaf, green and vibrant and special on its own, but in the last few days it's burst into dazzling bloom.

The roots are still there, and the sturdy stalk, the leaves that unfurled as we grew up together. But these blossoms are here now, too, bright and full and absolutely gorgeous. Maybe I needed them all together before I could be ready.

It's with this feeling, this certainty, that I step closer, pressing myself against Junior, fitting my chin right into the space between his neck and shoulder as we sway inexpertly back and forth.

He lets out this little contented sound, and then coughs like he didn't mean to do it out loud. I hide my smile in his shoulder, not teasing for once, because I feel just the same way.

Over his shoulder I can see the rest of the dance floor, and something catches in my heart when I see Lita, looking at Cole like he's a field of fireflies lighting up just as dusk falls. How did it take her so long to see what was right in front of her?

As Junior clears his throat, I realize maybe I don't really have a leg to stand on in that department.

I pull back a little, wanting to tell him about Lita and Cole, but there's a look in his eyes that keeps me quiet.

"Chicky," he says, his voice the kind of formal that tells me he's nervous again.

"Junior," I reply, equally formal. But he doesn't smile.

"Remember when you asked me who I'd be if I could be anyone?"

"Yeah, you mean right before Cole punched Royce and I came out to the whole school?"

"Ha-ha, right," he says haltingly, and it occurs to me that he's practiced what he's about to say, to the point where improvisation isn't really an option.

My heart squeezes in my chest, and I just listen, maintaining eye contact even as his eyes dart everywhere, from the trees to the lights to the people around us, but always coming back to rest on mine.

"Well, I think I know now, if you still want to hear it."

"Of course I do," I say, though this once all-important question isn't really that important to me anymore. Maybe it was always more about our hearts getting to know each other's than a list of answers to a list of questions.

But what do I know? I'm sixteen years old, and until two weeks ago I didn't even have a real friend.

Or at least, I thought I didn't.

"Okay," he says, laughing at his own nerves. "Well, I don't think I want to be anyone else. I like being me. But I think . . . maybe . . . if I could be anyone? I'd like to be me-with-you."

There it is again, the Coca-Cola fizz, but this time it's all over.

"I'm better with you, Chicky. You're my best friend. You make me laugh, and you make me brave, and you make me think I might be headed for more . . ." He smiles again, that same, nervous smile I saw for the first time when he asked if I wanted to be partners for ring toss in sixth-grade gym class and I said yes just because I was so surprised.

"And I know you're not sure about me, or about us, but I've always . . ."

He pauses. And it's not the perfect moment. It's not even one of the six movie moments we've had in the past week. But it's *the* moment. It's our moment. Something in me just knows.

So I don't wait for him to find a way to finish telling me how I wasn't sure, because it doesn't matter anymore. I'm sure now. I've never been so sure of anything.

And in the eye of this halting, stuttering, over-rehearsed, cute-as-hell storm, I cross the last few inches of distance between Junior Cortes and me, and I do my best to kiss him right.

It's probably not the most cinematic kiss in the world. We bump noses, and our lips seem confused about what goes where, and we're smiling too much to really get traction—but we're certainly not lacking for enthusiasm, and that's what makes it perfect.

"Wow," he says again, when we pull apart. "I am *great* at that."

And I swat his arm, and I'm laughing so much, and he's laughing, and he doesn't even wait until we stop before pulling me in again, so we're half kissing and half just giggling against each other's lips. I think another meteor (meteorite?) could hit right now and I'd go out happy, because no one has ever been happier than this.

Something surprising about Junior Cortes: his lips are the softest thing in the world. And look, I don't know much about kissing, and I would never admit this to him, but I think maybe he *is* good at this—even though I know he's never done it before.

The way he knows just when to switch angles. The way he slides a hand to the small of my back and pulls me in closer until my breath catches in my throat.

He smiles when he feels it. That breath catching, right against his teeth. And that's the moment I realize there aren't any secrets between us anymore. That he even knows how I breathe when someone's kissing me. That he's the only one who knows.

Around us, I'm aware that people are still dancing. Swaying. Laughing. Celebrating and mourning and living. And maybe we are too. Maybe a kiss, after waiting this long, is all of those things wrapped into one.

I slide my hands up his chest, up his neck, until they're pressed against the sides of his face. One continuous kiss becomes a hundred smaller ones. My top lip between his, his bottom lip between mine. We're learning. We're not laughing anymore. And like the clouds are parting in front of me, some unknown future spooling out between our small hiccups of breath, I know this is going to be the first of many, many kisses between Junior and me. And I'm glad. I'm so, so glad.

"Okay," comes a high, breathless voice from behind us, and we pull apart reluctantly, staying attached everywhere but the lips.

Lita and Cole are standing in front of us, and they're not

touching, but the space between them seems lit up somehow, and I'm already looking forward to later when Lita and I lie across my bed and dissect every last moment of this night.

Like friends.

Like *best* friends.

"First of all, I'm so glad you guys are finally doing that, trust me," Lita says, gesturing to the way Junior and I are intertwined. "And you know I wouldn't interrupt it lightly. But I just had the most amazing idea, and I'm going to need your help."

And I know from the way Cole's eyes are all the way open, and Lita's joy seems to be vibrating from her very core, that things are somehow about to get even better.

Probably stranger, too, but we're used to that by now.

LITA

BRUJA LUPE IS lighting a few more overly perfumed candles.

I hesitate on my way out the door. It's been a few days since the pageant, a few days since my body turned back to the brown that makes up Lita Perez. But I can tell Bruja Lupe is still getting used to the idea of not losing me, something wonderful but strange, unsettling, like the cactuses blooming all at once.

"Go," she says, blowing out the match.

"But . . ." I pause at the threshold.

I have been Bruja Lupe's prop, her girl from the stars, for so long. My eyes are the oracles her customers gaze into.

"My first appointment of the day wants a spell to make sure she looks better than her bridesmaids at her wedding," Bruja Lupe says. "I think I can manage."

Bruja Lupe is not a hugger. But she is my mom, and I am her daughter. That means sometimes she'll have to put up with it.

"Thanks," I say, letting go of her and dashing out the door.

I take my bike, streamers flipping and sparkling in the sun as I speed toward the center of town.

I can't be late today.

"Lovely day, isn't it, Señora Barrel Cactus?" I call out to the side of the road. "Top of the morning to you, Sir Purple Prickly Pear!" I yell as I speed past. "Give my best to the wife, Mr. Mountain Ball! Looking good, Mademoiselle Claret-Cup!" And then, as I pass the first one I ever made my acquaintance, "Wish me luck, Señora Strawberry!"

A half hour later, a crowd of visitors is following me out the doors of city hall.

I know very well that the city council only let me start these tours because they thought no one would come.

Now that they're one of the biggest attractions in Meteor, they can't stop me. And considering I bring more traffic not just to Bruja Lupe and Selena's and the Meteor Meteorite Museum, but to the whole town, I don't think they would even if they could.

"And that's the curb that Vice President Hubert Humphrey tripped on right after giving his address to the newly founded town," I tell the tour group. "We're in the process of designating this curb a local landmark."

(Buzz has been quizzing me on local history.)

I give the tour group time to take pictures with the

386

Humphrey statue, still sporting my gold antennae. I stop in front of city hall, waiting until everyone has gotten photos of the rocket clock.

"You've probably noticed by now that I haven't been saying the name of this town you've all come to visit," I tell them. "And that's because, as you might know, there is some small debate about this town's name."

The debate over the name is probably why at least a few of them are here, the ones drawn by wanting to see a town that's two towns on paper.

"The two sides of the debate are those who call this town Meteor, and those who call this town Meteorite. By a show of hands . . ." I ask them to vote first for one, then the other. It's about an even split.

"Now you see the problem," I say.

They laugh again, more at ease this time.

"As the official town tour guide," I say, not bothering to tell them I appointed myself, "I must remain impartial. But as a lover of astronomy, I also must tell you that I think there's an easy way to solve this, because the two names mean two different things. A meteor is an object flying through the atmosphere, that, through friction and heat, becomes a streak of light."

Thank you to Cole and his dictionary for helping me prepare the wording.

"You've probably seen them during meteor showers," I say. "A meteorite, on the other hand, is debris that has survived that trip through the atmosphere enough to land on Earth, like our beautiful space rock, which you can view in the Meteor Meteorite Museum. Mention this tour for a discount at the gift shop."

The Meteor Meteorite Museum now has a dazzling new midnight-blue velvet rope in front of the space rock and new bulbs in its roadside sign. Part of my first runner-up prize money well spent.

"So as you can see, what appears to be a matter of politics is simply an astronomical discrepancy," I say. "Do we mean the rock as it streaked through the atmosphere, or as it is now? One town meeting about what we wanna name this place after and we'd have it solved. I'm gonna do what I can, but you know civic bureaucracy, so check back in about another fifty years and we'll see if we've settled it."

I can tell who's a city worker in their own towns by who laughs hardest.

"If you look around"—I lead them down the main street, gesturing to the town and the desert beyond—"you'll see that this is a place surrounded by beauty. Our desert sky. The rock formations rumored to have been left by the very same visitors who brought our cherished space rock. The majestic crater where our town would have been founded if surveyors hadn't declared it geologically unsound for the weight of major structures."

I lead them to Selena's, which has a newly refurbished neon

moon in the window, so bright it glows in daylight.

More prize money I can't imagine doing something better with.

What's left might have to go toward surprising Bruja Lupe with a new upholstered chair in the living room. Hers has been due for replacement for a while, and she's had so much new business lately, I might have time to get it inside without her even noticing.

"And speaking of beauty," I say as the last of the group comes into the diner, "let me momentarily direct your attention to Fresa Quintanilla, former Miss Meteor Second Runner-Up."

Fresa gives a beauty queen wave.

Uva and Cereza trade wary smiles.

"She's going to be insufferable now," Cereza whispers.

Then they're back to their tasks, Cereza to her nursing school textbooks, Uva to taking orders. Selena's is as busy as the last pageant night.

"We couldn't be prouder of the talent in our town," I say. "A perfect example is the spectacular mural you're standing in front of, painted by local artist Junior Cortes."

Junior's here with Chicky on one of their sort-of-dates where she's both working and flirting without knowing it.

He greets the group. With a quick, embarrassed wave, but he does do it.

Good. The more people see the new mural, the more he's going to have to get used to this.

"As you probably noted from the sign, you're currently in Selena's, a longtime anchor of this town's business community," I say. "There is a rumor that almost every landmark astronomical discovery in the last ten years started with an idea a scholar had in this very restaurant." I lean in to the group and lower my voice. "And as much as I'd like to tell you names, the International Astronomical Union forbids it."

"Did she just tell them a total lie?" I hear Junior whisper.

Chicky smiles at him, and they sink back into that place where they always meet each other.

But not before she touches the purple star I embroidered on her new jean shorts. The first birthday gift I've had a chance to give her in years.

At the end of the tour, Cole slides up next to me. "There's a rumor about that, huh?" he asks.

"What?" I say. "There is. I just started it."

"You really made all that up, didn't you?" he asks.

"Yes, I did," I whisper, nudging his healing arm with my shoulder. "And if you ever wanna get lucky again, you won't breathe a word of it."

"Word of what?" he asks.

"Exactly."

"'Maple Street, USA,'" Chicky calls across the diner, not caring who hears. "'At the sound of the roar and the flash of light, it will be precisely 6:43 p.m.'"

Something in me twists back to life at these words, a quote from our favorite episode of *The Twilight Zone*, one Bruja Lupe used to let us watch over and over if it wasn't too close to bedtime.

"'Meteors can do crazy things, you know,'" I quote back.

She grins, because even though these are borrowed words from an old TV show, we both know them to be true.

By now, the radio waves of that first broadcast of "The Monsters Are Due on Maple Street" have probably gone as far as Wolf 1055, and Pegasus, and Vega, and so many other stars we have named because we are not close enough to ask them their names. Every movie and song stretches out into the universe like that. Everything travels out and eventually reaches the stars.

So maybe the part about the astronomical discoveries is something I made up. But our universe is full of so many more unlikely things. Many of them found us here, just in the last few weeks.

A diner about to close became a place that holds a hundred voices all at once.

A town believed all the possibilities held in swirls of crater rocks.

Four friends made those swirls of crater rocks, sharing the same desert night.

A girl spoke the truth of herself so loud a whole town heard her.

Another girl came back from stardust.

So maybe it's not exactly true, about astronomers getting their big ideas at a diner in a tiny desert town.

But it could have happened.

A lot of things happen here.

ACKNOWLEDGMENTS

Thank you to everyone who helped make this story of Selena, stardust, and small towns into a book, including (but certainly not limited to): our agents, Taylor Martindale Kean and Jim McCarthy; Claudia Gabel, Camille Kellogg, Stephanie Guerdan, and everyone at HarperTeen; Lily Anderson, Candice Montgomery, Aiden Thomas, and Lindsay Eagar; and everyone who supported us on Chicky and Lita's journey.